An Anointed Woman

Tabitha & Wolf Historical Mystery Series

Series

Book Twelve

Sarah F. Noel

ISBN - 979-8-9919192-4-1

Cover design by: HelloBriie Creative
Printed in the United States of America

Also by Sarah F. Noel

Tabitha & Wolf Historical Mystery Series

A Proud Woman

A Singular Woman

An Independent Woman

An Inexplicable Woman

An Audacious Woman

A Discerning Woman

An Indomitable Woman

An Intrepid Woman

A Patient Woman

An Enigmatic Woman

A Valiant Woman

The Continental Capers of Melody Chesterson

A Venetian Escapade

Mischief In Morocco

The Amsterdam Enigma

ACKNOWLEDGMENTS

I want to thank my wonderful editor, Kieran Devaney and the eagle-eyed Patricia Goulden for doing a final check of the manuscript.

To Trang, Randy, and Drew, you're all I miss about my corporate life, but I do miss you.

FOREWORD

This book is written using British English spelling. e.g. dishonour instead of dishonor, realise instead of realize.

British spelling aside, while every effort has been made to proofread this thoroughly, typos do creep in. If you find any, I'd greatly appreciate a quick email to report them at sarahfnoelauthor@gmail.com

CHAPTER 1

September 1898

"Wolf, you promised me you would not try to wrap me in cotton wool," Tabitha protested. "Yet, here we are again. Dr Pauls has been checking in on me regularly and believes that I am past the most dangerous stage for potentially losing the baby."

Tabitha felt as though they were having the same debate, in one form or another, nearly every day. She understood Wolf's concerns; given her history of losing two babies early in pregnancy, it would be foolish to overexert herself in any way. Tabitha was fully aware of how miraculous it was to have conceived and carried this child for more than four months. Yet, did this mean she should be imprisoned in confinement for the next five? That was an almost unbearable prospect. More importantly, it was not what Dr Pauls had recommended.

They were eating luncheon, and Wolf was reading his most recent correspondence. The letter that had precipitated this instance of their now regular dispute was still in Wolf's hand.

Noting this, Tabitha continued, "You have not even told me the details of the invitation, and yet you have already declared I will not be attending. Can I at least hear what we have been invited to and why?"

The expression on Wolf's face indicated a desire to find a reason even to deny her that. Still, he began to read the letter:

Arundells, The Close, Salisbury

September 12, 1898

My most honoured Lord and Lady Pembroke,

It is with feelings of the sincerest joy and, if I may add, the deepest humility, that I take up my pen to congratulate Your Lordship and Your Ladyship upon the extraordinary and providential discovery lately made in Pembrokeshire. News of this event, which I can only describe as a triumph of intellect and perseverance, has travelled with remarkable pace to our quiet city, where it has caused no small degree of scholarly commotion. Indeed, many of my esteemed colleagues have already expressed their conviction that such a revelation could only have been vouchsafed through the singular talents and devotion of Your Lordship and Ladyship, and I confess myself entirely of their opinion.

It would therefore be the most distinguished honour of my life if you would graciously condescend to honour with your presence a modest gathering of clerics, scholars, antiquarians, and other persons of refinement, organised by The Sarum Antiquarian and Ecclesiastical Society, under my unworthy auspices. This auspicious occasion is to take place on the evening of the 23rd of September at our Chapter House here in Salisbury, where a learned discourse shall be delivered on early charters and the Church's role as their protector through the ages.

The distinction of your presence, my Lord and Lady, would not only lend an incomparable lustre to the proceedings but would assuredly inspire all present with new zeal for their studies. Moreover, should it accord with Your Lordship's convenience, I would esteem it the highest privilege to extend the humble hospitality of my own residence here in the Close. Though my roof is but modest, I flatter myself that my hospitality has been found by many to be of notable excellence.

Trusting most fervently that this invitation may find favour in your noble eyes, and assuring you of my most profound respect,

I remain with the truest devotion,

My Lord and Lady,

Your obedient and most grateful servant,

Edmund Elliot

Canon of Salisbury Cathedral

"Oh!" was all Tabitha could think to say.

"Indeed," Wolf agreed. "The letter is rather effusive, to say the least. When I suggested to Mr Goodge that I sponsor the continuation of James Truegood's search for a long-lost Magna Carta, it never occurred to me that I would be credited for its discovery, should that happen."

Tabitha smiled fondly. She could easily believe that her modest, unassuming husband would not see that the men who worked hard for such a discovery, pouring their sweat and tears into it, wouldn't be credited, but rather the man who merely paid their wages. Even Mr Goodge, as a mere amateur local antiquarian, would likely be a footnote in history. Luckily, the Pembroke historian would have all the notoriety he desired with the upcoming publication of his article on the find in The Journal of the British Archaeological Association.

"I am glad that Mr Goodge made a point of giving James Truegood full posthumous credit in his paper for locating the likely site of the buried document and for his belief that it even existed," Tabitha nodded in agreement.

During their investigation into James Truegood's death, it became apparent that Jeremiah Goodge harboured a professional rivalry, possibly bordering on jealousy, towards his younger mentee. At one point, Tabitha and Wolf had even considered this a potential motive for murder. Given this, they were relieved to discover that Mr Goodge could set aside any resentment and not only complete the work begun by his supposed protégé, but also give the younger man appropriate credit.

Now that she had heard the full extent of the invitation, Tabitha remarked, "Wolf, it is hard to imagine how listening to a lecture amongst a group of ecclesiastical scholars will harm me or the baby in any way." Wolf could hear the irritation in her tone, even though she spoke the words gently.

"I worry about the trip to Salisbury. While it is not as far as Pembrokeshire, it is not a trivial journey," was his reply.

"We will get the train, and I will do nothing but sit for two hours."

"And then we will need to hire a carriage, which will probably not be as comfortable as the Pembroke carriage. And what about once we are in

Salisbury? If you have any medical issues, Dr Pauls will be unable to reach you quickly."

Tabitha saw that she could not mollify Wolf in any other way than by suggesting solutions. "Why do we not send Madison on ahead of us with one of our carriages? He can meet us at the train station in Salisbury and ensure that I am transported in appropriate comfort and splendour for the duration of our stay."

Wolf looked as if he would have liked to find a reason to counter that suggestion, but he said nothing. Tabitha pressed on, saying, "I will ask Dr Pauls to recommend a medical colleague in Salisbury, and he will ensure that this doctor is aware of my medical needs."

Again, this was hard to argue with, though Wolf would have if he could have thought of anything. Finally, looking for something to stand firm on that might persuade his wife to stay home, he said, "And it will just be the two of us."

He saw doubt and worry cross his wife's face and felt terrible for causing it. Still, Wolf knew this was his only chance to win the argument.

Pressing his advantage, Wolf continued, "The children will remain in London with Mrs O'Leary. We will not invite Langley, and I will personally assume responsibility for explaining the situation to Lady Pembroke."

Tabitha gasped at this last statement. "You are going to attempt to ban Mama from attending?"

Hearing it spoken aloud made Wolf appreciate the magnitude of what he was undertaking. Still, he remained undeterred. "Yes, I am. This invitation was addressed to the two of us, no one else. And I know how her ladyship adds to your stress and worry. The only way I will allow you to attend with me is if all possible external concerns are left behind."

"Melly is not a concern, Wolf. You know that," Tabitha protested.

"Not when she is here, perhaps. However, when we travel, I know you fret about her, and I want to ensure there is nothing to cause you worry."

Even though Tabitha knew she would accept Wolf's conditions, she felt obliged to point out, "Wolf, you cannot keep me from all harm or anxiety. Melody is our child now, and it is the nature of motherhood to worry. I will still be concerned about her even if she is not with us; perhaps even more so."

Nevertheless, her words were in vain. Tabitha could have argued the point further, asserting her independence and reminding Wolf that he had pledged to respect her autonomy when he proposed marriage. She could have done so, but she knew that his concerns stemmed from love; Wolf understood what it meant to her that she had managed to conceive a child. He cared little for himself, but he did care about Tabitha's wish for a child of her own.

As much as Melody had filled the vast void in Tabitha's life caused by years of fruitlessly praying for a child, Wolf knew that Tabitha still longed to have a child with him. Having a son to inherit meant nothing to Wolf. However, after all the heartache and shame of being unable to provide Jonathan with an heir, it mattered to Tabitha. She knew that Wolf understood this and that it was at the forefront of her husband's mind when he became overly protective, as he was now. This realisation tempered her irritation at his mollycoddling.

Somewhat.

Wolf stood and moved to Tabitha's chair. Pulling her up and into his arms, he pressed her to his chest and kissed her hair. "All I want is to keep you safe, Tabitha. You and the baby."

Tabitha felt her husband's heartbeat beneath her cheek. There, in his arms, she did feel safe. More importantly, she felt safe without feeling trapped; that was the power of Wolf's love.

Pulling away from him enough to look up into his kind, handsome face, she took her hand and cupped his cheek. "I know, my love. I know. We will find our way through this. I promise you that I will not be fool-hardy if you promise that you will trust me to make those decisions."

Taking the hand that held his cheek, Wolf planted a soft kiss in its palm. This was his promise.

Tabitha hated interrupting this loving moment with a practicality, but something needed to be decided. "Given that we need to leave in a few days if we are to attend, perhaps you should break the news to Mama this evening at dinner," she suggested.

Wolf sighed in acknowledgement of the wisdom of her suggestion, but also in anticipation of the lion's den he was walking into. "Yes, it must be done," he agreed, however reluctantly.

The couple stood there, locked in their embrace for a few minutes longer, before the demands of the day called them both.

The dinner had been planned earlier in the week as an intimate family gathering of Tobias, Lily and the dowager. Tabitha considered whether to suggest that the newlyweds skip the dinner, but hoped they might provide something of a buffer to the dowager's likely ire. And anyway, as the dowager countess's godson and granddaughter respectively, there was little about the woman that would surprise either of the young people.

Finally, Tabitha decided to send a note to the couple's new Grosvenor Square home and give them the courtesy of deciding. She had kept the note brief and to the point:

Lily, Wolf and I have been invited to attend a lecture in Salisbury. We are not inviting Mama and will be telling her at dinner. Feel free to rescind your acceptance.

In reply, Tabitha received a similarly brief note:

Thank you for the warning, but we would not dream of abandoning you.

Tabitha's overall feeling upon reading this note was that, if Wolf genuinely wanted to spare her stress, he should have thought about what it would be like to tell the dowager she wasn't invited to Salisbury. It might have been less stressful to include her than to endure announcing her exclusion.

CHAPTER 2

Did the dowager possess some sixth sense about such matters, Tabitha wondered. Certainly, unless Lily and Tobias had warned her, and Tabitha very much doubted that, then how on earth did the dowager infer the nature of the conversation Wolf wanted to have with her?

Of course, Tabitha realised, the dowager couldn't know the substance of the discussion because she was unaware of the invitation to Salisbury. Yet, from the moment she entered the drawing room, it was evident that the canny old woman sensed that a scheme was afoot to exclude her from something.

Certainly, Tabitha wouldn't have recognised such a thing two years ago. However, she hadn't known the dowager countess nearly as well back then. Now, Tabitha noticed the woman's slightly raised eyebrow as Wolf hurried towards her and kissed her hand. Had he been too effusive? Perhaps that was it. Certainly, Lily and Tobias had very guilty expressions on their faces.

Given how often, at least in the past, Tabitha and Wolf had tried to keep the dowager out of investigations, perhaps it was unsurprising that this was the first suspicion that entered the woman's mind. Of course, this wasn't an investigation; in that regard, she was mistaken. Tabitha only hoped this would lessen the dowager's anger somewhat.

"May I get you a glass of sherry, Lady Pembroke?" Wolf asked in a much more strained voice than it should have been, given the seemingly innocent question.

"Am I likely to need my nerves thus fortified this evening, Jeremy?" she replied tartly. Wolf's awkward bark of a laugh at this unfunny reply was all the confirmation the dowager needed. She glanced at Tobias and Lily, then turned to face Tabitha. "Out with it," she demanded.

"Mama," Tabitha protested, "Whatever do you mean?"

"Do you suppose I cannot see through such a tissue of nonsense? I have not lived to this advanced age without learning to smell a falsehood. Now, out with it!"

Wolf had hoped to delay this conversation until they were at least two courses and hopefully a few glasses of wine into dinner. However, he could see that attempting to put her off would only irritate the dowager when he finally reached the point.

Still hopeful that the woman might be somewhat mollified, Wolf poured a glass of sherry and handed it to her. "Let us all sit, Lady Pembroke, and I will explain the favour I do wish to ask of you."

"Ha!" the woman said triumphantly. "I knew it. It is hard to believe that any of you still think you can pull the wool over my eyes. About anything."

"Indeed, Mama," Tabitha said, in what she hoped was a reassuring but not condescending voice. "No one would ever imagine such a thing of you. We merely hoped to enjoy some of our evening first." As soon as she said this, Tabitha appreciated what a foolish comment it was.

The dowager settled into her usual armchair by the fireplace, sipped her sherry, and confirmed her suspicion. "Really, Tabitha. Did you hope to conceal an unpleasant truth with cut crystal and candlelight? Do you think a roast pheasant, a glass of claret, and a tasty pudding will improve my temper?"

Given that that was exactly what Tabitha and Wolf had hoped for, neither had a suitable reply. Luckily, as was often the case with the dowager, it had been a rhetorical question.

"Out with it! Evidently, this is less of a favour and more of an

8

unpleasant request, and I would prefer to hear it before I eat, rather than have it give me indigestion after." Wolf glanced at Tabitha, who gave him an almost imperceptible nod; whether this was the ideal time to have this conversation, there was no escaping it now.

Now, Wolf had to handle this situation with kid gloves; he needed to minimise the invitation to Salisbury in a way that was believable, at least to the dowager, while also emphasising his concerns about Tabitha. Of course, this was perhaps the most challenging part. The dowager did not see herself as anything less than a delight to be around, so any suggestion that she might cause stress for an expectant mother would instantly put her on the defensive.

Tabitha watched her husband chew his lip as he considered how best to phrase his request. Although they had discussed this earlier, they had agreed that anything too rehearsed would work against them. Now, Tabitha was second-guessing that decision.

Wolf began by explaining the invitation to Salisbury. Tabitha had suggested that he keep the letter ready and read it aloud; there was no doubt that, under normal circumstances, the gathering of antiquarians was something the dowager would find unworthy of her time and notice.

Of course, the dowager knew they believed this and was immediately suspicious about why they thought she would want to join them. At that moment, Tabitha immediately perceived what a strategic mistake they had made. She attributed it to her delicate condition; normally, she was much more adept at managing the dowager than this. If they had simply mentioned the invitation, perhaps even invited her to join them, there was little doubt she would have rebuffed them. Instead, their reluctance to broach the subject initially had aroused her suspicions, and now that they were heightened, there was no turning back.

When Wolf had finished reading the letter, they all waited. The dowager said nothing. In fact, she took so long to answer that Tabitha wondered if she was going to at all.

Finally, after taking another sip of sherry, the old woman asked, "And why would you think I would want to join you, Jeremy? Because I must assume this ridiculous charade is leading up to a request that I not attend."

Again, Tabitha felt like slapping her forehead in dismay. What a green-horn's mistake, she thought.

Deciding that she should take the reins at this point, Tabitha said as carefully as possible, "Given your role in helping us solve the murder in Pembroke, and because this discovery is at least tangentially related to the earldom through William Marshal, we thought you might wish to partake in your share of the honour."

Tabitha could tell she was walking a fine line; if they didn't make the invitation sound sufficiently illustrious, the dowager would assume ulterior motives in their wish to exclude her. However, she would insist on joining them if they made it sound too grand.

As it was, she narrowed her eyes as she stared at Tabitha. "And so, if you believe I might wish to be one of your party, what is the request you wish to make of me?"

While she could see Wolf ready to jump in and answer, Tabitha thought this question was also best handled by her. "Initially, Wolf was reluctant to allow me to join him; he is worried that the journey will put too much strain on me."

The dowager gave a bark of a laugh. "She is expecting a child, Wolf, not suffering from consumption. She is increasing, not wasting away."

Wolf hesitated to argue but did not want to undermine the point they were hoping to make. Instead, he said, "While that is true, you will understand my concern about Tabitha placing herself under any more strain than usual, Lady Pembroke. However, while she insists that she is fit for the journey, I intend to make certain arrangements to minimize Tabitha's discomfort and worry. One of these is that we will go alone. We will not be taking Melody with us, even."

Now the dowager understood. In a tone that was ice cold, she said, "And you believe that my inclusion in the party will be one of the things that might unduly strain your wife's composure? Is that correct?"

Glad to answer somewhat truthfully, Wolf said, "Tabitha worries about you. While we know that you have the vigour of someone far younger than your years, you can understand her concern."

This was a tough one for the dowager. She despised being perceived as weak and incapable, but this line of argument did exploit one of the few cracks in her armour: her need to be the centre of attention.

Finally, after considering all her options, she decided she had no wish to sit through a long, dull historical lecture. The dowager shrugged and said, "Perhaps if you are so concerned for my well-being, you can hurry your staff along and we can sit down to dinner."

Tabitha and Wolf sighed in relief. Despite a rocky start, they seemed to have escaped by the skin of their teeth.

For the most part, dinner was a pleasant enough affair, at least to begin with. To the untrained eye, it might appear that the dowager was over her snit. Well, over that snit at least.

As the soup plates were being cleared, Tobias announced, "Lily has been accepted into University College London to study botany!" The pride on the young husband's face and voice was heart-warming.

From the moment that Lily had accepted Tobias's offer of marriage, Tabitha had worried that the brilliant young woman had done so for the wrong reasons: Lily believed that the besotted young viscount would allow her more freedom to pursue her academic studies than her father was willing to. Mostly, those fears were now assuaged. When Lord Williams, Tobias's father, was arrested for murder and the wedding was nearly cancelled, it became clear how sincere Lily's love for her fiancé truly was.

The other concern Tabitha and Wolf shared was that Tobias's enthusiasm for Lily's education might diminish once she became his wife. It appeared that, at least for now, it hadn't.

While Tabitha and Wolf might be pleased with Lily's news, the sour expression on the dowager's face showed she felt differently. "Lily, you are a viscountess and will be a countess someday; surely you have better things to do than play with plants."

Lily had endured some form of this debate with her grandmother so many times that she no longer saw the point in replying. Still, the dowager's sullen mood lingered for the rest of the evening. Tabitha only hoped their earlier chat about the trip to Salisbury wasn't part of the reason.

CHAPTER 3

Although Tabitha would never have admitted it to Wolf, the journey from Waterloo Station to Salisbury was more tiring than she had expected. She could not understand why switching from a plush carriage to a first-class train compartment and then back into a comfortable carriage felt so draining. She carried nothing more than her reticule and did little aside from reading a book and staring at the countryside outside the window, yet by the time the train arrived at Salisbury Station, she was barely able to suppress her yawning.

While Tabitha might have believed she had concealed her exhaustion from Wolf, he had kept a keen eye on her from the moment they left Chesterton House and was aware that the journey had been draining. At least they didn't have to change trains. Nonetheless, he was pleased they had sent Madison ahead the day before so their comfortable carriage would be waiting for them.

The train came to a stop with a final burst of steam. As Wolf descended to the platform before helping Tabitha out, porters bustled around them, calling to one another as they lugged valises and trunks. Wolf flagged down one of them and directed the man to fetch their luggage and bring it to the front of the station, where Madison would be waiting with the carriage.

With that taken care of, Wolf led the way down the platform and out of the station. The clatter of carriage wheels echoed outside the station gates, where a line of hansoms and larger four-wheelers were waiting for passengers. He glanced around for Madison for a few moments before spotting the driver. Wolf settled Tabitha in the carriage, ensured the luggage was loaded, and then got in himself. A moment later, the horse set off at a steady trot, hooves striking rhythmically against the cobbles as they departed the station yard.

The road curved almost immediately, gently climbing towards Fisherton Street. As they drove, Tabitha gazed out of the window and watched the ancient city of Salisbury unfold before her. She had read that it was a beautiful example of a well-preserved medieval cathedral city, and now she saw for herself how true that was. However, it was also a bustling mercantile centre for the region. Shops lined either side of the thoroughfare: grocers with baskets of apples and carrots spilling onto the pavement, drapers displaying bolts of cloth in their windows, a baker's shop releasing the warm aroma of fresh bread, and everywhere she looked, there was lively bustle as people went about their business.

The carriage rattled past the Wyndham Arms, its painted sign swinging gently in the wind, then across Fisherton Bridge, where the Avon rippled beneath, swollen from recent rains. As they entered the High Street, more of Salisbury's character and charm were revealed; gabled timber-framed houses leaned against later Georgian facades, with their upper storeys jutting over the shopfronts below, the different architectural periods blending beautifully.

The street's cobbles shone with the dampness from a brief midday shower. Ladies with their parasols at the ready in case of another downpour hurried across the road, their hems lifted to avoid the mud. Errand boys wove between carts delivering milk and coal. The clop of the horse's hooves echoed between the buildings, mingling with hawkers' cries and the faint toll of a church bell marking the half-hour. The overall scene was charming, and although she had difficulty hiding her yawns, Tabitha was glad she had accompanied Wolf.

"Look," Wolf said.

Tabitha followed his direction and saw the cathedral's spire ahead, visible above the shop roofs. At first, only the tip could be seen, but the spire became more visible as the carriage drew nearer. It was a marvel of stonework that seemed to defy gravity. Madison turned the carriage onto St Ann Street, which was narrower and quieter than the High Street. Rows of modest houses lined the way, their gardens walled and tidy, many filled with late-summer blooms. Now, the noise of commerce faded somewhat.

Soon, they reached St Ann's Gate, a medieval archway that had guarded the entrance to the cathedral Close for centuries. The carriage slowed as its wheels clattered over ancient, worn paving stones beneath the gateway. The passage was narrow, enclosed by thick stone walls, and it felt like stepping back in time. On the far side, the Close opened out in a sweep of green, with broad lawns stretching towards the cathedral itself. The sudden sense of spaciousness after the crowded town was breathtaking.

Although Tabitha had seen many splendid buildings in London, there was something truly awe-inspiring about Salisbury Cathedral standing in the centre of the Close. The enormous height of the spire drew the eye upward as it vanished into the overcast sky.

As magnificent as the cathedral was, the Close was also quite grand. Around its edges stood an array of very fine houses, each with its own character. Some were timber-framed survivors from earlier centuries, leaning and crooked, while others displayed the red brick and symmetry of Georgian taste. Gorgeous gardens, moss-covered walls, and wrought-iron gates enclosed the area. Gentle smoke curled from chimneys, and the air carried the blended scents of damp earth, cut grass, and early autumn leaves.

The carriage turned left, tracing the curve of the Close. They passed a dignified house, whose Queen Anne façade was almost severe. They continued along until Madison slowed the carriage to a halt. At the corner where the Close opened towards the water meadows, the canon's house, Arundells, came into view. Tabitha's first thought was that it was graceful rather than ostentatious. A long brick, perfectly symmetrical façade stood behind a sweep of lawn bordered by clipped hedges. The rooms at the front of the house looked as if they would enjoy the most wonderful view of Salisbury Cathedral.

For much of their journey, Tabitha had been wondering about their host, Canon Edmund Elliot. Considering the pompous, ingratiating letter the man had sent, she was curious how they would find him in person. When they agreed to accept the invitation, Wolf had replied, saying they would arrive the day before the lecture to see something of Salisbury and rest after their journey. In return, he had received a letter that, if it were possible, was even more self-important and obsequious.

As the carriage came to a halt, Tabitha's questions were about to be answered. Almost immediately, as the horses stilled, the front door swung open, and a man, whom she assumed was their host, hurried out, his black cassock fluttering, a wide-brimmed hat clutched in one hand, and an umbrella in the other, even though the rain seemed to have ceased some time ago.

Canon Elliot was probably around forty, a tall beanpole of a man with little else to distinguish his appearance. Coming down his front steps, waving his arms, and with his cassock billowing behind him, he looked like a large, flapping crow.

"Lord Pembroke! Lady Pembroke!" the canon exclaimed, bowing so deeply that the hat slipped from his grasp and rolled down the steps. He lunged after it, umbrella nearly toppling him headfirst, then straightened himself again, cheeks florid, spectacles askew. "Welcome, welcome to Salisbury! It is a most singular honour to receive you under my humble roof. Indeed, Providence itself must have decreed this happy conjunction."

Wolf was helping Tabitha out of the carriage when this proclamation was made, and they locked eyes. He quirked his lips in amusement.

When Tabitha had safely descended, Wolf turned, composed himself, inclined his head graciously, and replied, "Her ladyship and I are grateful for the invitation and hospitality."

"Might I lead the way in, your lordship?" Canon Elliot intoned solemnly. Tabitha did her best to suppress a smile, while Wolf indicated their host should lead the way.

As they entered the house, their host continued breathlessly, "I have taken the liberty, my lord, of arranging a small collation, no more than a modest repast, of course, though I flatter myself the syllabub is particularly fine, that you may refresh yourselves after your arduous journey."

While their cook, Mrs Smith, had packed a basket of food for their trip, Tabitha hadn't felt like eating on the train. Now, she was hungry and, more to the point, in need of some sustenance to keep her strength up. However, she also needed to wash the grime of the road off her.

"Thank you, Canon Elliot," she replied. "I assume my maid and his lordship's valet made it here safely earlier?"

"Indeed, indeed. I believe they are both unpacking your trunks as we speak."

While Tabitha and Wolf had travelled with some luggage, most had been sent earlier with Ginny and Thompson. Wolf would have happily travelled with far fewer clothes and without his valet, but knew how horrified Thompson would be at the mere suggestion; this trip and the lecture were the kind of public display of aristocratic splendour the man thrived on.

Tabitha knew that the always efficient and organised Ginny would have already selected an outfit for her to change into. "Might we be shown to our bedchambers? I would like to refresh myself before our repast."

She had assumed that she and Wolf would be allocated separate rooms, and it seemed she was correct. As expected, Ginny had a dress ready for her and had even had the forethought to order a tray of tea and toast. Gratefully, Tabitha sank into an armchair.

"M'lady, you look quite pale. Let me pour you some tea."

As much as she did want to wash her face and hands, Tabitha wasn't sure she would have the energy for even that without a restorative cup of tea and a couple of bites of toast. Had Wolf been right in wishing her to remain behind instead of accompanying him, she wondered?

CHAPTER 4

O nce she had washed her face, changed her outfit, and drunk two cups of tea, Tabitha felt sufficiently restored to face Canon Elliot.

Based on what she had seen of the house so far, it was as grand and well-maintained inside as it was outside. As she descended the stairs and looked at the sparkling crystal chandelier hanging above the gleaming oak staircase, she wondered how a clergyman could afford the upkeep of such a home. While she knew that bishops usually lived in quite grand residences as a perk of their position, it was hard to imagine that a lowly canon, even of Salisbury Cathedral, had similar benefits.

Even if the cathedral owned the house, someone was paying for all the servants she had already seen scurrying around. There was even a footman, which seemed quite excessive for a canon. Tabitha was intrigued to learn more about their host. She could hear voices and headed in the direction they were coming from.

The voices led her into a drawing room that wouldn't have looked out of place in Mayfair. While it wasn't as grand as the one at Chesterton House, even the dowager wouldn't have turned her nose up at its elegant, tasteful furniture and silk furnishings.

Canon Elliot leapt to his feet as soon as Tabitha entered. Rushing forward, he took her hand and bowed deeply over it. "Lady Pembroke, I sincerely hope you are sufficiently recovered from the ardour of your travels. I am well aware of the physical and emotional strain long journeys can impose on the gentler sex. Please, allow me to escort you to the most comfortable chair in the room while we await luncheon to be announced."

Tabitha had to resist the urge to roll her eyes at this speech. It was fortunate the dowager had been dissuaded from joining them. Tabitha could only imagine how quickly she might offend their host with her sharp tongue.

Their luncheon was marked by the same elegance and refined display of wealth seen throughout the house. Once again, Tabitha wondered how unusual that was in a clergyman of Canon Elliot's rank. If nothing else, it seemed he could afford an excellent French chef. If there had been any concerns about an earl and a countess lowering themselves to stay in the home of anyone less than a bishop, those would have been dispelled by the luxury and comfort with which they found themselves surrounded.

Tabitha found Canon Elliot to be a fascinating mixture of pomposity and obsequiousness.

As they were served a delicate salmon mousse, the canon explained, "Of course, I am a senior canon of Salisbury Cathedral, but I organised the lecture as one of the leading members of the Wiltshire Archaeological and Natural History Society. Since my early days at Oxford, I have been interested in early medieval manuscripts and Anglo-Norman history. It is one of the reasons I was so glad to be appointed to a role at this cathedral; for someone with my deep intellectual fascinations, there can be few places in Britain as fascinating as Old Sarum."

"Old Sarum?" Wolf inquired.

"Indeed, your lordship." Canon Elliot put down his fork, and his face adopted an expression of profound reverence. Then, in a tone more suited to addressing a lecture hall, he intoned, "Old Sarum was once both fortress and cathedral, a place where bishop and soldier shared the same high walls uneasily."

Tabitha tried to appear interested in the canon's words, but found her mind drifting.

Pulling herself back to the conversation, she found that Canon Elliot was still lecturing them. "At last, in the early 1200s, Bishop

Richard Poore obtained permission to move his seat to the valley below, where Salisbury Cathedral now rises in all its splendour. To construct it, much of the stone was carried down from Sarum's ruined keep. And so Old Sarum fell into ruin, yet it remains inseparable from Salisbury's story; the hill and the spire, the ruin and the glory, forever bound together."

This speech sounded so formal and rehearsed that Tabitha wondered whether they were receiving a preview of the introduction the canon planned to deliver before the main lecture the following evening.

For all Canon Elliot's romantic vision of Old Sarum's history, reading between the lines, Tabitha discerned that what he was actually saying was that the matter had been far more practical: Old Sarum was an inconvenient and inhospitable site for a cathedral, so the clergy moved to the valley. The canon made it seem as if he was describing something similar to Malory's *Le Morte d'Arthur*, but in reality, it was simply common sense.

Tabitha had one question: "I am still unclear as to the connection between Old Sarum and the Magna Carta. And is this what the lecture will be on tomorrow?"

It seemed she couldn't have asked a better question as far as their host was concerned; he appeared almost visibly to puff up in front of them. To Wolf, the meal felt far too similar to the dullest lectures he'd attended at Oxford, with dons who droned on with little concern for engaging their students. He inwardly groaned at the thought that Tabitha's question might prolong the canon's monologue.

As soon as Canon Elliot started to answer her, Tabitha had the same awful realisation as Wolf: Why had she asked that question?

In a voice tinged with even greater affectation and self-importance, if that were possible, the canon explained, "While it has to be studied extensively, there are hopes that the copy of the Magna Carta you uncovered might be regarded as the noblest surviving copy to date. Given this, it is only appropriate for this very charter, which links our liberties to this land, to reside in Salisbury. Old Sarum, though now a ruin, once housed both fortress and cathedral, a seat where bishop and king's officer stood shoulder to shoulder. From such uneasy unions arose the demand for law over tyranny."

This was one of the rare occasions when Tabitha missed the dowager's propensity to interrupt such recitations, often with a comment about her advanced age as an excuse for her rudeness.

Without the dowager, there seemed to be no way to cut the canon short. So, he continued, "And it was at Runnymede, yes, where the great document was signed, but upon these same chalk plains that the barons mustered, and here that their cause was nurtured. The very soil of this place nourished the liberties of England."

Tabitha and Wolf exchanged glances; a silent mutual agreement to try their best to change the subject.

However, it seemed they would only receive a temporary reprieve, at best, when Canon Elliot announced, "I will not say any more for now. I do not wish to ruin your enjoyment of our dinner conversation."

What on earth did the man have planned? Tabitha wondered.

"I hope it was not too presumptuous of me, but I thought you might enjoy meeting our speaker, Mr Leland, ahead of tomorrow's talk. I am sure that he is eager to meet you both to discuss the great find you helped to discover. Of course, Bishop Wordsworth will be in attendance. I am certain that someone as erudite as your lordship will particularly appreciate the conversation. Bishop Wordsworth is deeply academic and has a special interest in the early Church and comparative liturgy."

Tabitha's heart sank; it seemed that the conversation at dinner might be even more turgid than this one. Wolf felt much the same and was tempted to plead a respite for the evening on Tabitha's behalf. However, the canon was attempting to be a gracious host, and Wolf knew that swearing off the dinner plans would be impolite.

"Are you hosting Mr Leland at Arundells?" Wolf asked.

The canon looked shocked at such a suggestion. "Milord, I would never presume to impose such a lowly commoner on your lordship and ladyship. I am honoured that you agreed to stay in my humble abode when someone of your rank might expect to be hosted by the bishop himself."

It had never occurred to Wolf to expect such deference to his rank, though it rarely did. However, the canon seemed to expect some kind of response, and so Wolf nodded along in what he hoped was received as agreement.

The canon, encouraged by Wolf's nods, warmed to his subject and continued, "I suggested that Leland stay at the Red Lion Hotel. It seems he has been quite a regular visitor to Salisbury over the years and was familiar with that establishment."

Tabitha wanted to ask why it was not offensive to ask them to have dinner with the speaker, but would be to ask them to share a breakfast table, but she had no desire to give the man more fodder for a pompous lecture.

Eventually, the meal came to an end. Tabitha wanted to walk to the cathedral and see its interior. However, she found that she couldn't summon the energy. At last, she surrendered to the need for a nap, rationalising that if she rested for an hour or two, she would be better prepared to explore the cathedral later.

For his part, Wolf wanted to do all he could to escape from Canon Elliot. He was worried that their host would feel compelled to keep him company while Tabitha rested, and that was the last thing Wolf wanted. He hoped to forestall that eventuality, saying, "I believe I will stroll around the town while her ladyship rests."

"Walk? You will walk around Salisbury, milord? Do you think that's wise?"

One of the things Wolf missed most about his life as a humble thief-taker was walking. Usually, he and Bear had walked everywhere because they couldn't afford to do otherwise. However, he'd always found strolling through London a great way to clear his mind and gather his thoughts. While Wolf still walked on occasion, particularly if he was dressed in his thief-taker clothes, the dowager had made her feelings very clear on the Earl of Pembroke perambulating as if he were a commoner.

However, the dowager wasn't with them, and Salisbury wasn't London. Rather, it was a small, charming town that Wolf was sure was best explored on foot. He expressed this thought to the canon, who looked very dubious about such an idea.

Still, Canon Elliot needed to make one final effort to ensure the earl's safety. "Milord, I must insist on sending a man with you. This may not be London, but we still have footpads and pickpockets. A man, bedecked as you are in sartorial splendour, will be an easy mark for every ruffian in Salisbury."

Wolf had no intention of explaining his history as a thief-taker in

Whitechapel to the canon. Instead, he insisted he would take care and keep his wits about him.

The last thing he heard as he left Arundells was Canon Elliot muttering to himself, "Whatever will I tell the bishop if harm should befall his lordship?"

Salisbury was a small, charming town. Despite Canon Elliot's warnings, it appeared as peaceful and safe a place as one was likely to find in Britain. While he had no doubt there was some lawlessness, to someone who had spent years navigating the crime-ridden streets of London's East End, Salisbury seemed as innocuous as a church fête. Although Wolf stayed alert for pickpockets, as far as he could tell, the most serious hazard in Salisbury was a goose wandering into the road.

Wolf spent two pleasant hours wandering the streets of Salisbury before returning to Arundells. He hoped Tabitha had managed to rest during this time and felt concerned when he entered the drawing room and saw her sitting on a charming little sofa. To his relief, she appeared at least somewhat more refreshed.

Tabitha could easily read Wolf's worried expression. She smiled and reassured him, "I managed to sleep and only just came downstairs." Wolf glanced around the room. "I have not seen Canon Elliot yet," Tabitha said quietly.

Approaching and speaking softly, Wolf said, "Given the dinner he has planned for us, perhaps we should take advantage of his absence to leave the house quietly and at least make a quick visit to the cathedral." Tabitha nodded her agreement and, after slipping upstairs to retrieve her hat and reticule, the two sneaked out of the house. In the end, they decided to postpone their visit to the cathedral to the following day and just strolled around the Close, admiring the houses.

CHAPTER 5

L ater that day, Tabitha sat beside Wolf in the drawing room at Arundells, sipping a sherry and waiting for the other guests. Canon Elliot appeared unable to relax; he stood by the mantelpiece, shifting from foot to foot impatiently. Whenever he heard the sound of wheels on the cobblestones outside, he would rush to the window.

Finally, they could hear what sounded like a coach coming to a halt. A minute or two later, the footman entered and announced, "The Lord Bishop of Salisbury."

If they'd thought Canon Elliot was agitated before, now the man seemed to quiver visibly. He hurried towards the newcomer. "Lord Bishop, I cannot tell you what it means to have you grace my humble abode this evening."

The bishop was a man of middle years, medium height, with a spare frame. He had a long, intelligent-looking face, a high forehead, and an aquiline nose. His thinning hair was silvery-grey and worn quite long at the back in the clerical style. He possessed a neatly trimmed full beard and a moustache that was greying at the edges. Clear, piercing blue eyes observed Canon Elliot with what, at least in Tabitha's view, appeared to be wry humour.

"Canon Elliot. Thank you for organising this dinner. Apologies if I am late; I had a meeting outside of Salisbury," the bishop explained.

At this moment, Wolf and Tabitha approached. The canon, puffed up with pride at being their host, said, "My lord, let me introduce you to the Earl and Countess of Pembroke."

Bishop Wordsworth extended his hand, gripping Wolf's with a steady, deliberate hold. Bishop Wordsworth was aware of his authority. As a bishop, he held a seat in the House of Lords and was the Earl of Pembroke's equal in his own way. His glance towards Wolf suggested he recognised this parallel in their statuses, but he was not one to trumpet it. Wolf instantly warmed to the man.

Everyone sat and exchanged pleasantries as they waited for Mr Leland to arrive. A few minutes later, the footman re-entered the room and announced, "Mr Jacob Leland."

A man much younger than Tabitha had anticipated bustled into the room. There was something quite dishevelled about him. His hair was windswept, and his clothes, although clean and pressed, showed signs of wear in spots. His hazel eyes sparkled with excitement, and his mannerisms and speech exuded a rather frenetic energy.

Everyone rose. Mr Leland hurriedly approached them, nearly tripping on the carpet in his eagerness, exclaiming, "My Lord Bishop! Canon Elliot! And you must be Lord and Lady Pembroke. An honour indeed, a singular honour."

"We are pleased to meet you, Mr. Leland," Tabitha said, smiling at his unguarded enthusiasm.

The footman poured the latest arrival a glass of sherry, and the group retook their seats.

Leland clasped his hands together and continued with the same enthusiastic energy. "Your discovery in Pembrokeshire! Extraordinary. Positively extraordinary. You cannot imagine how it has set the antiquarian world in motion. I have had three letters from colleagues in as many days, each with a theory more ingenious than the last."

Canon Elliot cleared his throat. "Mr. Leland," he said, "we shall reserve scholarly disputation for the table."

"Of course, Canon, of course. Forgive me. But you must understand, the implications are…"

The bishop raised a placatory hand. "We shall hear all in good time. For now, let us enjoy this excellent sherry."

As much as Wolf appreciated the efforts to manage Leland's exuberance, he felt he needed to clarify something. "I do not believe I deserve much credit for the discovery. The original impetus to search for a buried version of the Magna Carta belongs to James Truegood, a young antiquarian taken from us too early. A local Pembroke antiquarian, Mr Jeremiah Goodge continued his work. All that I did was to provide the funding."

"No, no, your lordship," Leland insisted. "Please do not belittle your significant contribution. If you had not believed in Mr Truegood's vision and then ensured that its execution could take place, we would not now have this momentous discovery. Having an idea is one thing, but the spoils go to he who executes it."

Wolf wanted to continue arguing but understood it was probably pointless; if nothing else, an antiquarian like Jacob Leland probably saw a benefit in fawning over a potential benefactor of his future work.

Dinner was announced, and Canon Elliot led the bishop into the dining room as if escorting a king to his throne. The table gleamed with candlelight, which caught the gilt on every plate and highlighted the copious amounts of highly polished silver. Every piece of glass sparkled, every napkin was folded into elaborate fans, and swan-necked ewers of flowers crowded the centre of the table.

Tabitha, who had dined in many noble houses, could not help but admire the effort, although she thought it rather heavy-handed. One might have believed the Queen was visiting. Their host appeared determined to impress.

Wordsworth sat at the head of the table, with the canon to his right. Wolf was seated at the opposite end, with Tabitha on one side of him and Mr Leland, who appeared unable to stop fidgeting, on the other.

The first course was a delicate consommé, poured from a silver tureen. The bishop murmured a blessing, and the company bowed their heads. No sooner were the spoons raised than Leland leaned forward, eyes shining.

"Lord and Lady Pembroke, you must allow me to say again how

thrilling it is to have you here. Your discovery overturns half a century of settled opinion."

Once again, Wolf wanted to remind everyone that it wasn't his discovery. However, he was pre-empted.

Canon Elliot set down his spoon with a deliberate click. "Not overturns, Mr. Leland. Confirms. The Pembrokeshire charter is a vindication of what the Church has always maintained: that it was through clerical custody that these documents endured. Elias of Dereham, himself a Salisbury man, bore one from Runnymede. It is no accident that our Chapter House possesses the finest copy. The Pembrokeshire find merely enlarges the evidence."

"Enlarges, yes!" Leland cried, delighted. "That is precisely the point. If one is forgotten in Pembrokeshire, who shall say what Old Sarum may conceal? I have long been fascinated by the area around Salisbury and the history associated with its ancient inhabitants, but this discovery opens up a new, even richer, vein of possibilities. I intend to visit the site tomorrow to begin sketching my thoughts on the subject. Drafts, variants, and confirmation; why, the hill is riddled with history. Imagine a charter with clauses more daring than the canonical text. A demand for wider consent in taxation, perhaps, or stronger common rights. What if the first thoughts of the barons were bolder than the final compromise?"

Elliot stiffened. "To claim that the Church's sacred holdings are merely drafts is to encourage chaos."

Mr Leland enthused, "Yet drafts are the footprints by which we trace the road. The footprints matter, Canon. They show us how men thought before they agreed to what could be kept. If a variant clause survived at Sarum..."

Canon Elliot's voice cut across him sternly. "If, if. Speculation is not history. It is peril. You would have the public believe that the liberties of England lie not in the solemn charter kept in our Chapter House, but in some tattered scrap buried in the earth, contradicting the whole. Sir, if I had anticipated the heresy you speak, I would never have encouraged you to come to speak to our gathering. In fact, your words confirm my worst fears about this Pembrokeshire find."

Bishop Wordsworth cleared his throat, his tone conciliatory. "Surely, we may allow Mr Leland his enthusiasm without mistaking it for assertion. Let us not quarrel over phantoms."

However, Mr Leland was not to be restrained. "Phantoms today, discoveries tomorrow! The Pembrokeshire charter was a phantom until Lord Pembroke facilitated its discovery. Why not Sarum? Why not here, in the very place where bishop and baron once contended side by side?"

"Because," Canon Elliot said coldly, his long fingers tightening on his glass, "Old Sarum is a ruin, abandoned by God and man. It is a lesson in what comes of discord. To rummage among its stones for scandalous drafts is to slander the Chapter that preserved the true text."

Tabitha empathised with the younger historian and couldn't help but step in, saying softly, "Surely, Canon, to seek is not to slander. If something were found, it would only expand the story. The Church and the Salisbury Chapter would still be its guardian."

Canon Elliot looked at her, a flicker of something like pity softening his severity. "While your intention is generosity itself, milady, your words threaten to fan the flame of heretical beliefs. The charter in our care is the law. I will not see it diminished by idle talk of variants."

"Idle talk today," Leland said, "but proof tomorrow. I go to Old Sarum at dawn. I have been in touch with an excavation foreman at Stonehenge. He'd worked under an antiquary a decade ago at Old Sarum, helping clear ditches or expose foundations of the cathedral ruins. He tells me the ground will yield marvels if one knows how to look. His words leave me to believe that both sites may yet yield even more."

The bishop set down his knife with quiet emphasis. "Mr Leland, I would hope you know better than to trust the ramblings of a workman who is likely merely looking for coin. However, if you persist in your research, I would caution appropriate restraint and respect for what has gone before. Let us not give the newspapers cause to imagine scandal where there is none."

Leland flushed, half-abashed, half-exhilarated. "Of course, Lord Bishop. I meant no offence. Only to say that the past is not done speaking."

For his part, Canon Elliot looked less than thrilled as his bishop seemed to condone, at least somewhat, Leland's investigation. His eyes narrowed. "Some voices are better left unheard." Just as Tabitha and Wolf hoped the debate was over, the canon added, "And talk of that pagan temple, Stonehenge, in the same breath as the holy relics the Church guards, is the greatest heresy of all!"

The next course was served: salmon in aspic, and the moment seemed to pass. The conversation drifted to less contentious topics. However, by the time a magnificent side of roast beef was served, they had again returned to the charters. The subject appeared to exert a magnetic pull on Mr Leland that he couldn't resist, despite the seemingly undeniable ire of their host and the cautionary words of the bishop.

Leland sparkled and stumbled by turns, too captivated by the possibilities to notice the danger in his words, even as Canon Elliot grew visibly more irritated. Bishop Wordsworth tried to soothe the waters, but Tabitha, watching, saw in Elliot's stiff posture and Leland's reckless fire the outline of a quarrel that would not be easily forgotten. It did not bode well for the historian's talk the following evening.

When they eventually rose from the table and moved to the drawing room for coffee, the air of civility had been somewhat restored, but beneath it lurked something that caused a sense of unease that Tabitha could not shake. The Pembrokeshire charter, the shadow of Old Sarum, and the talk of hidden clauses seemed to her like tinder piled too close to the flame. She only hoped that she and Wolf would not be present when it finally ignited.

CHAPTER 6

T he following morning, Wolf could tell how drained Tabitha was, even after a night's sleep.

"You look pale, my love," he said softly, stroking her face.

"I did not sleep well," she confessed. "As much as I wish to tour the cathedral, would you mind if we postpone it to later?"

"Mind? I insist. In fact, I do not want you to leave this bed. I will have Ginny bring up tea and toast, and I want you to rest all morning."

Wolf spent his morning reading in the canon's library and managed to avoid the man himself. Tabitha had her midday meal in her room, but afterwards she decided it would be best to dress and make an effort to do something with her day. She wanted to attend the lecture that evening and didn't believe a brief stroll around the cathedral would prevent her from doing so.

Although Wolf wasn't convinced that such a walk wouldn't drain all of her energy, he knew well enough that Tabitha needed to make the final choice. After one last attempt to persuade her to stay with her feet up for the afternoon, he accepted her decision, and they set off across the Close to visit Salisbury Cathedral.

As they left Arundells, Tabitha looked across the wide green towards the cathedral. It was an impressive piece of architecture, not least its spire, which was the tallest in England.

Wolf tilted his head back to admire the height of the spire. "You could see that from miles away."

Tabitha nodded. "While there are equally impressive buildings in London, the cathedral dominates the entire landscape in a town such as Salisbury."

They crossed the green at what Wolf ensured was a leisurely pace for Tabitha. Up close, the details of decorations carved into the façade of the cathedral became clear: saints and bishops lined the west front, their faces weathered but still recognisable.

Tabitha paused to look more closely at the pointed arches and the tracery above the central doorway. "Thirteenth-century hands created all this," she said. "Imagine the skill and patience required." Wolf's eyes swept over the façade as he agreed.

Passing through a side entrance, they entered the cathedral's cloisters. The covered walkway enclosed a square of grass, bordered by stone arches open to the garden. It was easy to imagine generations of monks enjoying the shadows of the cloistered walk as they meditated, studied, and prayed. Tabitha slowed down, gently running her hand along the cool, ancient stone. She looked out over the grass, where a single tree rose at the centre. It was a peaceful place, conducive to contemplation and prayer.

Wolf spoke softly, echoing her thoughts. "This is where a man of God might quiet his mind."

Tabitha smiled faintly. "There must have been many prayers sent to the heavens from within this cloister."

They wandered along the length of the arcade, pausing at intervals to look out. The tranquillity of the garden silenced their conversation, leaving them content to contemplate the place's history.

Finally, they reached the doorway leading into the central part of the cathedral. The transition from the cloisters to the cathedral proper was striking. They stepped into a vast space where pointed arches drew the eye upwards, and the slender columns appeared almost too fragile to support the weight above. Light streamed through tall windows, cast across the stone floor, and illuminated the ribbed vaulting overhead.

Tabitha exhaled softly. "It is humbling, is it not?"

Wolf chuckled. "I believe that was the point; to leave a congregant in awe of the majesty and might of the Church." Despite his words, Wolf couldn't help but feel a similar sensation. He stood still, his gaze tracing the line from the floor to the vaulted ceiling, then to the spire's base far above.

They strolled up along the nave, their footsteps echoing on the ancient stone floor. Up ahead, near the choir screen, they noticed a figure kneeling in the pews. Since it was a house of worship, the sight was not particularly surprising. Moving as quietly as possible, Tabitha and Wolf continued their walk.

When they reached the figure, they were surprised to see it was the bishop himself, robed in plain black rather than ceremonial dress, with his head bowed in prayer before the altar. His hands were clasped, and he seemed unaware of everything around him.

Tabitha lowered her voice. "We should not disturb him."

Wolf inclined his head in agreement. Together, they stopped, letting the majesty of the great cathedral envelop them.

At that moment, the bishop crossed himself and stood. They must have made more noise than they realised, because he turned around and caught sight of Tabitha and Wolf standing watching him.

"Apologies, my lord. We did not mean to disturb your prayer," Wolf said.

"Not at all, Lord Pembroke. My prayers have been sent upwards." Bishop Wordsworth approached them and said, "I was praying for a dearly departed soul, taken from this world too soon." The man paused, then lowered his voice. "Actually, might I request a private audience with you?" He glanced around him. "I would prefer not to speak of this matter in public."

Although no one appeared to be nearby, it was clear that the cathedral's design meant any conversation would probably be echoed throughout the nave. Wolf nodded in agreement, and the bishop led them back to the cloisters.

"If you do not mind, I believe it would be best if we walked across the Close to the Bishop's Palace and spoke there," the bishop explained. Wolf would have preferred to save Tabitha the walk, however short it was. A quick look at her face assured him she would not be left out.

A few minutes later, they approached the opposite side of the Close from Arundells, heading to the Bishop's Palace. They entered through wrought-iron gates onto a wide gravel driveway. The interior of the house was as elegant and dignified as its exterior. Oak panels lined the walls, while portraits of solemn-faced past bishops gazed down at the visitors. The bishop led them into his study and firmly closed the heavy oak door behind them.

Once they were all seated, Bishop Wordsworth shook his head sadly. "It is with great sorrow that I have to inform you that Mr Leland is dead. The Wiltshire Constabulary visited me earlier today." Whatever Tabitha and Wolf had expected to hear, this wasn't it. They sat in shock, absorbing the news.

The bishop continued, "Apparently, a shepherd boy found the body at dawn. He thought it was a bundle of cast-off cloth until he came nearer. According to the police inspector who visited me, it seems as if the cause of death was a stabbing, followed by a fall to the rocks below. He said that the body lay at the foot of the rampart, twisted where it had landed."

Wolf was the first to speak. "So, he was murdered!"

"The knife wound can only indicate foul play," the bishop said, rubbing his eyes wearily. "I cannot believe we were breaking bread with the young man only hours ago. What a terrible loss of life. Even if his enthusiasm sometimes got the better of him, Mr Leland was a bright and energetic young man."

Tabitha was curious and asked, "What made the police visit you?"

"They found a letter of introduction to me in the young man's jacket pocket," the bishop explained. "It appeared he had not known he would be meeting me last night and had made the request of a mutual ecclesiastical acquaintance in Oxford. When they described the body, I confirmed that it must be Mr Leland. They then asked me if I knew why he was visiting Salisbury. I told them about the talk tonight and the dinner we had last night."

As he uttered these words, a realisation struck the bishop. "I must alert Canon Elliot; tonight's talk must be cancelled." Then, another, more despairing thought appeared to cross his mind. "Heavens! What if this death entangles the Chapter in scandal?"

"Why would it?" Tabitha asked.

"Given Mr Leland's rather controversial theories on the charters and Old Sarum, I could imagine how a line might be drawn to someone in clerical circles who might want to suppress such heresy."

Wolf wasn't entirely sure what the bishop was suggesting. "My lord, are you worried that the police might be suspicious of Canon Elliot?"

The notion that such an academic disagreement about a subject as dry, at least to Wolf, as the provenance of historical documents, could lead to a suspicion of murder seemed absurd. Though even as he thought this, Wolf acknowledged that one thing he'd learned from all their investigations was that one man's absurdity could easily be another's motive.

Bishop Wordsworth nodded forlornly. "Certainly, Canon Elliot, or perhaps another of my brethren who knew of Leland's views and anticipated the talk he was to give tonight." He smiled faintly. "You must understand that I wish justice to be done and the murderer to be found and punished. However, I worry about the reputational damage that might be done in the meantime, even to the innocent."

Wolf turned his head slightly and caught the meaningful look Tabitha was giving him. He sighed. "Bishop Wordsworth, my wife and I have some experience in such investigations. Would it help soothe your concerns if we offered our assistance to the Wiltshire Constabulary and made sure that this is handled with appropriate sensitivity?"

The bishop's relief at this offer was palpable. "Lord Pembroke, that would be an enormous weight off my mind. I see you are an educated man of sense and compassion, and I would rest assured that the investigation is being conducted with an eye to protecting the Church's reputation."

These words gave Wolf pause; he had no intention of helping to cover up a crime to manage the Church's reputation, nor did he want to give the impression that he would. He debated briefly whether to voice this concern, then chose to wait and learn more about the crime.

However, by this time, it was early afternoon, and Wolf knew that if he was to take on this investigation, it was best to start as soon as possible. "I believe that the first step is for you and me to speak to the local police superintendent and make him aware of my involvement," Wolf said.

Even as he spoke these words, Wolf could feel Tabitha's hackles rise; he had very clearly spoken in the singular and excluded her. He knew they'd be having a difficult conversation as soon as they were alone.

Bishop Wordsworth replied, "I will summon the superintendent here now. It is a journey of only a few minutes."

Over the years, Wolf had learned a thing or two about forcing his involvement in local police matters. "My lord, I believe it would be best if we made our way to the police station. Since the superintendent has full jurisdiction over the matter and is not obliged to engage with me, it is prudent to extend such a courtesy, rather than summoning him across town."

"Superintendent Wallis may not be obliged to work with you, but a request from Salisbury's bishop carries considerable moral and social, if not legal, weight. The superintendent will understand the importance, including for his career prospects, of not antagonising the Chapter and its leaders." This was spoken with a somewhat imperious air. Then, the bishop smiled and continued in a softer voice, "However, your point is well made. One catches more flies with honey than vinegar, after all."

"Excellent. Will you excuse me, my lord, while I walk my wife across the close and back to Arundells?" Wolf could sense Tabitha seething at his words, but he didn't care. He was happy to take advantage of her reluctance to argue with him before the bishop.

The walk across the Close was brief and tense. "I will not be excluded, Wolf," Tabitha hissed.

Wolf kept his voice controlled but firm. "I am not excluding you. I am merely concerned that you conserve your energy. Speaking to the superintendent is something I am perfectly capable of doing alone. There is no need for you to exhaust yourself unnecessarily."

Deep down, Tabitha knew Wolf was right. There was no denying she lacked her normal stamina, and pretending otherwise was foolish. If she insisted on being involved in every conversation and expedition, she might not only exhaust herself but, more importantly, endanger her unborn child. Yet, she could not yield fully. Tabitha felt her status as Wolf's equal partner in their investigations was too hard-earned, and giving even an inch now could set a precedent that everything would change once she became a mother.

Without Tabitha needing to say a word, Wolf understood all. He also knew that he couldn't allow his beloved wife to do anything that might put herself or the baby she was carrying at risk. Somehow, he had to find a way to assuage both of their concerns.

"I am going to telephone Bear and ask him to join us." Tabitha noticed his use of us rather than me, but she wasn't mollified. However, she had one thought that needed to be expressed before arriving at Arundells. "Despite the bishop wishing otherwise, we must consider the possibility that Canon Elliot is our killer."

"Certainly," Wolf acknowledged, uncertain where Tabitha was heading with this line of thought.

"Given that, should we truly continue to remain under his roof?"

It was a good question that Wolf hadn't considered until then. "In many ways, it gives us a perfect opportunity to investigate the man far more surreptitiously than if we announce our suspicions by moving out," he pointed out. "Though you are correct; it also inhibits us in other ways."

After further consideration, he suggested, "I think we should remain as the canon's guests for now. If nothing else, it will keep him off his guard about being considered a suspect. However, Bear should stay elsewhere, perhaps at an inn in town, and we can use his lodgings as our main base for the investigation." Then, Wolf added, "If the man is the murderer, and becomes aware of our suspicions, then staying may become dangerous. If at any point I believe that is the case, we will leave immediately."

This made sense, and the couple walked in tense silence back to Arundells.

CHAPTER 7

S alisbury Police Station was a two-storey brick building, plain yet sturdy. It had barred windows on the ground floor and a small yard at the rear for the lock-up. Inside, the front desk was staffed by a constable in a tunic and helmet, who had a ledger in front of him for recording visitors.

The constable looked up in surprise as the two distinguished visitors entered the station. Like most people in Salisbury, he recognised the bishop by sight, and the well-dressed man with him was clearly a toff of some kind.

Bishop Wordsworth took the lead in the conversation. "Please inform Superintendent Wallis that the Bishop of Salisbury and the Earl of Pembroke wish to meet with him."

The constable's eyes widened, but he said nothing, merely nodded and hurried away. A few minutes later, he returned and signalled for them to follow him. The police constable led them upstairs to a door marked "Superintendent Wallis". He gave one quick knock and then opened it.

The door swung open into a utilitarian room, furnished with a large oak desk and a few chairs for visitors. One wall was lined with shelves holding ledgers and reports; another displayed a map of the Salisbury Division with pins marking patrol beats.

Sitting behind the desk was a man of perhaps forty, heavyset in build. His thinning hair was greying at the temples, and worry lines furrowed his brow. He wore a dark tunic with silver buttons and a high collar, displaying rank insignia.

Superintendent Wallis rose and greeted his visitors before dismissing the constable. "My Lord Bishop and Lord Pembroke, you do me a great honour. Please, sit. May I assume this visit relates to the recent serious occurrence at Old Sarum?"

The bishop quickly made his supplication. While he spoke, the superintendent's face revealed no hint of his thoughts or reaction to such an unconventional request.

When the bishop had finished speaking, Superintendent Wallis turned to Wolf. "Lord Pembroke, I can assure you that the Wiltshire Constabulary is more than capable of managing this situation. While it might be a small, rural force compared to the Met, Salisbury is one of its largest divisions and has ample manpower and skills to handle this investigation."

Wolf fought back a sigh; he wasn't surprised by the direction of the conversation. He decided to allow the bishop to take the lead in trying to persuade the superintendent; he didn't wish to push his assistance where it was unwelcome.

It appeared Bishop Wordsworth was not to be undeterred. "A man lies dead beneath the ramparts of Old Sarum. I cannot change that sad fact, but I will not tolerate whispers of murder that could in any way implicate the Church. The Salisbury Chapter must remain free of scandal."

Superintendent Wallis looked as if he was also working to suppress a sigh as he answered tersely, "Bishop Wordsworth, I appreciate fully the need not to drag the Chapter into a murder inquiry unless absolutely necessary." He paused. "However, I feel confident that my men and I are capable of doing so without amateur assistance or oversight from outside the department."

As much as Wolf didn't want to be drawn into this argument, he felt compelled to speak. "Superintendent, while I very much understand your hesitance to accept my assistance, I feel I must tell you that my wife and I have been instrumental in solving multiple murder inquiries, including one in Pembrokeshire recently. We have worked closely with the

Metropolitan Police on occasion to bring murderers to justice in London."

Wolf felt a little guilty about making this last statement; he wasn't sure if working with Bruiser informally truly counted as working with the Metropolitan Police. Nevertheless, he knew this would help strengthen their credentials, and the number of cases he and Tabitha had solved was no lie.

His words seemed to give the superintendent pause for thought. He remained silent, pursing his lips as he thought over what Wolf had said.

Finally, Superintendent Wallis appeared to reach a decision. "Of course, if Lord Pembroke's assistance is welcomed by the Met, then the Wiltshire Constabulary would be willing to accept it as well."

While it was impossible to ignore how grudgingly this was said, Wolf chose to accept the offer as graciously as he could. Turning to the bishop, he said, "My Lord Bishop, I believe you can safely leave this matter with the superintendent and me now."

Bishop Wordsworth appeared to understand this hint as Wolf intended. He expressed his thanks and rose to leave.

When the door closed behind the bishop, the superintendent raised his eyebrows slightly, surprised that Wolf hadn't also left. "We will keep you informed of our progress, milord," he said, in what he hoped was a tone of finality.

Wolf could see where this was heading; Superintendent Wallis intended to uphold his agreement in the loosest possible sense. If he didn't say or do something now, Wolf would only get occasional, vague updates that might be no more than the bishop himself could request. While he might not have wanted to get dragged into this investigation, now that he had been, Wolf intended to be involved to the fullest extent.

Shifting his posture and tone just enough to emulate his grandfather, the late earl, Wolf replied, "That will be insufficient, superintendent." The shock on the other man's face indicated how easily he had expected to run roughshod over the earl. Taking advantage of this, Wolf pressed harder. "I intend to be involved in this investigation every step of the way. My investigative prowess is known and acknowledged by the Home Secretary, and if I have to appeal to Whitehall to be fully included, I will."

Wolf hated being that man. He despised flaunting his title, wealth, and connections in front of those less fortunate, but over the past year and a half, he had learned how effective it could be. He consoled himself with the knowledge that he never did so for his own benefit. Still, sometimes it was a necessary tool during an investigation. He momentarily doubted whether this was truly one of those times, especially since he had been dragged into it so unwillingly. Nonetheless, having agreed to help the bishop, Wolf felt he had little choice but to make full use of his ability to wield power and connections.

It seemed his words achieved their goal; the superintendent's face took on a look of weary resignation as he said, "That will not be necessary, Lord Pembroke. We will involve you in any way you wish."

"Excellent. Then let us begin with you telling me everything you have learned so far about our victim and his murder."

Twenty minutes later, Wolf left the Salisbury Police Station and strolled back to the Close. While he and the bishop had made the journey there in the bishop's carriage, Wolf was happy for the walk on the return trip. He always found walking conducive to reflection and wanted to think through what he had learned at the police station.

From their conversation with the bishop earlier that day, the police already knew as much about the victim as Wolf did. He'd added his observations about the young man, such as they were. The superintendent asked about their dinner the night before, and Wolf gave an honest, if simple, account of the evening. Bishop Wordsworth seemed to have mentioned the debate between Canon Elliot and Mr Leland. Still, he appeared to have done his best to portray it as nothing more than a lively exchange between fellow antiquarians. Certainly, nothing had been said that aroused any suspicion towards the canon.

Wolf hadn't contradicted the bishop's version to Superintendent Wallis, but now, he wondered if he should have mentioned something about the seemingly excessive passion the conversation evoked in the canon. Of course, Bishop Wordsworth had asked him to involve himself in the investigation to ensure the Church wasn't touched by scandal. While Wolf would not commit himself to that promise, he'd held back from saying more of the canon's behaviour, both out of a sense of obligation to the bishop and to avoid fanning the flames unnecessarily.

It appeared the police surgeon wouldn't provide his full report until the following day. Still, his initial observations aligned with what the bishop had explained: Leland had been stabbed, followed by a fall from the ruins onto the rocks below. They were unsure which of the two had actually killed the man.

There were two new details. The first was a hasty supposition by the police surgeon based on his first, cursory view of the body. The stabbing wound was clean and deep, and slightly curved and likely not made with a blade of any common knife. The second detail was the time of death. All signs pointed to Jacob Leland having died either late the night before or, at the latest, in the early hours of the morning. Wolf recalled the man mentioning a visit to Old Sarum the morning after the dinner, but why was he there in the middle of the night?

The superintendent had described how the body had been found with an uneven circle scrawled on the chalk around it. He described the scrawl as a broad ring scratched by a blunt tool, uneven in width and broken where the soil crumbled away. He suggested that whoever had drawn it lacked either patience or knowledge: the lines wavered, sometimes overlapping, sometimes spreading wide, so that it looked less like a sacred figure than a careless sketch.

Within the ring lay bones, either sheep or goat by their size, scattered with a hint of order. Some were arranged in pairs, as if to resemble limbs; others were laid end to end to form rough spokes across the circle. The superintendent knew little about such things, but even to his eye, the effect was theatrical rather than solemn, the work of a hand eager to suggest ritual, but unaware of its symbols. But why? The only conclusion Wolf could reach was that the killer wanted more than Leland's death. In fact, was the actual victim significant, or was the purpose simply to have a corpse whose death pointed the finger at someone or something?

The superintendent had given Wolf a drawing made by one of the police constables of the circle and symbols. Wolf carried it in his pocket, unsure whom to ask about it. Under other circumstances, the most obvious person would be Canon Elliot. However, could they trust his answer? This reminded Wolf that they needed to inform the canon that they would be taking advantage of his hospitality for a few more days, at least. Wolf wasn't sure how full a reason to give. Finally, he decided to say nothing more than that the bishop had asked him to keep an eye on the investigation.

The final detail the superintendent had shared was that an unusual odour lingered on the body. While they had struggled to identify it initially, the police surgeon had suggested that it might be juniper smoke. Wolf had filed that detail away.

CHAPTER 8

As much as she had resisted when Wolf insisted on visiting the police station without her, once Tabitha returned to Arundells, she found she barely had the energy to climb the stairs to her bedchamber. All she had done was walk across the Close to the cathedral, take a brief and leisurely stroll through the cloisters, visit the bishop's Palace and then amble back across the Close. How could she be so drained after so little exertion? Dr Pauls had warned her she might not have her usual stamina during the first part of the pregnancy, but she'd hoped that would be over by now.

The temperature suddenly dropped that afternoon, leaving no doubt that autumn had arrived. A fire blazed in the drawing room's hearth as Tabitha sat with a book on her lap. She had been sitting there for over thirty minutes, yet she hadn't even read a page; her thoughts were too consumed by the latest investigation they seemed to have become involved in. Although she initially agreed with Wolf's reasoning for why they should remain guests of one of their suspects, she now second-guessed that decision; was there more to lose than gain in such a plan?

Certainly, removing themselves from under Canon Elliot's roof would immediately raise his suspicions that they viewed him as a suspect. There was little doubt that it was better to keep the man unaware of their thoughts on the matter and, potentially, let down his guard. By remaining at Arundells, they could monitor conversations and perhaps even look through the canon's study if necessary.

All these points supported their current strategy. However, remaining also complicated the investigation, making discussions about it between her and Wolf difficult. Was there a polite way to decline the canon's hospitality without arousing suspicion?

Tabitha felt her eyelids growing heavy and must have dozed off. The next thing she heard was the sound of a door opening and closing as Canon Elliot entered the room. The armchair Tabitha was sitting in faced the fireplace, so the canon hadn't noticed Tabitha sitting there until he was already in the room and staring into the fire.

The canon was alerted to Tabitha's presence as she startled awake, causing the book to drop to the floor. "Lady Pembroke, please excuse me. I had no idea you were in here."

"No excuses needed, Canon Elliot. I must have fallen asleep."

Tabitha had no desire to share the reason for her exhaustion with the canon. Fortunately, his ingrained prejudice provided the man all the explanation he required. "The fairer sex must rest where they can and leave the burden of labour to their husbands while they indulge in nothing more than the most delicate of activities."

As he made this pronouncement, the canon nodded and smiled at his own sagacity. He seemed unaware that a life of purely delicate pursuits was not a reality for most of the women in Britain who worked in factories and fields, while also bearing all the responsibility for cooking, cleaning, and raising children.

Just as she was dozing off, it had occurred to Tabitha that the canon might not yet know about Mr Leland's death. This question was now put to rest as he said, "I just came from a meeting with the bishop. I trust his lordship has laid this sad matter properly before the constabulary?"

What did Canon Elliot consider a proper conversation? Tabitha wondered.

"Lord Pembroke has not yet returned. However, I believe he is meeting with the police superintendent, at the bishop's behest." Tabitha observed the canon's face. What did he make of his bishop making such a request?

Elliot gave a short, almost impatient nod. "Excellent news. Someone must ensure that the authorities are not swayed by village gossip. The moment a body lies at Old Sarum, the common folk prattle about Druids and sacrifices, as if we had regressed to the dark ages. That the victim is someone in any way associated with the Church will only add fuel to the fire."

It seemed that Canon Elliot knew all the particulars of the murder. Was that because he had been told them by the bishop, or because he was the killer? While it seemed implausible that the murderer would claim to be grateful for Wolf's oversight of the investigation, Tabitha could think of multiple reasons for such a sentiment. It seemed unlikely that the canon was aware of all the investigations Tabitha and Wolf had helped solve, and perhaps he imagined a dilettante aristocrat muddying the waters for the police. Beyond that, this would not be the first time that they had encountered someone who feigned horror at a murder to cloak their own guilt.

Elliot's eyes narrowed, and he continued. "And to leave bones and scratchings around the body is nothing more than a childish trick. Bones from a butcher's midden, chalk lines scratched like a schoolboy's game. If the constables have any sense, they will dismiss it as a parody."

He spoke with such certainty that Tabitha frowned. "You sound very sure of the arrangement." Even as she said this, she suppressed a shudder, which was her instinctive reaction to this disturbing detail of the murder.

"I have been told," Elliot said quickly. "The bishop himself described it. The man lay with one arm outstretched, as if in mock supplication. I find the details grotesque."

Tabitha studied him. The bishop had not spoken so plainly to Wolf and her earlier. How much had Elliot truly seen? Or was it merely the bishop's reticence about speaking of such things in front of a woman?

Canon Elliot paced to the window and stood looking out on the Close. "The greater danger," he went on, "is not the deed itself but the suspicion it throws upon us. Mr. Leland and I disagreed, yes, publicly, even heatedly. Now he is dead, and the world will say, 'See how the Church silenced him.' It is intolerable."

A question had been nagging at Tabitha since the previous evening's dinner. Now, she couldn't help but ask, "Canon Elliot, forgive me if I speak plainly, but why extend the invitation at all, if you found Mr.

Leland's views so offensive? As far as I understand it, you invited Mr Leland to Salisbury, yet seemed surprised by the details of his planned talk. Were you not aware of his beliefs on the topic?"

Elliot stiffened at the question. He paused for so long that Tabitha thought he might refuse to answer. Finally, he said, "Lady Pembroke, when I issued the invitation, I knew Mr Leland by reputation only. His earlier writings spoke of cathedrals and charters with proper reverence, and I took him to be a man who would confirm, not confound, the truth. I did not imagine he would allow his fancy to run riot once he reached Salisbury. Indeed, his first letter to me was all compliments: praise for our Magna Carta, praise for the spire, praise for my own poor efforts to preserve Sarum's memory. I was deceived, yes; flattered, perhaps, into believing he and I were of one mind. Only when he sat at my table did I hear the extent of his heresies. By then, alas, the mischief was done, and it was my name on the invitation."

Tabitha wondered if the man realised that he had just provided a perfect motive for the murder; once Leland gave the planned talk, his "heresies", such as they were, would be inextricably linked to the man who issued the invitation to give the talk.

Letting this pass for now, Tabitha returned to Canon Elliot's earlier statement. "Your concern at his death seems focused on how it will reflect on the Church. Yet surely, the greatest sorrow is that a young man has been taken before his time." Her words were provocative, but the occasion to ask them had arisen so organically that Tabitha felt she couldn't let it pass. She also suspected that the canon's obvious contempt for women might cause him not to take her challenge seriously and let his guard down.

"I show the sorrow proper to a fool's end," Elliot retorted, then softened his tone, catching himself. "Forgive me, Lady Pembroke. My heart is for the cathedral. It is there my grief lies at the stain cast upon her honour by even the appearance of association with such a man. However, of course, you are correct; one must always regret the loss of life. Any life." Tabitha wasn't sure she considered this an appropriately compassionate and loving response from a man of God.

Tabitha felt she had heard enough for the time being. She wanted to escape the self-righteous, pompous man before her. Perhaps more harshly than she intended, she said, "You are right about one thing, Canon. Appearances can be important. Do you not worry how such a lack of feeling towards Jacob Leland, a man who was a guest in your house mere hours before his death, might appear?"

For a heartbeat, Elliot looked struck, as though she had touched a nerve. Then his expression hardened, and he inclined his head with stiff courtesy.

"You are very plain spoken, Lady Pembroke," he observed. "While I am not sure it becomes a woman of your rank, I cannot forbid it. But remember this: I have given my life to the cathedral. If men choose to doubt me now, let them. God sees what they do not." Tabitha thought the canon was finished speaking, but he added, "Of course, I am happy to offer you both my hospitality for as long as Lord Pembroke is needed for the investigation."

With that, Canon Elliot bowed awkwardly and withdrew, leaving Tabitha alone with the echo of his words. Had she taken her questioning too far and alerted the canon to their suspicions? He had sounded so very certain. Tabitha could not decide whether she had been speaking to an innocent man misunderstood, or to one who was so sure of his divine mission to protect the Church that he might defend it by any means possible.

CHAPTER 9

Before Wolf left the police station on Salt Lane, he asked the constable where the post office was and for the name of the best hotel in town. Now, he began walking up Castle Street towards Market Place, where the police officer had told him he would find the post office.

After a few minutes, a broad square opened before him, busier than the narrow lanes he had just left. Stalls were being packed up for the day, carts rattled across the cobbles, and apprentices hurried by with baskets under their arms. On the corner, he saw what he assumed was the red-bricked frontage of the post office. A pair of clerks in dark coats stood near the entrance, speaking with a telegraph boy who leaned his bicycle against the rail.

In the post office, Wolf sent a telegram to Bear, asking him to catch the first train to Salisbury and bring weapons. He wouldn't need to say more than that for his friend to understand what was required and why. He added that he planned to reserve a room at the Red Lion Hotel.

Wolf then left the post office and continued in the general direction the police officer had suggested. When Wolf arrived on Milford Street, he noticed an inn with a timbered frontage and a grand archway leading into its court-yard. A carriage was just inside, the driver tending to his horses while a porter hurried forward with a traveller's trunk. Wolf slowed his pace and examined the sign hanging outside the inn: The Red Lion Hotel. This was the hotel the constable had directed him to. He believed that this was also the hostelry Canon Elliot had deemed suitable for Jacob Leland. Did the police know this was where Leland was staying? Wolf wondered. Had they searched the room?

Wolf considered what he should do; he had never before entered into a partnership with the authorities on an investigation. Perhaps partnership wasn't the correct word; what he and Superintendent Wallis had agreed to could be called an uneasy alliance, at best. He wasn't at all confident that Wallis would be forthcoming with information if he didn't need to be, and, given this, what obligation did Wolf have in return?

Despite the novelty of the situation, Wolf knew enough about human nature to understand that the first indication that he and Tabitha were being anything less than forthcoming with clues would enable the superintendent to justify being equally circumspect.

As Wolf drew nearer to the inn, he decided to search the room first and determine what to share based on what he found. When he entered the inn's courtyard, his initial instinct was to sneak up to the bedrooms and break in, but he didn't know which room Leland had occupied.

If Tabitha had been with him, this would have been yet another time when she would have pointed out that he was no longer a scruffy thief-taker but was an impeccably dressed earl who could command people's attention and obedience. As it was, he pushed open the heavy oak door from the courtyard into the inn's hall, uncertain as to what to do. The hall was an oak-panelled room with a beamed ceiling and a blaze roaring in the grand fireplace that dominated the space.

A clerk looked up from behind the polished counter, straightening as Wolf approached. The man wore a smart black coat and had an air of practised discretion. A pair of porters lingered nearby, ready to carry trunks or see to horses.

Wolf removed his hat and set it lightly against his thigh. "Good day to you," he said in a voice that, while not his impersonation of his grandfather, was certainly closer to that than his usual mild-mannered tone. "I am inquiring after a gentleman staying here by the name of Jacob Leland."

The clerk consulted a large leather-bound register, running a finger down the page. "Mr. Jacob Leland, sir, yes. He arrived yesterday." While the clerk might not usually be so forthcoming about a guest, it was clear that the impeccably dressed man standing before him was a man of consequence and, therefore, to be handled with kid gloves.

Wolf had experienced enough obsequiousness in the face of his wealth and rank to recognise it immediately. Now, he faced another dilemma: how candid should he be with this clerk regarding Mr Leland's demise and his own reasons for wanting access to the room? He doubted that the murder was common knowledge yet and had no desire to be scolded by the superintendent for making it such.

Finally, Wolf decided to see if he could gain access without disclosing this information. "I am the Earl of Pembroke. I am visiting Salisbury as the guest of Canon Elliot's. Mr Leland is also here at the invitation of the canon."

Using his title and his connection to the canon ensured Wolf had the clerk's full attention now. "How might I assist you, milord?"

"I wonder, is Mr Leland available?" he asked, knowing the answer full well.

The clerk hesitated, then acknowledged, "Mr Leland went out late last night and has not returned, at least as far as I am aware. I apologise, milord."

Wolf leaned a little closer, lowering his voice. "That is very unfortunate. Perhaps you can assist me. Mr Leland's business in Salisbury concerns a matter of scholarship in which I, too, have an interest. His sudden absence is inconvenient, and there are points I must confirm without delay. I would be obliged if you allowed me to step into his chamber, simply to see whether the papers I expect are in order."

The clerk appeared uneasy. "Ordinarily, milord, we would not permit..."

Wolf set his hat on the counter and fixed the man with a steady gaze. "This is a matter of consequence to the bishop himself. You may be certain no harm will come to the gentleman's property. I give you my word."

He realised he had put the man in an impossible situation; permitting Wolf to enter a guest's room would be an extraordinary breach of etiquette. However, to refuse an earl, especially one connected with the bishop, might be an even greater offence. Wolf could see the dilemma play out on the man's face and knew the moment he reached a decision.

The clerk nodded, his usual discretion overridden by the importance of Wolf's title. "Very well. If you will follow me."

He led Wolf up a staircase, along a corridor where the floor sloped and the beams revealed their age. Stopping at a narrow door, he produced a key and opened it. The room was modest but tidy. It contained a neatly made bed, a washstand with its jug of water, and a small desk pushed against the window.

The clerk hesitated in the doorway. "Would you like me to wait, milord?" he asked, clearly hoping for a positive response that would allow him to ease his conscience a little. He was visibly disappointed when he received a blunt negative reply.

"Very well then," the clerk responded grudgingly. "I shall wait below, milord. Take all the time you require."

Wolf waited for him to leave, closed the door, and inspected the room. Since Mr Leland had only arrived the day before and had almost immediately gone to dinner at Arundells, it was no surprise that the room had hardly been disturbed. A somewhat battered Gladstone bag was on the floor by the wardrobe, and on the desk, some papers lay stacked alongside what appeared to be a worn leather diary.

After flicking through the papers, Wolf saw nothing but some rather dry-looking academic theses. He picked up the diary and turned to the last entry. It was dated 19 September, the day before. Did Leland write it before or after the dinner at Arundells? A quick look at the first few lines made it clear that it had been written after.

My upcoming lecture at the Chapter House has stirred more unease than I expected. Canon Elliot's courtesy was genuine enough, yet I cannot ignore the worried glances and comments when I spoke of the rites beneath the chalk. They whisper "heresy," but the truth will not be denied.

After reviewing the bones Edwards sent me, I am certain the fragments at Old Sarum will confirm my suspicion: the site was once more than just a stronghold. The circle of stones nearby was no coincidence of heathen superstition but a purposeful design, aligned with the solstice and sacrifice. In fact, I believe even more strongly than before that the missing evidence is not at Stonehenge but at Old Sarum itself.

There is a pattern to be uncovered, a union of Druidic rite and early Christian sign, that others would rather leave buried. I have reason to think the Church concealed this union centuries ago. If I am correct, the find would overturn their neat histories.

Tomorrow, I will walk to Old Sarum stones at first light. There is danger in this, I know. Already, I sense eyes upon me. Yet I cannot turn back. If the truth rests beneath those sarsens, I must be the one to find it.

Wolf flicked back through the other entries, but realised he needed more time to review them. Certain that he was now definitely going against the spirit of the arrangement he'd made with Superintendent Wallis, Wolf guiltily slipped the small book into his jacket pocket.

Jacob Leland had brought little with him: what was probably his best suit for the lecture, a few other clothes, and that was all. There was nothing else of interest, so Wolf slipped out of the room and returned to the front desk. There was one more thing he needed: to make a reservation for Bear.

As he continued his walk back to Arundells, he thought about his next move. The diary entry confirmed what Leland had said at dinner. If he had planned to visit Old Sarum that morning, why was he there during the night? The mention of someone called Edwards was intriguing; was this the excavation foreman from Stonehenge? Wolf assumed so. He remembered Leland mentioning a meeting with him that morning, which clearly hadn't taken place. Wolf's next step seemed to be to visit Stonehenge.

CHAPTER 10

Tabitha and Wolf spoke briefly as they changed for dinner. Even if the canon wasn't guilty of murder, it seemed Tabitha's frankness had rubbed him the wrong way. She had apologised to Wolf about possibly going too far and unnecessarily antagonising Canon Elliot. He had assured her she had done nothing wrong, although secretly he wished they'd managed to keep the canon ignorant of their judgement for as long as possible.

Unsurprisingly, dinner that evening was quite tense. The canon seemed not to have recovered his composure after Tabitha's frankness. Or was his discomfort caused by more serious reasons? It would have been a significant breach of etiquette for him not to offer them his continued hospitality. However, what if he was the killer, had he arrived at a similar realisation as Tabitha and Wolf: that it would be easier to investigate him from within his own home?

The uncomfortable silence was still preferable to the canon's verbosity and pomposity. Given this, Tabitha ate her meal and was grateful not to endure another dull lecture while she dined. They were just beginning their dessert when the footman entered the room, looking quite flustered. He approached and whispered something in the canon's ear. Whatever the news was, it seemed to unsettle Elliot almost as much as it did his manservant.

Canon Elliot wiped his mouth with his napkin, then said in a tone that suggested he wished he'd never invited them to Arundells in the first place, "Lord Pembroke, it seems you have a quite imperious visitor. She demanded entry into my drawing room and, apparently, is waiting there for you, tapping her stick in what my man describes as a threatening manner."

Tabitha and Wolf looked at each other and sighed simultaneously; this description only suited one person they knew. Whatever was the dowager doing in Salisbury?

Wolf stood and explained, "I believe the visitor may be the Dowager Countess of Pembroke."

"This is your mother?" the canon asked.

"No, she is the mother of my cousin, the late earl," Wolf said. If the canon didn't know that Wolf had married his cousin's widow, he felt no need to reveal that information.

"Would you like me to accompany you?" Tabitha asked, torn between the two equally disagreeable situations: sitting alone with the canon, or facing the dowager in whatever high dudgeon she had worked herself into.

Wolf considered that this was precisely the kind of scene that he wished to shield Tabitha from as much as possible. As uncomfortable as remaining with Canon Elliot might be, it was almost certainly the less stressful of the two choices. He indicated that she should finish her meal, and he would attend to the dowager.

As he walked from the dining room to the drawing room, Wolf tried to imagine what might have brought the dowager to Salisbury. Pausing by the door, he took a deep breath before pushing the door open. He could hear the impatient tap tap tap of her stick on the floor and sighed once more.

"Ah, Jeremy, at last," were the first words that greeted him. The dowager was seated with her lady's maid, Withers, hovering behind her. "Can you believe that footman had the temerity to suggest I wait on the doorstep like a common debt collector? Apparently, this Canon Allion, or whatever his name is, does not like to be disturbed during his dinner."

Well, that explained the high dudgeon, or at least Wolf hoped it did.

Choosing not to address the footman's behaviour, Wolf asked, "What are you doing here, Lady Pembroke?"

Now, the woman's expression grew even more sour. "It seems you are in the midst of an investigation that you wished to exclude me from?" Wolf's first thought was to wonder how she knew about Leland's death. He was spared asking such a question when the dowager continued, "If I had not been at Chesterton House when your telegram arrived for Mr Bear, I might never have known."

Wolf hesitated to ask what she was doing at his home while he and Tabitha were away, knowing it would only inflame the situation. Instead, he spoke as calmly as he could. "Lady Pembroke, the body was only found this morning, and my assistance was requested just a few hours ago."

Of course, as soon as he said this, Wolf realised the trap he had stepped into. The dowager gave him a smile of feline satisfaction. "So, you were planning to inform me and request my assistance but had simply not got round to it?"

There was only one correct, more to the point, safe answer. "That goes without saying, Lady Pembroke."

The harrumph he received in reply revealed what the dowager thought of his response. However, the wily old woman understood the position of strength she was now in. "Yes, without saying, of course, Jeremy," she murmured. "Well, it is a good thing I took matters into my own hands and made the trip here. I have not eaten dinner. However, I am weary from travel, so I will take a tray in my room. Can you send someone to show me the way?"

Before he could think better of it, Wolf blurted out, "You mean to stay here?"

"Where else would I stay, Jeremy? I believe this home belongs to some sort of cleric. It is far from ideal, but I will make the best of it. Let it not be said of Julia Chesterton that she is hard to please."

Wolf bit the inside of his lip to prevent his face from giving away his thoughts on this statement. Apart from having to ask a favour of the canon, who might be their primary suspect at present, Wolf could only imagine how the man would rub the dowager the wrong way, and even worse, how she was likely to reply to him. He wasn't sure how to progress.

Luckily, the footman re-entering the room to check on the situation resolved this problem.

While he wasn't sure what danger the footman feared a petite septuagenarian might pose for a hale and hearty young man such as Wolf, the servant's appearance was a relief. Wolf knew that the mannerly thing to do was to speak to the canon first before agreeing that the dowager would stay at Arundells. However, there was little doubt that the toadying canon would be delighted to have another aristocrat under his roof, at least to begin with. Furthermore, the idea of what the dowager might say if Wolf attempted such a move was enough to prompt him to tell the footman that the Dowager Countess of Pembroke would be staying and to show her to a guest room and make sure a tray was brought to her.

The footman's inscrutability was worthy of the finest Mayfair butler. Nothing of what he thought about this request showed on his face. Instead, he led the dowager and Withers away. It hadn't even occurred to Wolf that a room might not be available or at least ready, and he breathed a sigh of relief as this potential problem was resolved.

Once the dowager left the room, Wolf remained standing and pondered what he would say to Canon Elliot. Although the man's general sycophancy suggested he wouldn't protest the imposition, the uncomfortable atmosphere at dinner made clear that the bloom was off the rose when it came to the canon's feelings towards his guests.

Finally, deciding there was no way to make the news anything less than an imposition, and one that would only be increased once the dowager and canon met, Wolf shrugged and returned to the dining room.

It was clear from the strained look on Tabitha's face that the atmosphere hadn't improved while he was out of the room.

Addressing Tabitha first, Wolf said, "As you might have expected, the visitor is indeed Lady Pembroke."

Turning to Canon Elliot, Wolf attempted to modulate his tone to be as apologetic as possible. "It seems that the dowager countess decided she wished to hear the planned talk after all."

Of course, given the late hour of her arrival, this didn't quite make sense, but the canon didn't question it. Instead, as expected, or at least hoped for, the canon's ingrained servility kicked in automatically. "Of course, her ladyship is more than welcome to a pillow in my humble abode on which to lay her head."

"Thank you, canon. In anticipation of your great generosity and hospitality, I asked your footman to show her to a bedchamber. Lady Pembroke is an elderly woman, and the journey greatly fatigued her." Wolf saw Tabitha raise her eyebrows at this description of the dowager as a fragile creature.

Fortunately, the canon, with his reflexive disdain towards women, was all too willing to believe that a two-hour train journey would overwhelm any woman, especially an elderly one.

It seemed that Canon Elliot was no more desirous of extending their evening together than Tabitha and Wolf were. As soon as dessert was finished, he excused himself and hurried out of the room.

"Perhaps we should retire to our room," Tabitha suggested. Her meaning was clear: where we will have more privacy to talk.

Once they were in their bedchamber with the door securely shut behind them, Wolf recounted to Tabitha all the details of his conversation with Superintendent Wallis and then his search of Leland's room. He produced the journal, and Tabitha glanced at the last entry.

"I read no more of it. I did not want to give the desk clerk any reason to come back and start asking questions," Wolf explained.

Tabitha then provided Wolf with more details of her afternoon conversation with the canon. "I certainly discombobulated him," she said thoughtfully. "His discomfort could not have been more evident during dinner."

Wolf agreed that it had been one of the most awkward meals he had sat through in quite some time. "The question is: was he disturbed because he is guilty and fears we suspect him? Or is it mainly that he was offended by your candour?"

Tabitha reflected on the tangent of her earlier conversation with Canon Elliot. "Perhaps Mama being here will turn out to be a blessing in disguise."

Wolf started at her words. "You will have to explain that logic to me, my love."

Tabitha smiled. "Yes, I know she will complicate the investigation somehow. However, you cannot deny that no one sets the cat amongst the pigeons quite as she does. Perhaps that is what we need at this moment."

While Wolf conceded her point about the dowager's likely impact on the Arundells household, he remained highly sceptical that the imperious, difficult elderly woman would turn out to be the boon that his wife optimistically anticipated.

He changed the subject slightly and said, "In a little while, I intend to slip out and visit Bear. I asked him to bring weapons, and I would like to fill him in on everything we know. I am going to ask him to visit Stonehenge with me tomorrow."

These words brought Tabitha up sharply. "Can I take it that you intend for me not to travel with you?"

Wolf sighed; he should have anticipated this argument and approached the subject with more delicacy. "I only plan to track down this foreman, Edwards, and inquire about his dealings with Leland."

"You speak as if this were only a minor diversion in the investigation. This man was supposed to meet Jacob Leland this morning. Did he see the body? Did he see anything else? I will not be left out."

This was said with such determination that Wolf decided to hold his fire. If this investigation wasn't resolved quickly, there might be more strenuous and dangerous situations he would want to keep Tabitha away from. It was better to concede now and stand firm later.

CHAPTER 11

The Pembroke carriage left Salisbury by the western road, its wheels clattering over the cobbles before giving way to the softer thud of packed earth. The beginning of autumn had sharpened the air, and the hedgerows alongside the lane were laden with blackberries. Tabitha sat opposite Wolf and Bear, with a lap rug tucked about her knees. Wolf might not have convinced her to remain behind at Arundells, but he was determined to keep her as safe and comfortable as possible.

The horse team crested a low rise, and the city disappeared behind them. Ahead lay Salisbury Plain, rather desolate, with hardly a tree in sight.

Tabitha stared out of the window. "It seems like quite a lonely, almost ominous place."

"A fitting stage for a site no one quite understands," Wolf suggested.

Madison urged the horses on, and the carriage rocked as they left the lane for a track across Salisbury Plain. Chalk dust rose around the wheels, coating the harness and the hems of the horses' manes.

It was nearly eleven o'clock when the stones came into view. At first, Tabitha thought them an optical illusion: grey shapes against the sky, half lost in haze. The day was overcast, and its gloom enhanced the illusion. As the carriage drew nearer, the stones resolved into their true forms: towering, massive, irregular uprights, crowned with lintels, and scarred by time.

Tabitha's breath caught. "They look..." She hesitated, searching for the right word. "As though the earth itself had pushed them upward. How did they ever get here?"

Wolf regarded the stones with equal amazement. "Perhaps giants set them here for sport," he said only half-jokingly. "It is hard to believe that men raised those so long ago without sorcery."

"I wish I'd brought my charcoals," Bear said. "I will have to return to draw these before we leave. There is something quite haunting about it all that I would love to capture and perhaps even paint once we return home."

The closer they came to Stonehenge, the more awe-inspiring it became. It wasn't difficult to see why the stones inspired legends and drew people for mysterious rituals.

Wolf exclaimed in wonder, "No wonder men speak of Druids and sacrifices. A place like this demands stories to make sense of it."

The carriage slowed to a halt a short distance from the site. A wooden fence encircled the stones, barely offering a barrier to the wind that swept across the Plain. Inside the fence, they could see trenches cut into the turf, the raw chalk exposed, and piles of earth heaped beside them. Tents sagged in the wind, and tools lay scattered where workmen had left them.

Wolf stepped down first, offering his hand to Tabitha. She carefully descended, her boots sinking slightly into the chalky soil.

The scale of the stones was more overwhelming on foot. Each upright one stood taller than the Pembroke carriage, with lintels so massive they could serve as bridges. Weather had eroded them into strange shapes: hollows resembling eyes, ridges like brows. Tabitha felt as if a company of silent giants was watching her.

They wandered along the fence, searching the encampment for signs of life. A kettle hung cold above a ring of stones, and a line of washing fluttered in the wind, but no men were visible.

"Where are the workmen?" Tabitha asked.

Wolf pointed south, where a low line of huts and sheds huddled against the wind. "Likely eating an early meal under cover. Let us hope we find Edwards there."

They headed towards the sheds. The ground was uneven, churned by boots and wheelbarrows. Even more chalk dust clung to Tabitha's hem, and she held Wolf's arm tightly for fear she'd lose her footing. As they drew nearer to the huts, voices drifted on the wind: coarse laughter, the scrape of stools. Wolf motioned for Tabitha to wait with Bear and stepped forward alone.

He pushed open the door of the largest hut. The laughter stopped abruptly. Inside, a dozen men sat at rough tables, their bowls half empty, mugs of ale in hand. At the far end, a stocky man rose slowly, his shoulders broad, his face weathered by the sun and wind. He sized up the well-dressed man who had appeared among them without warning.

"Can I help you?" he asked brusquely.

"I am looking for the foreman, Mr Edwards," Wolf said.

"Who is looking for him?"

"I am Jeremy Chesterton, the Earl of Pembroke," Wolf replied.

"And what would an earl want with the likes of me?" the man asked suspiciously.

"Are you Edwards?"

"Perhaps I am. Depends why you want to know." Wolf could sense the energy in the tent shift and was relieved he had taken his revolver from Bear and kept it in his pocket. He understood the men's sentiments. It was unlikely that an aristocrat had come looking for a lowly foreman for any reason that would benefit the man.

Wolf realised he needed to get straight to the point. "I am investigating the death of Jacob Leland."

The foreman's reaction was hard to read. Something flickered across his face, and his tone grew even more wary. Was this because it was the first time he was hearing about the man's demise? Wolf knew that the murder had been reported in that morning's newspapers, but there was no reason to believe the foreman would have had time that morning to read the news.

"And who's he when he's around?"

Edwards's response was too sharp, and he narrowed his eyes. What was the man hiding? Wolf wondered. He did not doubt it was something.

Deciding to stop beating about the bush, Wolf replied, "I had dinner with Mr Leland the evening before his death, and he mentioned some correspondence with you, and that he planned to meet you at Old Sarum early yesterday morning. Instead, he was found dead there."

Wolf's words immediately inflamed tensions in the tent. "Are you accusing me of something?" Edwards snapped.

"Not at all. I merely want to ask you a few questions," Wolf said in the most placatory voice he could manage. "Is there somewhere we might talk privately?" Deciding to play his trump card, he added, "I am working with the Salisbury police on this matter. If you prefer, I can return with Superintendent Wallis this afternoon."

These words appeared to be enough, and Edwards said in a resigned tone, "Come with me. There's a supply tent we can talk in." He gestured for Wolf to follow him as he left the tent.

Edwards stopped short when he saw Tabitha and Bear waiting outside the tent. It was likely that Bear's enormous size had at least something to do with this. "They with you?" the foreman asked.

"This is my wife, Lady Pembroke, and our associate, Mr Caruthers," Wolf explained. Then, turning to Tabitha, Wolf continued, "Mr Edwards is happy to answer a few questions and was just taking me somewhere we could speak privately, if you would care to join us." He glanced briefly at Bear, sure the man would understand the look; Wolf wanted him to stay where he was and monitor the situation in case the other workers took it upon themselves to intervene.

There was only one chair in the tent, so Wolf and Edwards stood while Tabitha sat down, grateful at the chance to rest.

Edwards's first words were to spit, "So, you're working with the coppers, are you? Why do they need a toff like you?"

Wolf didn't feel the need to explain himself to the man. Still, he wanted to ease the tension between them if he could. "I do not know if you are aware of why Mr Leland was visiting Salisbury, but he was here at the invitation of Canon Elliot of Salisbury Cathedral. Because of this, the bishop himself asked me if I would assist with the investigation."

The foreman laughed with a harsh bark. "Want to make sure they don't get tainted by any of it, does he?"

Given that this was largely correct, Wolf simply nodded and then said in a matter-of-fact tone, "Let us dispense with the notion that you did not know Mr Leland, and instead you can tell me how you met him."

It seemed as if Edwards was about to continue denying any knowledge, then his shoulders slumped, and he admitted, "Yes, I knew the man. What of it?"

"And you met him how?"

"He was hanging around the dig earlier in the year, asking questions. Gave me his details and asked me to write to him if I found anything that I thought might interest him."

Tabitha couldn't help but ask, "Would not any relics found here belong to the patron of the excavation?" While she didn't know who owned the land that Stonehenge was on, she assumed the dig was being conducted with their permission and that there was a procedure for what happened to anything found.

Her assumption was confirmed by the foreman's sullen look and shrug of his shoulders. "He just wanted to know about anything we found that particularly interested him. Animal bones, antler picks, and the like. Sir Edmund doesn't care about things like that. He just wants the coins, bits of pottery, and such. What does he care if someone else gets a load of old animal parts?"

Neither Tabitha nor Wolf knew enough about such digs to judge the truth of the foreman's claim. They assumed that Edwards wasn't doing this out of charity and that he'd been promised payment for anything he discovered for Leland.

Instead of challenging Edward's statement, Tabitha asked, "And is that what Leland was hoping to find at Old Sarum as well?"

The foreman shrugged. "No idea. I assume so. I remember mentioning at some point that I used to work on a dig there and was telling him about some of the things we'd found. He asked if I could show him where. That's all I know."

"And that was what you were going to do yesterday morning?" Wolf asked. Edwards nodded. "Yet, he did not show up," he pressed. "I assume that you did not see his body."

"I told him a place to meet me, and I waited there for a while. When he didn't turn up, I left."

"What time was that?" Wolf asked, wondering how far Old Sarum was from Stonehenge. "And were you not supposed to be here?"

Edwards shrugged again. "I'm the foreman. I can do what I want. I was supposed to meet him at about nine or so." This was late enough that it was plausible the police had taken the body and left the site by then. "That's all I know," he said, with a defiant crossing of his arms.

It appeared they wouldn't get any more information from the foreman, at least for now. Wolf thanked him for his time, and they left the tent.

CHAPTER 12

The dowager slept later than she had intended. Worried that Tabitha and Wolf might try to slip out of the house to investigate without her if she wasn't at the breakfast table first thing, she had planned to rise early, or at least early by her standards. Unfortunately, she forgot to tell this to Withers, who knew better than to wake her mistress before ten o'clock without good cause.

When she finally opened her eyes, the dowager sensed it was later than she had expected. She sat up straight and called for her maid.

Almost immediately, the much-imposed upon Withers entered the room. "What time is it?" the dowager demanded.

"About half-past nine, milady," Withers answered warily. After nearly forty years working for the termagant, the maid had a sixth sense about when she was about to be berated for something.

"I wanted to wake earlier than this," the dowager complained.

Withers knew better than to argue with her mistress or overtly point out the many contradictions in her speech and actions. However, her long employment had given Withers a certain temerity or at least a sense of how far she might defend her position before being accused of impudence.

After assessing the dowager's mood, Withers responded, "Is half-past nine not earlier than your usual time to rise, milady?" She was aware she was treading a fine line; while the dowager rarely left her bedchamber before noon on most days, it was never wise to remind her of this.

There were few people whose feelings the dowager cared to consider, but somewhat surprisingly, Withers was one of them. The dowager suspected that the maid was considering retiring to a cottage by the sea, near where her sister lived. The thought of breaking in a new maid at her age made the dowager more careful about how she treated Withers than she might otherwise.

With just a quick sniff, the dowager changed the subject. "I will wear the grey silk today, I think. What have you learned of the master of this house?" The dowager was well aware of how much servants gossiped. She also recognised the value of a maid who listened more than she spoke and kept her finger on the pulse of the servants' hall, especially when they were guests elsewhere.

"It appears Canon Elliot is the third son of a wealthy merchant," Withers said.

"Ha!" the dowager exclaimed. "Well, that explains the house. It is far too extravagant for a mere canon."

"Indeed," Withers agreed. "There is a far more extensive household staff than expected." The woman paused, then added conspiratorially, "Though, none of them seem to think much of their master."

The dowager rubbed her hands together with glee; despite her frequent rude remarks about her gossiping friend, Lady Hartley, this was exactly the sort of kitchen tattle and maids' chatter she relished. She had long ago realised that if you wanted to know what someone was truly like, it was best to learn how their servants spoke of them. Shockingly, she had never wondered what her household staff said about her.

"Do tell, Withers," the dowager said, sitting up straighter in bed.

"Well, the man is rather pompous," Withers confided. "Let me think how the footman put it now... yes, he said, the master carries on as if he were the bishop already."

"Is that it?" the dowager asked petulantly.

"No, milady. The fancy French chef was complaining this morning that the canon has money enough for French wine, but they never see a rise in wages."

Pompous and close-fisted. The dowager couldn't wait to meet Canon

Elliot. She almost bounded out of bed, or at least as much as a woman of her age could and was dressed surprisingly quickly.

Withers had assumed her mistress would want her to fetch tea and toast to the room, but the dowager was determined to sally forth and meet her host as soon as possible. Unaware of the canon's new status as the prime murder suspect, the dowager saw him merely as fresh fodder for her withering comments. She'd been feeling somewhat out of sorts recently, and the opportunity to heap wit-laden scorn on someone who, by all accounts so far, deserved it and was a member of her most reviled group, the clergy, had her bright-eyed and bushy-tailed.

"Instruct the kitchen that I will breakfast downstairs and ensure that word is sent to this Canon Elliot that his presence is required." As she said this, the dowager sat at the dressing table and contemplated her reflection. While even she felt her diamonds were too much before noon, she wondered which jewels might strike an appropriate level of awe into the canon's heart.

Withers left the room to carry out her tasks, and in a mere twenty minutes, the dowager was at the breakfast table, spreading jam on her toast and sipping tea. Of course, the canon might have been at the Chapter House or the cathedral. However, the dowager had not worried herself over such possibilities. She assumed that wherever the man was, his staff would understand the urgency of sending him word to return to Arundells. Luckily for his servants, the man was in his study, and they did not need to be caught between their master and the outrageous expectations of his unexpected houseguest.

The dowager was just finishing her second slice of toast when the door opened with an unnecessary flourish, and in swept the tall, lean, black-clad figure of Canon Elliot. His cassock hung from his gaunt frame, and he had a book he'd been reading in one hand, the other fluttering nervously at his side.

While some men might have been shocked, perhaps offended, to be summoned by someone who had invited herself to partake of his hospitality, the canon was far too overawed by the presence of a dowager countess under his roof to take umbrage. While Wolf was correct and the charm of their presence had very much thinned, nevertheless, the canon still had high hopes for the dowager countess.

"My dear Lady Pembroke!" the canon exclaimed, bowing so deeply that his spectacles slid perilously down his nose. "Permit me to extend the warmest felicitations upon your presence here in our humble Close. It is, I assure you, an occasion of no ordinary significance, for seldom has Salisbury been so distinguished."

He took a step towards her too quickly, nearly colliding with a side table, then caught himself with a strained laugh.

"I am Canon Elliot, Edmund Elliot, at your service. I blush to speak of my modest efforts on behalf of this venerable cathedral, yet, if Providence has graciously chosen that I should welcome you, I accept the duty with the utmost grace and gratitude. Indeed, it has been remarked, by others, not by myself I should add, that hospitality is among my more notable qualities."

The dowager was delighted; the man was even more pompous and absurd than Withers had led her to believe. She eagerly anticipated multiple delicious opportunities to sharpen her wit on this Canon Elliot.

While she didn't stand, as that would be an unacceptable acknowledgement that his rank as a senior clergyman was in any way equal to her own, the dowager extended a hand and offered her new supplicant a regal smile.

Taking the offered hand, the canon beamed as if the handshake itself were a benediction and said with solemn earnestness: "Ah! To clasp the hand of one whose noble family has ever stood as a bulwark of our realm is a privilege I shall long treasure."

"Indeed," the dowager rejoined coolly. "That is as it should be." The woman walked a fine line when it came to sycophancy; she despised anyone who humbled themselves to such a level of subservience, but believed she was worthy of it from almost everyone she met. In this regard, Canon Elliot immediately became both a figure of ridicule and a subject of pity; to her aristocratic eyes, he epitomised the lower clergy, ambitious yet lacking refinement, striving for a grandeur he would never attain. She decided that this was going to be a very entertaining visit.

The dowager indicated that the canon was allowed to sit at his own breakfast table, which he did with many snivelling words of gratitude. She regarded the man in front of her. How best to utilise him, she wondered.

Deciding to set her own amusement aside for a moment and be practical, the dowager asked, "I understand there has been a murder that Lord Pembroke has been asked to investigate. However, I have no more details than that. What do you know, Canon Elliot?"

Of course, she didn't know there had been a murder, only that there had been an unexpected death and that some sort of investigation was underway. Nonetheless, the dowager couldn't imagine that Bear would have been summoned for anything less than a murder inquiry and felt quite assured in her assumptions.

The dowager hadn't anticipated the pall that seemed to overwhelm the canon at her words. The man's already deathly pale skin took on an ashen hue as his mouth formed an unconvincing, and indeed rather unpleasant, attempt at a smile.

"Lady Pembroke," the canon said with an air of marked condescension, "I have already assured the other Lady Pembroke that this is not a matter for the fairer sex to concern themselves with. These matters are best left to the constabulary and to gentlemen more suited to handle them."

The dowager's face should have been all the warning the canon needed about how his words had been received and the tongue-lashing he was about to get. "The fairer sex, Canon? Spare me such nonsense. It is women who have buried husbands, sons, and brothers, held households together through war and ruin, and endured griefs you could scarcely name. Yet you presume we should be sheltered from the sight of a single corpse? Your misplaced attempt at gallantry is an insult." More than the words themselves, the tone in which they were delivered would have struck terror into a more sensible man.

While he didn't realise the hornet's nest he had just stumbled into, the canon sensed that further conversation with this ornery old woman would not be to his advantage.

He stood up suddenly and blustered, "I regret I do not have the time to give you the particulars of the unfortunate death. I am sure that Lord Pembroke will return shortly. I must hurry to the Chapter House for a meeting." Before the dowager could reply, he had made his escape.

CHAPTER 13

O n the journey back from Stonehenge, Bear said, "Today is market day in Salisbury. I was thinking of visiting and talking to some of the market traders. Word of the murder must have reached the townsfolk by now. Given the rise in occultism and the fascination with Druids, Freemasons, and the like, I wonder if superstitious rumours will spread with the news."

Tabitha considered Bear's words. It was an interesting thought. It was obvious that there had been an attempt to suggest such an association. What would people make of that information? Would the murmurings throw up any useful gossip?

While Bear's suggestion was sound, perhaps it would be more efficient for them all to visit the market. As luck would have it, she and Wolf had dressed plainly for their outing to Stonehenge. While there could be no doubt that they were well-off, they might have been mistaken for a prosperous merchant and his wife. It wasn't unbelievable that such people might visit the market. Or at least, that was what Tabitha hoped.

Wolf's thoughts shifted to more practical matters; he wanted to ensure that Tabitha had something to eat before they walked any further. He knew such a suggestion wouldn't be well-received and would be seen as more fussing.

Instead, he said as casually as possible, "Would you mind if we stopped for something to eat before we headed out to the market?"

It was almost noon, and Wolf realised that the market would start winding down within at least a few hours. Tabitha was equally aware of this and quirked one suspicious eyebrow at the suggestion, but she didn't argue. Bear suggested they eat at the Red Lion Hotel, close to Market Place, and no one could think of any reason to disagree.

They ate a hearty but quick meal due to the time constraints. Shepherd's Pie was on the menu. This was one of Tabitha's favourite working-class meals. She ordered it, declared it delicious, and ate the entire serving, to Wolf's relief. He couldn't remember the last time he had seen her eat so well, and he made a mental note to make sure they returned to the hotel for at least one more meal before leaving Salisbury.

After their meal, the threesome left the Red Lion Hotel and walked the short distance to Market Place. Even before they arrived, Tabitha could feel the hum of activity ahead. Entering the market, she was quite overwhelmed by the press of bodies, the cries of hawkers, and the clatter of wagons. The Saturday market was the main market day in Salisbury; traders came from all over Wiltshire. It was bustling, noisy, and at times, shoulder-to-shoulder with shoppers. The Poultry Cross rose at the centre, its worn Gothic spire pointing to the overcast autumn sky.

Bear gave a low whistle. "Now this," he said, surveying the scene with a thief-taker's instinct for opportunity, "is where a man could lose his purse in the space of ten paces." Acknowledging his friend's words, Wolf slipped his pocket watch into his jacket's inner pocket with his leather wallet.

As soon as they entered the main market area, Bear parted from the group to avoid attracting unwanted attention; his size always drew a lot of notice. Tabitha and Wolf walked side by side between the stalls. Wolf kept his hands in his pockets, shoulders relaxed, suggesting he was observing everything without seeming to.

Tabitha looked around her, captivated. Having lived a pampered life, she had first visited markets like this when she met Wolf. She stopped briefly at a fruit seller's stall to admire the mound of mottled pears.

To their right, pens of sheep and pigs stretched out, bleating and squealing in protest. A boy no older than twelve shouted bids for his father's geese, which flapped their wings furiously inside a wicker crate. To their left, the butchers displayed their wares: sides of beef hung from hooks, mutton joints laid out on boards, and the sawdust beneath their feet already stained dark. Knives flashed as cleavers fell, punctuating the drone of haggling voices.

In between, flowed a river of humanity: farmers in smocks, women with shawls pulled tightly, apprentices balancing baskets, children darting underfoot with sticky buns clutched in their fists. The market was so busy that no one batted an eye at the toffs walking amongst them.

Tabitha and Wolf wandered around for some time, hearing nothing of interest. Around them, the market went about its business. Housewives bargained over cabbages still clotted with earth; an apprentice boy struggled with a jug of milk sloshing dangerously near the brim; a baker's boy carried a tray of buns still steaming, their glaze shining in the afternoon sun.

Suddenly, the voices of two women at the next stall caused Tabitha to stop walking. She pretended to examine some potatoes while trying to listen in on their conversation. The women were bent over onions tied in ropes, but their heads were close together, and their tone was more secretive than the matter of vegetables required.

"Murder, I hear! Can you believe it? I always said there was something going on up there. My Tom said he heard that there were lights on the hill again," the first woman muttered. "He said they'd seen 'em clear as day. Lanterns moving along the ridge, and voices too. Chanting, he said."

"Poachers," the other woman replied, though without much conviction.

"Poachers don't chant, Bess. And now there's been a killing. My Tom said he thinks it was a human sacrifice."

The second woman, Bess, gasped. "Human sacrifice! You don't say. And it's a full moon soon, you know. There's bound to be more of it."

Then, one of the women noticed Tabitha and Wolf standing rather close and listening to their conversation. She elbowed her friend, gestured with her head, and the two women walked away to continue their conversation.

"Well, that was interesting," Wolf remarked in a low voice.

"It does seem as if something has been going on at Old Sarum.

Though, of course, it may end up being no more than tomfoolery by local young men." Even as Tabitha said these words, she wondered if she believed them true. After all, a man had been murdered, and there had been an apparent effort to tie his death to ancient rites.

They wandered the market for another half hour but learned nothing else of note. Although they overheard some mutterings about the murder, Leland wasn't a local and Old Sarum wasn't Salisbury; people didn't seem to feel threatened in any way. Eventually, they spotted Bear and made their way over to him.

"I think we should return to Arundells," Wolf suggested. "We have been gone for some time, and the dowager countess is likely to have worked herself into quite a state of indignation by now."

Bear looked a little shamefaced at this. "I am sorry I wasn't able to dissuade her from joining me," he admitted. "I didn't even see her on the train, so I hoped that she'd thought better of the adventure."

"Do not berate yourself," Wolf said kindly. "When her ladyship gets an idea in her mind, it would take an act of the Almighty himself to dissuade her." Bear chuckled at the truth of this statement.

As they returned to the carriage, Bear admitted that he hadn't heard of anything useful and asked what Wolf wanted him to do for the rest of the day.

"See what you can find out about the canon. How is he regarded in Salisbury? Also, these lights that have been seen at Old Sarum, ask around and see if you can gather any clues about what they are. I believe we will need to go up there for the full moon. If those women are correct, that is an ideal time for any rituals that might occur." Even as Wolf said this, he glanced at Tabitha from the corner of his eye. He was determined she would not join such a late-night, potentially dangerous outing. Now, he just had to decide how best to persuade her.

At the Pembroke carriage, they parted ways with Bear, who planned to return to the Red Lion Hotel before setting out to see what he could discover. He'd decided to have a tankard of ale or two at one of the local inns and see who he could strike up a conversation with. His experience was that offering to buy a man a drink usually loosened his tongue.

In anticipation of another extremely uncomfortable dinner with the canon, they agreed to meet later for a meal at the Red Lion and then return to Bear's room. He had taken the trouble to bring the corkboard with him, and Tabitha was eager to start writing up notecards for what they had learned so far.

Once they settled in the carriage and headed towards Arundells, Tabitha asked the obvious question, "What are we going to do about Mama? She will not tolerate being sidelined; in fact, I am sure she is already outraged by our early departure without her this morning."

"Well, that is not a conversation I want to have with her if there is any chance the canon might overhear us. I suggest we invite her to join us this evening and let her give us whatever tongue-lashing she desires in private." This was a sensible suggestion, and Tabitha only hoped that the dowager could be persuaded to postpone venting her spleen.

CHAPTER 14

Their reception upon returning to Arundells was everything they had expected and more. By then, it was already past three o'clock in the afternoon. During that time, the dowager had worked herself up in a state of such irritation, at least partially fuelled by boredom, that she almost leapt on Tabitha and Wolf when they entered the drawing room.

"Finally!" she proclaimed. "Are you expecting me to believe that whatever you went to do this morning took all this time?"

"Shh, Mama," Tabitha whispered. "We can have no expectation of privacy here." She hesitated to explain further. However, she was also worried that if she didn't say more, the dowager would push the matter so forcefully that the canon might be drawn into the room by the commotion.

Tabitha went and sat beside the dowager on the elegant silk couch and said very quietly, "We will explain everything later. We are all to meet Bear for dinner and then move to his room, where he has the corkboard set up. I am begging you to hold your fire for now. There is a good reason we cannot say more here."

Now, the dowager's ire was replaced by something even more worrying; the woman's eyes lit up with glee. "That horrible little man is a suspect? How delicious."

This response was precisely what they had hoped to avoid. Tabitha shushed the dowager again and said, "I am going to rest before we leave." Turning to Wolf, she asked, "Can you inform the footman that we will not join the canon for dinner and will be out for the evening?"

"Well, what am I supposed to do in the meantime?" the dowager asked petulantly.

Tabitha had to work hard not to roll her eyes; they hadn't asked the woman to join them, yet now they were somehow responsible for entertaining her.

Fortunately, Wolf intervened. He was relieved to hear that his wife was going to rest and wanted nothing to disturb that. "Lady Pembroke, perhaps I can walk you around the Close. We might even step into the cathedral. It is quite a sight to behold."

The look on the dowager's face left no doubt about what she thought of such a suggestion. Still, it was the only option on offer, unless she wanted to attempt to read one of the turgid books of sermons in the canon's library. She accepted Wolf's offer with a mild eye roll of her own. Tabitha shot him a grateful look and escaped to their room for her nap.

Some hours later, they met in the hallway and made a hasty exit to the carriage before the canon could walk by, forcing them to extend a reluctant invitation to join them. While Wolf was sure their host had no more interest in breaking bread in their company than they did in his, better to be safe than sorry. Not for the first time, he wondered whether it might be better, all things considered, to take up lodgings at the Red Lion Hotel with Bear.

Once they were settled at a quiet corner table in the restaurant, Wolf wasted no time informing the dowager of all the details of the murder and their investigation so far.

"Ha!" she declared. "I knew that odious man was guilty of something. He has very shifty eyes."

"Mama," Tabitha admonished, "we know no such thing. All we know is that the conversation at dinner with Mr Leland indicated a conflict of academic opinion. That does not mean the canon is guilty of murder."

Despite her words of caution, there was no containing the dowager's enthusiasm for their prime suspect. Tabitha wished they had more evidence of the canon's innocence to share. Yet they didn't. They also had little evidence of his guilt. All they had were strong words, and words were not weapons.

Once they finished dinner, they retired to Bear's bedchamber, and Tabitha began to write out notecards. As she did so, she came to the disheartening realisation that they didn't have much evidence of any kind.

"We know so little," she said in frustration.

"Let us look at what we do know," Wolf suggested. "We know that Mr Leland had an interest in ancient rites at Old Sarum and Stonehenge, and that some in the Church disapprove of such research."

"Particularly Canon Elliot," the dowager interjected with unnecessary enthusiasm.

Not for the first time that evening, Tabitha wondered exactly what had occurred between the dowager and the canon to have created such enmity in so short a period. She was loath to open that Pandora's Box and kept her question to herself. After all, it was hardly shocking that the dowager found the canon distasteful; that it had taken no more than a brief exposure to the man to surface was also not a surprise.

Instead of asking that question, Tabitha acknowledged that Canon Elliot disagreed with Jacob Leland but added, "However, was he the only cleric to do so? We know this was not his first time in Salisbury because he had met with the foreman, Edwards, previously. Who else did he encounter then?" She wrote this rhetorical question on a notecard and pinned it to the board.

Now that the subject of the foreman had been raised, they shifted their discussion to him. "The man was not pleased to see us," Wolf observed. "Yet, is that really so surprising? The average working man seldom gains from attracting the attention of men of wealth and rank."

"Yet, there was something else," Tabitha admitted. "Though I cannot quite pinpoint what it was. Certainly, the idea that he turned up at Old Sarum, observed nothing, waited half an hour, and then left seems odd. It is hardly a quick journey from there to Stonehenge. It is clear that the man has either been receiving financial compensation for the artefacts he passes along or expected to. That does not seem to me an expectation one might simply shrug off. Did Leland tell Edwards he was going to stop buying artefacts from him, and in a fit of rage, the foreman killed him?" Everyone nodded at her words, and she wrote up another notecard."

"Then, there is the gossip of lights being seen at Old Sarum late at night and talk of ancient rituals being revived," Tabitha said.

"Oh poppycock," exclaimed the dowager. "The ignorant masses are always ready to imagine such things."

"I am sorry to contradict you, your ladyship, but given the increasing interest in the occult and ancient ceremonies, I do not believe we can ignore this," Wolf said carefully.

"Such things are the nonsense of our age. Every decade brings its own follies. In my day, it was table-turning; now it is moon-gazing Druids. A bunch of young men in bedsheets pretending to cut mistletoe!" The dowager said this in a voice that left no doubt about her opinion about such fads.

Bear was reticent at the best of times, but around the dowager, he usually kept his opinions to himself, only sharing them with Tabitha and Wolf once the old woman had left the room.

Given this, it surprised everyone when he said, "Lady Pembroke, the folly is not confined to the young. Learned gentlemen have put their names to such pursuits. Recently, I read of a gathering at Anglesey, white-robed 'Druids,' they called themselves, meeting at dawn to welcome the solstice. Somehow, the newspaper had got wind of it."

No one was more taken aback by Bear speaking than the dowager. She was so startled that she had no immediate reply. As it happened, he was someone the dowager respected, not merely because his enormous size struck fear into her neighbours' hearts whenever he visited.

Seizing on Bear's words, Wolf said, "Yes, what about that group, The Golden Dawn? I remember reading about them now that you mention it. They are one of those occult societies that have sprung up in London. Not mere table-tipping, but elaborate ceremonies, candles, swords, and robes, blending Egyptian gods, the Kabbalah, and supposed Druid rituals. They call themselves restorers of ancient wisdom. Poets, actors and actresses, even barristers, have joined their ranks. To some, it might be dangerous folly to dabble in such things, but it seems that, to others, it is the height of fashion."

The dowager sniffed with disdain. "Fashion? Fustian, more like. Poets in nightgowns, lawyers playing at magicians, and actresses pretending to be priestesses of Isis; what utter rubbish. If this is the height of London society, then heaven help us all."

Despite her previous scornful words, the dowager adopted an almost gossipy tone, adding, "Of course, I have heard of such things. It is one of the many bits of nonsense I often must tolerate at society teas. Only the other week at a particularly insipid tea hosted by Lady Hartley, I heard whispering about so-called Egyptian mysteries. Then, there was absurd girlish giggling as though they had all been initiated into some secret priesthood."

"So, even you have witnessed this fascination people have with such things," Wolf said pointedly.

"And what does that prove? That some people have too much time on their hands and are gullible fools. So many ladies in society whisper about every kind of nonsense merely for the thrill of the so-called secret itself." The dowager said this as if she expected her opinion to be the final word on the matter.

"Lady Pembroke, that these things are being spoken of quite openly in Mayfair drawing rooms is proof of serious interest. The Golden Dawn counts W. B. Yeats among its members, and he takes it most seriously. When a poet lends his pen, the thing acquires weight in certain circles."

Now, the dowager just gave a dismissive bark of laughter. "Weight? Feathers tied to a balloon, more like. I suppose next we shall learn that Parliament itself has been consulting the spirits." She paused, then, with an evil grin, added, "Though this might explain some of the legislation passed recently."

Tabitha could see that this conversation might easily spiral out of control. In an effort to steer it back to the matter at hand, she said, "Bear and Wolf are right to raise this issue. The Golden Dawn and similar orders flourish because educated men and women wish to believe the world holds more than what their eyes can see. They conceal their hopes in ritual and symbols. That hope might be foolish, but it can also be dangerous. Given that, we must take seriously the talk of possible ritualistic activities at Old Sarum. Perhaps Mr Leland stumbled across them."

Wolf pointed out, "Or perhaps he was involved in them." Both were questions worth writing on notecards.

One outstanding question was whether the canon had the opportunity to kill Leland.

Bear asked, "Is there any reason to believe Elliot couldn't have slipped out at some point in the night?"

Wolf considered the question. "I do not believe he keeps a carriage. We are not even able to keep ours at Arundells. He must have either hired a fly or keeps a gig at a local stable. Madison has the carriage and horses at a public livery stable just off Market Place. Can you find him and, between you, ask around about both options?"

"Of course," Bear agreed, adding, "I did ask the front desk clerk about what transportation they offer, and it seems they have flies and dog carts for the use of guests. Apparently, Leland made use of one of them to get himself to Old Sarum. I talked to one of the ostlers and he told me that Leland took a dog cart out at about eleven o'clock."

"I assume that the police have already talked to the man," Wolf asked. Bear nodded.

The final agreement the group reached before disbanding for the evening was that they would attend Sunday services at the cathedral the next day. Tabitha had suggested it might be a way to find out what the canon's fellow clerics thought of the man, as well as to gauge feelings about the murder and the potential rites at Old Sarum and Stonehenge.

While everyone was pleased to see that Canon Elliot still seemed to be doing his best to avoid them, they did need to know what time services were in the morning. Luckily, the footman appeared able to provide the needed information and told them that Matins started at eleven o'clock. He said that the canon usually left earlier than that to prepare for his role in the service, which was a relief.

CHAPTER 15

While dressing for Sunday services the following morning, Wolf asked Tabitha, "How much do you think we should read into the canon's evident desire to avoid us?"

She considered the question, though it was one that she had been reflecting on since the uncomfortable dinner two evenings prior. "Truly, I do not know. There is no doubt that my conversation with him on Friday discombobulated him in the extreme. The question is why? Certainly, on its face, it does not seem to be the behaviour of an innocent man. However, is he guilty of murder or a lesser sin that he fears will come to light?" Then, in a lighter tone, she added, "Perhaps, it is nothing more than a sensible desire to avoid Mama."

Wolf smiled at her last statement. However, the overall question was a serious one that they needed to unravel. They both hoped that their visit to Sunday services would help illuminate the answer.

Canon Elliot did not join them for breakfast. He seemed determined to continue avoiding their company unless he had left very early for morning services. Tabitha wondered if he even realised that they intended to attend Matins.

Tabitha had dressed stylishly, yet conservatively. She had chosen a beautiful, high-necked, pale blue Worth gown and complemented it with a double strand of pearls. The ensemble made a clear, yet subtle statement of wealth and social standing. Neither she nor Wolf harboured a hope that the dowager would display similar restraint.

Their expectations were fully met when the woman swept into the room resplendent in diamonds and furs. As was often the case when she hoped to instil awe in the masses, her outfit was more suited to an audience with the Queen. Since Tabitha had anticipated nothing less, she didn't bother commenting. Though as she watched the woman regally sweep into the room, she wondered if the dowager's determination to ensure that others knew her wealth and importance at first glance might help for once. Only time would tell.

Once the dowager had seated herself and had taken her first few sips of tea, Tabitha asked, "What is our plan of action for today?"

The dowager leapt in. "Find incriminating evidence on the weasel, of course."

While Tabitha was grateful the dowager had not uttered the canon's name aloud, she shushed her. It was better to discuss this when they were outside and walking across the Close.

Wolf must have had a similar thought, because he said, "We can talk more as we walk to the cathedral." While the walk wasn't far, the dowager wasn't fast, so it wouldn't seem odd if they took their time.

The bells of Salisbury Cathedral began their sonorous toll shortly after ten o'clock, rolling across the Close in deep, sombre waves. The sound echoed against the large houses and rolled into the narrow lanes of Salisbury. Tabitha could hear the bells clearly from the breakfast room, as the city was called to worship.

The dowager finished her tea, ate some toast, and then pronounced herself ready. It was just before half past ten, and so a leisurely walk that took them to the cathedral a little early was perfect.

As the group exited the front gate, the dowager asked impatiently, "So, what is the plan?"

People were walking across the Close to the cathedral from every direction, so Wolf kept his voice low as he replied, "Given that the bishop asked me to oversee the investigation, I see no reason to be coy about why we are in Salisbury. We know that Leland has been in Salisbury before. While Canon Elliot seemed unaware of some of the man's more, shall we say, heretical views, I do wonder if that is true for all the Chapter members. Given this, I think that one priority is to raise the subject of the murder and try, very subtly," and as he said this, Wolf looked pointedly at the dowager, "to discover the general view of the man. To the extent there was one."

The dowager didn't find that task the best use of her talents. "And what about the Weasel, as he shall now be named?"

"There is no doubt that our second priority is to discover what Canon Elliot's peers in the Chapter make of him." While he knew his following words would not be received well, Wolf felt he had no choice but to add, "However, Lady Pembroke, this line of questioning must be handled delicately. We cannot have the canon more wary of our suspicions than he already is. And, if he turns out to be entirely innocent, it would be unconscionable to have raised doubts about the man's character through the cathedral."

This caution was received as well as Wolf expected. "Jeremy, is there a particular reason you believe me to require such a lecture?" Without waiting for a reply, she continued, "I am more than capable of conducting myself with appropriate discretion."

Given that neither Tabitha nor Wolf was sure she was, they made no reply. The dowager's response to their silence was an indignant sniff. Then, she commented, "I assume we will be invited to dine with the bishop for luncheon."

Wolf hadn't given the matter any thought. However, now that the dowager had raised the subject, he assumed she was likely correct. "That might be a perfect time for casual conversation," he said. "Though I would assume Canon Elliot will also be invited. So, again, we need to exercise appropriate caution."

They crossed the green, joining the stream of townsfolk and visitors making their way toward the cathedral that loomed above them. The morning sunlight caught the lancet windows and gilded the tracery so majestically that Tabitha could not help but draw a breath of awe. Even after so many grand buildings visited on their travels, this Cathedral possessed an air of ancient, serene authority.

The bells were still pealing when Tabitha, Wolf, and the dowager reached the cathedral's west front. There was already quite a crowd of parishioners gathered there, indulging in gossip and judging each other's Sunday finery. A tall, thin verger in a flowing black gown stood just inside the threshold, guiding the stream of worshippers with brisk efficiency. He looked up as they stepped into the cool hush of the nave.

"Good morning, sir, madam," he said, inclining his head. "May I enquire your names so I may direct you to your place?" This was said politely, after all, they were very well dressed, but the man's impatience was obvious.

Tabitha hesitated, glancing at her husband. Still uncomfortable with the formalities of his rank, Wolf did understand the importance of using it under circumstances like these. Reluctantly, he replied, "The Earl and Countess of Pembroke, and the Dowager Countess of Pembroke."

The verger's eyes widened, and his demeanour changed instantly. His back straightened, and his tone deepened into deference. "Your lordship and ladyships, my apologies for not recognising you immediately. The bishop mentioned that you might attend services and directed that you be shown the best pews."

"As it should be!" the dowager said rather unnecessarily.

They were led along the south aisle, then turned toward the choir screen where the carved stalls began.

As the verger led them to their place, he said to Wolf, "I understand you are guests of Canon Elliot's."

"Indeed," was all Wolf replied.

"Watch yourself there, milord," was the cryptic response he got in return.

At the front of the nave, pews stood reserved for visiting dignitaries. The verger gestured for them to sit in one such pew, close enough to see the canons across the screen and hear every word of the lessons.

"Here, my lord, my ladies," the verger said softly, "the most fitting of seating areas." He offered a final nod, then slipped away to usher in another stream of visitors.

What on earth had the verger meant? Wolf wondered. He made a mental note to mention this to Tabitha later.

Their seats were just beyond the choir screen, close enough to see the clergy processing in. Tabitha folded her gloves neatly in her lap, her eyes wandering over the intricately carved stalls and gazing beyond to the altar.

Within a few minutes, the procession started. The choirboys led the way, their surplices bright white against the dark wood, their voices clear and high as they sang the opening introit. Behind them came the clergy in procession: deacons and canons, including Canon Elliot, robed in a black cassock and white surplice, his jaw set a little too firmly. Tabitha watched him closely. Something about his manner suggested nervous pride, as though the grandeur of the service was almost a burden.

Finally, the bishop himself entered, vested in cope and mitre. Bishop John took his seat, watching his congregation with an air of dignified paternalism.

The congregation rose as an officiant began the service. The words echoed through the nave, resonant beneath the high stone vaults. Morning Prayer unfolded with a stately rhythm: confession, absolution, the Lord's Prayer. The choir sang the Venite, their voices rising in lyrical waves, bringing Tabitha a great sense of peace. She followed along in her prayer book, though her attention often wandered to look at the rest of the congregation. She noticed the rustle of silk gowns among the families of the Close, sitting together in the front pews. There was the muffled cough of a tradesman behind them, and the small drama of a child who dropped his hymnbook that a parent hastily retrieved. These details brought life to the solemnity of the service.

Wolf, in contrast to his wife, fixed his gaze upon the clergy. He observed how the bishop leaned forward attentively and how Canon Elliott fumbled slightly with his book before regaining his composure. When it was time for the psalms, Elliott's voice joined the choir, deeper and rougher than the pure trebles.

The first lesson from the Old Testament was read by a minor canon, his voice clear but unremarkable. Then the choir sang the Te Deum, filling the cathedral with soaring praise. Tabitha felt a shiver run down her spine. Although she was not a regular churchgoer, listening to the music seemed to lift her above the petty troubles of the investigation and into a higher realm.

Canon Elliott read the second lesson. He mounted the lectern with a deliberate step, and for a moment his eyes swept the congregation. When they met Tabitha's eyes fleetingly, she thought she saw something like defiance or perhaps fear. Then he began to read. His voice was strong, if somewhat overemphatic. It was the cadence of a man determined to impress. From St. John's Gospel, he read words concerning light and darkness, truth and falsehood. In another setting, they might have gone unnoticed, but in the context of their investigation, they carried an unsettling resonance.

The Benedictus followed, then prayers for the Queen, the nation, and the Church. Finally, it was time for the sermon. On this Sunday, the bishop himself ascended the pulpit. His sermon was brief but thoughtful, emphasising vigilance in uncertain times and the importance of truth in an age tempted by spectacle. He spoke with deliberate precision, yet his words conveyed warmth. Tabitha sensed why he was so respected; the man combined intellect with genuine pastoral care.

The service was not long, but it was certainly compelling. Even so, Tabitha sensed the dowager fidgeting next to her in the pew. In a moment of exasperation, she felt she would get better behaviour sitting next to five-year-old Melody.

Luckily, the service soon concluded with final hymns and a blessing. The congregation rose as the procession withdrew, choirboys leading once more, followed by clergy and finally the bishop. The great organ roared as the people began to file out.

Outside, the sunlight had grown stronger, and Tabitha had to shield her eyes as they left the cathedral. The grass in the centre of the Close stretched wide and green, dotted with groups of worshippers pausing to converse. Gentlemen lingered in casual conversational circles. Ladies exchanged greetings, while children ran under the watchful eyes of nurses and concerned mothers.

"Any thoughts on where we should begin?" Wolf asked under his breath. Before she could answer, they were approached by the verger who had shown them to their seats. He conveyed the bishop's compliments and requested that they join him near the Palace gate. Following the verger's instructions, they crossed the Close, the spire casting its long shadow beside them.

Bishop Wordsworth was waiting for them beneath the elm trees that lined the path. He tilted his head with courtly grace. "Lord Pembroke and your ladyships. I trust you found the service edifying?"

Tabitha cast the dowager a sharp look, hoping she wouldn't say anything untoward. Luckily, she did not comment as Wolf tilted his head, offering a respectful "Indeed, Bishop. It was a moving and thought-provoking service."

The bishop smiled beneficently at this compliment. At that moment, Canon Elliott approached, bowing stiffly. "My Lord Bishop," he said in greeting, "and Lord and Ladies Pembroke." His tone was correct, yet Tabitha detected tension beneath it. The canon's hands were clasped too tightly in front of him, and his gaze flickered from the bishop to Wolf with something like unease.

The bishop placed a gentle, yet authoritative hand on Elliott's shoulder. "Canon Elliott has kindly offered to join us for luncheon today. I should be most pleased if you would do likewise."

Wolf accepted gratefully, unsure if the bishop meant more by the invitation than there seemed to be superficially.

The bishop continued, "We shall dine at the Palace shortly. But first, perhaps a few moments to enjoy the Close. You will find no lovelier prospect in all England than this green beneath the spire."

They strolled across the lawn, the bishop at the centre, Tabitha, the dowager, and Wolf to one side, Elliott to the other. Parishioners passing by bowed or curtsied, offering greetings. Some whispered among themselves, curious at their first glimpses of the Earl of Pembroke and his wife in the bishop's company.

CHAPTER 16

The bishop had stepped away from their group to greet an elderly parishioner, leaving Tabitha, Wolf, and the dowager to converse among themselves. For the dowager, this mainly involved making rude, overly loud comments about the fashion, or lack of it, in Salisbury.

Just as she was making one such particularly mean-spirited remark, the dowager paused mid-sentence and said, "Oh!"

Tabitha looked in the direction of the dowager's glance and saw a dignified-looking couple walking toward the bishop. The woman's bearing was at once gracious and composed. Her dark hair, streaked with silver, was pulled back beneath a smart bonnet trimmed with velvet ribbon. Her gown, of dove-grey silk with darker accents at the cuffs, was fashionable without ostentation, and her manner conveyed a quiet dignity. Everything about the woman's attire was entirely appropriate for church, yet signalled great wealth, but in such a careful manner that there was no doubt she was no parvenu.

The woman was on the arm of a tall, broad-shouldered man in his late fifties, his figure softened somewhat by years of comfortable living, yet still carrying a decided air of authority. His dark hair was silver at the temples, and his well-groomed beard framed a ruddy, weathered face that spoke of country pursuits and long rides across the Wiltshire downs. His attire, not unlike Wolf's, was sober yet impeccably tailored: a dark frock coat, waistcoat in a muted pattern, and trousers with a fine crease. He moved with the deliberate steadiness of a man accustomed to deference, pausing to exchange patrician nods with clerics and other parishioners.

The couple made their way to the bishop's side. The man inclined his head with grave courtesy and seemed to be received warmly. The couple exchanged a few words with Wordsworth before they all looked in Tabitha and Wolf's direction. A few moments later, the bishop began walking over to their group with the distinguished couple.

"Lord and Lady Radnor, may I present to you the Earl, Countess, and Dowager Countess of Pembroke. Lord Pembroke, the Earl and Countess of Radnor."

The Earl of Radnor inclined his head. "An honour," he said, his voice deep and deliberate, the kind of tone that made even casual remarks sound judicial.

The countess, in contrast, extended her gloved hand to Tabitha with graceful ease. "How delightful to meet you at last, Lady Pembroke," she said, her voice clear and musical. "We have heard you are newly arrived in Salisbury. I do hope the Close is proving agreeable."

The dowager pushed herself forward, apparently tired of being merely referred to. "Helen Adene! When last I saw you, child, you were scarcely out of the schoolroom, and altogether too fond of waltzing with unsuitable partners. How delightful to see you again. It has been far too long."

The other countess gave a soft laugh. "And you, Lady Pembroke, have altered not a whit. I recall you once decreed my gloves too short for Almack's, and I never dared shorten them again. I would have come sooner if I had realised you were one of the party."

"Sound advice then, and sound advice now," the dowager replied, clearly pleased to be remembered. The two women embraced. Tabitha caught Wolf's eye; would this be a help or a hindrance?

The countess added, "We were to attend Mr Leland's talk and were excited to meet the man who funded such an important discovery. What a terrible situation we now find ourselves in instead."

Just as Wolf wondered what Lord Radnor knew about the bishop's request that he oversee the investigation, he said, "The Lord Bishop tells me that you have some experience with such investigations and are remaining, at his request, to ensure the protection of the Chapter's reputation."

Wolf had to suppress a groan; that is not how he wanted his involvement to be characterised. He replied, "Yes, my wife and I have helped solve some investigations over the past year or so." Then, realising the fatal error he'd just made, Wolf quickly added, "And, of course, we have done so with great help from the dowager countess. Given this, Bishop Wordsworth has asked us to remain in Salisbury and provide what assistance we can to the local constabulary." Earl Radnor nodded sagely at this explanation.

"Are we all ready to make our way to the Palace?" the bishop inquired. It appeared that Lord and Lady Radnor were to be included in the luncheon party.

As the group began to move off, Tabitha took Wolf's arm and pulled him close. "Let us take this opportunity to learn how some local landowners view the Chapter." Wolf agreed. Gaining an outside view of Canon Elliot and his colleagues would be interesting. The earl might even know something of the supposed rituals taking place locally.

The bishop's dining room was cool despite the afternoon warmth. The September sun streamed through the long, elegant windows, highlighting the many portraits of previous prelates. A great oak table stretched the length of the chamber, already set with gleaming silver and crisp white linen. Footmen moved with hushed efficiency, pouring wine and bringing in food.

As the company filed in for luncheon, the order of precedence was observed with punctilious care. The bishop took the great chair at the head of the long oak table, beneath the portrait of a long-dead predecessor. On his right, he seated Tabitha, with Lady Radnor on his left. Canon Elliot sat next to Tabitha.

To balance the table, the Earl of Radnor sat at the opposite end. As the senior peer of the county, he was granted the place of honour facing the bishop. The earl had the dowager to his right, and to his left sat the Dean, ready with a learned, if dull, anecdote should conversation flag.

Wolf found himself midway down, with the Countess of Radnor on one side. From where he sat, Wolf had a perfect view of Elliot, something that perhaps was not lost on the canon, whose pallor seemed to increase with each course. Once everyone was seated and grace intoned, a clear soup was served.

The bishop, as host, began the conversation in his resonant tones, first addressing Tabitha on his right. "My lady, I trust you have found Salisbury to your liking? Few cities can boast such a mix of history and tranquillity."

Tabitha spoke warmly of Salisbury's beauty and charm, especially of the Close. The Countess of Radnor, sitting on the bishop's left, leaned in and said, "I am only sorry that your stay has been marred by this terrible murder." Tabitha was unsure what to say in front of the bishop, and so merely nodded and changed the subject.

After the soup, a sumptuous saddle of lamb was brought to the table, which the bishop began to carve with a skilled hand. Footmen moved silently along the table, filling glasses and placing each guest's portion before them. The large silver dishes steamed, and the air was filled with the aroma of rosemary and roasted meat.

Wolf sat, attentive but reserved. He replied courteously when addressed, yet his eyes often drifted to the earl at the far end. Radnor cut a solid figure, listening with judicial gravity, his occasional remarks measured and thoughtful. Wolf judged him to be the sort of man whose opinion carried weight not only in the courtroom but throughout the county and beyond. In many ways, the man reminded him somewhat of Langley.

On Tabitha's other side, Canon Elliott fiddled with his fork, contributing little to the conversation. When he did speak, it was usually to mutter an assent or a half-hearted remark. Wolf thought that his voice carried a faint tremor. Wolf noted every twitch, every restless glance towards the bishop, and filed it away.

Wolf waited until the footmen had withdrawn, then turned slightly toward the earl, pitching his voice so that it carried across the table's breadth.

"I have heard," he said with deliberate casualness, "that Salisbury Plain is not always as tranquil as it appears by day. Indeed, there is talk of gatherings at night and of strange ceremonies among the stones. I wondered, my lord, whether, as a significant local landowner and magistrate, you have heard anything of such things."

Radnor set down his knife and regarded him steadily. "I have," he admitted. "There are whispers of fires burning where none should be, of circles marked upon the turf. My bailiffs have found traces, wax, ash, and once, I am told, a hare laid out with curious precision."

The countess smiled. "Old wives' tales," she said lightly, "but they make for fine winter stories."

Her husband did not smile. "Perhaps. Yet enough to warrant watchfulness."

Beside Tabitha, Canon Elliott gave a short, nervous laugh. His fork clattered against his plate, and he bent quickly to retrieve his napkin. "Idle nonsense," he muttered too hastily. "There is no substance to such tales. Mere rustic fancy."

Wolf turned to him, eyes narrowing. "You think so, Canon?"

Elliott's cheeks flushed a blotched crimson. "Assuredly. The Church will have none of it. We must not dignify superstition by repeating it." He pressed his lips thin, and his knuckles whitened against the table.

"And yet," Radnor said, voice heavy with meaning, "rumours seldom persist without a spark." The canon made no reply.

Wolf leaned back, allowing the silence to stretch out. The canon's unease communicated as much as any words might have. The rest of the meal passed uneventfully. The Earl and Countess of Radnor were engaging, witty, and generally delightful company. They invited Tabitha, Wolf, and the dowager to dine with them again the following evening. Tabitha wasn't sure whether it was significant that they hadn't included Canon Elliot. However, he didn't seem bothered by the omission; perhaps he was just pleased not to spend another meal in their company.

After dessert was served, the company drifted from the dining room, chairs scraping and servants moving briskly to clear the dishes.

As the canon was rising from his chair, the bishop stopped him. "Canon Elliot," he said, his voice mild but carrying easily across the table, "perhaps you will remain back. There are matters of the Chapter I would discuss when our guests have departed."

Elliot stiffened, then swiftly bowed his head. "Of course, my lord. I am always at your service."

The Earl of Radnor murmured something to Wolf as they headed towards the drawing room, but Tabitha lingered long enough to steal a glance back. Elliot stood by his chair, hands clasped tightly before him, his expression a careful mask of dutiful attentiveness. Yet the set of his shoulders revealed something else: tension, perhaps even dread. Perhaps this was the man's usual demeanour, Tabitha wondered.

CHAPTER 17

As Tabitha, Wolf, and the dowager crossed the Close to return to Arundells, Wolf said, "I plan to search the canon's study while he is occupied with the bishop. I am going to tell the footman that I need to write some letters."

"What do you need me to do?" Tabitha asked.

"Sit in the drawing room and pay attention to when Elliot returns. Try to give me some warning, if possible. Perhaps you can join her, Lady Pembroke." Wolf knew there was no one better at causing an absurd scene than the dowager.

"You know, Jeremy, I play second fiddle to no one," the dowager said with a sniff.

It was fortunate they were walking side by side, because this time, Tabitha couldn't help but roll her eyes. "Mama, if we are to investigate as a team, then we must all accept that sometimes we are the lead, and sometimes we support."

"That may be all very well, Tabitha. However, I cannot help but feel that I am relegated to the chorus far more than I am cast as the leading lady!"

Fortunately, the walk to Arundells was brief, and they had almost reached the house, rendering the need to answer unnecessary.

Just before he opened the garden gate, Wolf added, "I want to go and check in with Bear in an hour or so. I do think it is too obvious if we all keep leaving together for long stretches of time. So, can I suggest the two of you remain behind?"

Even the dowager could think of no reason to argue with this, so the plan was made. As it happened, Tabitha wanted to take a more thorough look through Jacob Leland's journal, and that afternoon seemed a good time to do so. It occurred to her to take the journal to the hotel at some point; leaving it lying around the canon's home seemed foolhardy.

The footman opened the front door. Wolf handed him his hat and remarked casually, "I have letters to write and would avail myself of Canon Elliot's study. He has been kept behind by the bishop." Wolf made a point of not phrasing this as a question, even though his natural inclination to politeness pulled him to do otherwise. While he didn't claim that Elliot had allowed him the use of his study, there was no doubt that his statement might be seen as implying as much. All that Wolf really cared about was that no servant questioned why he was in their master's study and that he was left alone so he could search it thoroughly.

As he hoped, the footman was not inclined to challenge such an illustrious personage. Instead, he directed him to the study and asked if he would like coffee served. Wolf declined any refreshments but suggested that the ladies might like to take tea in the drawing room.

A few minutes later, Wolf opened the heavy oak door to the canon's study. It was a rather cramped, book-lined room that smelled of pipe smoke. While it was not uncommon for the master of the house to consider his study a sanctuary safe from excessive dusting and other ministrations by the maids, there was something particularly unpleasant about the canon's study. It wasn't that it was particularly messy or dusty, rather that, somewhat like the man himself, the canon's study had a dour, almost oppressive atmosphere.

The painting hanging on the wall behind the desk definitely contributed to the gloom. It appeared to portray the dramatic and brutal martyrdom of a saint. The martyr was on his knees, gazing skyward with a beatific expression. The men surrounding him were faceless shadows, their fists clutching jagged stones frozen in mid-strike, as if the painter had captured the moment just before the skull cracked and blood spilt. The background was a bleak landscape, as stark as Salisbury Plain.

The painting showed no angels and no mercy, and Wolf wondered how it would feel to be summoned to the canon's study and sit opposite that painting with its depiction of bloody judgment and punishment.

Shaking off his visceral reaction to the painting and his questions about what sort of man might want to highlight it in his home, Wolf made his way to the desk. He sat down, took some sheets of paper, and set them in front of him. If someone came in, he wanted there to be no doubt about the task he was busy with. He took the pen next to the inkwell, filled it, and wrote a few lines on the top sheet of paper to maintain the illusion of letter writing.

Wolf had closed the door behind him when he entered. There was a key in the lock, and it crossed his mind to use it. However, while it would allow him to search without interruption, if someone, including the canon, did try to enter, how would he explain having locked the door?

On one side of the desk was a tidy pile of what appeared to be sermons. Wolf inspected them but found nothing of interest. Next to them was a well-used Bible. Then he began to investigate the drawers. The top left-hand one held a household ledger. Wolf flicked through it, but nothing of note jumped out at him. His only observation was that the canon lived like a lord, but after a few days of eating the man's food and drinking his fine claret, he had already gathered as much.

The drawer beneath that was locked, usually a sign that something of interest was to be found. Wolf produced his lock picks and made quick work of opening it. Beneath a pile of sermon drafts lay a book bound in cracked calfskin, the leather blackened by centuries of hands. Wolf drew it out and set it on the desk. The thick parchment pages cracked when he opened them. Faded brown ink filled the pages, the letters broken by garish red initials.

Wolf bent closer. Someone had bookmarked certain pages with scraps of paper scrawled on in a heavy modern ink: *The priests of the stones did sprinkle blood upon the earth, believing thereby to bind their gods.* Another said: *Those who profane sacred ground must themselves be purged by whatever means necessary.* And a third: *They cast down victims from the high places, deeming the cries pleasing to the spirits.*

Wolf's jaw tightened. The words might have been a description of the body at Old Sarum. He glanced behind him at the painted martyr on his knees, waiting for stones to fall. Canon Elliot seemed drawn to torture and gory vengeance.

Closing the book with care, Wolf slid it back into the drawer. "So," he muttered under his breath, "If this is not the mind of a man who could kill, I'll be damned."

As Wolf searched the study, Tabitha and the dowager watched for Canon Elliot's return from the drawing room. As Wolf had requested, a tea tray was brought in. While they waited, Tabitha poured them each a cup.

As she held her teacup, Tabitha sat ramrod straight in her armchair, afraid to relax and risk missing the sound of the front door opening and closing. The dowager had told the maid to leave the door ajar as she left the room. If the young girl thought this odd, she likely just chalked it up to the eccentricities of toffs.

The dowager drank her tea and appeared quite unfazed by the situation, but after taking one sip from her cup, Tabitha placed it on the table beside her, fearing her hands were too unsteady.

"Really, Tabitha!" the dowager scolded, noticing her worried expression. "Do calm yourself. Nerves are for shopgirls and stage actresses, not for women of your standing."

Tabitha had no wish to argue with the woman, especially with the door open. Instead, she took a deep, calming breath and tried to gather herself. Wolf knew what he was doing, and, at least in theory, there was no reason he couldn't use their host's study to write some letters.

In an effort to distract herself, she began a conversation about Melody. The adorable five-year-old girl was someone the dowager was always happy to talk about.

"I believe she should be starting language lessons, Tabitha," the dowager said. "What languages does that tutor of yours speak? I would expect a child as bright as Melody to learn French and German, at the very least."

"Really, Mama? She is so very young." In truth, Tabitha didn't know which languages the tutor, Theodore James, spoke. When she hired him, language fluency hadn't seemed the top priority.

"One is never too young," the dowager insisted. "I continue to be appalled at how lax your mother was when it came to ensuring your competency in other languages."

Considering that Tabitha often wished she spoke German and French better than she did, and that she was the last person likely to defend her mother, she didn't disagree.

They managed to sustain a conversation about Melody for some time. Occasionally, they drifted onto the topic of Rat and his education under Lord Langley. Overall, it was a fine enough way to pass the time while they waited. Even so, Tabitha couldn't help feeling somewhat distracted as she kept one ear out for the canon's return and the other for the sound of Wolf leaving the study.

Suddenly, they heard the front door open and the footman welcoming his master home.

"Mama, he has returned. What do we do?" Tabitha whispered. Although she'd had time to think of a possible distraction, Tabitha had not yet decided what she might do if it were necessary.

The dowager raised one eyebrow, then took her nearly empty teacup and dashed it to the floor away from the Persian rug, causing it to smash onto the oak floorboards. With a loud crash, the fine porcelain shattered into hundreds of tiny shards.

Then, the dowager stood and, hand to her breast, her voice rising to a pitch that would carry through the house, announced, "Really! Must I risk life and limb in a house where even a cup cannot be safely borne? Is this what passes for service here?"

She swept into the hall, skirts swaying like banners in battle, and fixed Canon Elliot, who had just returned and was handing his hat to the footman, with her fiercest glare. "Your house is plagued with drafts, Canon. My hand was quite chilled, and the cup slipped clean away. A disgrace!"

Canon Elliot seemed quite taken aback by the dowager's seemingly irrational ire. "Lady Pembroke, I assure you that Arundells is not normally chilly. Was there not a fire set this afternoon?" Turning to the footman, who looked quite flustered by the whole scene, the canon demanded, "Jones, send for Sally and ensure a good blaze is going in the drawing room. "

While she could only imagine that the dowager was feeling quite smug about the ruckus she had managed to cause over nothing, Tabitha felt dreadful for the fuss they were making and the likely trouble some poor servant would find herself in for no reason. However, there was nothing to be done about it at that moment; they had wanted a distraction, and now there was one.

The footman hurried off to find Sally and ensure the porcelain shards were swept up. Canon Elliot escorted Tabitha and the dowager back into the drawing room with many solemn assurances that not a nip in the air would disturb the dowager for the rest of her stay. Just before she allowed herself to be shepherded into the room, Tabitha caught a glimpse of Wolf slipping out of the study unnoticed. Sighing with relief, she decided it was probably worth the scene the dowager had caused.

Tabitha tried to communicate to the dowager through her facial expressions that Wolf was safe. However, it didn't matter whether the older woman understood her meaning or not; the canon was now sufficiently riled up that they had to endure his fussing for ten minutes before he could be assured that the dowager was not about to succumb to a deadly chill.

Eventually, Tabitha managed to escape the canon's ministrations and retreat to her bedchamber, which shared a door with Wolf's adjoining room. She found him sitting in the armchair by her fire. He quickly and quietly shared what he'd discovered.

What did it all mean? Tabitha wondered aloud. Wolf expressed his earlier thoughts: if nothing else, the canon seemed to have a disturbing obsession with violent punishment.

"Does this make him the killer, though?" Tabitha asked. Wolf shrugged his shoulders. Certainly, it wasn't evidence that Superintendent Wallis would take particularly seriously.

"I am going to leave shortly to meet Bear," Wolf said, worried he would have to argue with Tabitha against her accompanying him. Surprisingly, she didn't even suggest doing so. The truth was that between the luncheon at the bishop's and the tension of keeping watch for Canon Elliot's return, she was quite fatigued and thought she would look at Leland's journal, then lie down, and perhaps take a nap. However, she also wanted to get the journal out of the house. Torn, Tabitha decided to keep it with her for the time being, but have Wolf return to the Red Lion sometime the following day to secure it with Bear.

CHAPTER 18

The Haunch of Venison was a crooked old public house just off Market Place, with low, dark beams and windows clouded with decades of smoke. Having passed by it a couple of times since arriving in Salisbury, Bear thought it was the kind of place where an offer of free ale might loosen tongues and where local townsfolk would gather to gossip on a Sunday afternoon. He ducked inside and looked around: stone floor, long oak tables worn smooth with use, a fire blazing in the hearth, and the air thick with pipe smoke and ale. As he'd hoped, there was a decent-sized crowd of barflies, many of them clearly quite a few pints in already.

The patrons were what he expected: mostly masons, labourers, and market traders, enjoying an afternoon off, and a group of younger lads hanging around the edges, not yet quite the ale-soakers they'd become in a few years. A few men looked up when Bear entered; his enormous size usually assured him of at least some attention.

Bear walked to the bar, placed a coin on the counter, and ordered a pint of ale. When the landlord set the tankard in front of him, Bear said, "Send a round over to those men by the window. And the lads next to them too. On me." Bear knew that free ale made friends quickly.

The landlord raised his brows but did as he was asked. The free ale was delivered to the surprised yet grateful patrons. Those by the window waved him over, and Bear joined them, tankard in hand.

"Cheers to you," one said. He was broad across the chest, and he looked like he was a mason who'd hauled stone since he was a boy. "Name's Tom. This here's Harry. You new to Salisbury?"

"Passing through," Bear said easily. "Work takes me to odd places. Thought I'd spend the afternoon in good company, and hear a bit about the town, if you don't mind talking."

"Plenty of that available here," Harry said, grinning. Bear took a sip of ale and continued casually, "I'm here with my master, who is staying with Canon Elliot at Arundells." Tom and Harry exchanged a glance. Bear noticed it and asked, "Is there something my master should know about the man?"

Tom shrugged. "Elliot preaches well enough, or so the wife says. Keeps himself to himself. Doesn't mix much. Eats better than most, so folk say. My Cathy has a cousin who works in the kitchen at Arundells. She says he lives grand for a canon."

Harry leaned in. "My brother's a watchman in the Close. Says he's seen Elliot walking about after midnight. Lantern in hand, like he's patrolling. Strange for a churchman."

Bear nodded as if it hardly mattered, though he stored the detail away.

The younger lads drifted over, tankards in hand. One, red-haired and freckled, spoke up before his friends shushed him.

"Couldn't help but hear you, sir. The ale is much appreciated. Who's your master?"

Bear considered whether there was any reason not to disclose Wolf's identity and decided that Salisbury was a small enough town that word might have already spread about the toffs staying in the Close. "I work for the Earl of Pembroke. He is here for a talk that was meant to happen last night, but the speaker was murdered."

The men all nodded; clearly, news of Jacob Leland's death had spread throughout Salisbury.

"I heard he was killed in one of them there rituals at Old Sarum," Harry said in a knowing voice.

Bear was pleased by how quickly and easily the conversation had turned to the matter he was most interested in. He nodded in encouragement, and Harry continued. "There's always been talk of strange goings on by the stones, but recently, there's been real odd things going on, if you ask me."

"What kind of things?" Bear asked.

"People say there are hooded men, and chanting. I even heard tell that local shepherds have lost sheep that they think are being killed in devil-worshipping ceremonies." Harry was becoming very enthusiastic in his storytelling, and Bear wondered how much he was embellishing now that he had a rapt audience.

Bear raised a brow and said, "Is that so?"

Harry took a long gulp and finished his ale. Bear called to the bar for another round. The prospect of more free drinks seemed to encourage Harry. "I heard that some lads went out there on a dare one night when there was a full moon. Jack Brown, who got it directly from one of them, said that they'd hidden in a ditch. He said they swore they saw men inside the stones. They were all hooded so that he couldn't tell them apart. They'd lit a fire in the centre of the stones. Then they did all this chanting, killed a sheep, and drank its blood."

The others laughed nervously, but none called him a liar.

"And what sort did these men think they were?" Bear asked. He doubted he would be fortunate enough to receive a description that was obviously the canon, but perhaps there might be a hint.

"Not farm all lads," the man said quickly. "One of 'em moved like a gentleman. Walked straight, boots polished. The lads said there was no real telling."

The landlord came by to collect empties. Bear caught his eye.

"You've lived here long?"

"All my life," the man replied brusquely.

"Have you heard about these so-called Stonehenge and Old Sarum gatherings?" Bear asked.

The landlord looked around, then lowered his voice. "There's always been tales up on the Plain. Truth be told, I have caught the sound of chanting myself, carried on the wind a while back. Not in English. Some sort of heathen foreign words."

Harry spat into the fire. "Churchmen, then. They sing in that gibber-ish, don't they?" Bear assumed this was a reference to Latin chants and anthems sung in the cathedral. Although he doubted that any of the working men he sat with could tell Latin from any other foreign language, or even absolute mumbo jumbo.

The table fell silent.

It wasn't long before the men finished the second round of ale. Bear ordered yet another, and their tongues loosened further. A carter joined the group, tempted by the hope of a free tankard for himself. He swore he'd seen Canon Elliot at Old Sarum at dusk, standing on the walls as if he owned the place. A shy young man, emboldened by Dutch courage, said one of the canon's maids had found scraps of parchment stuffed in the fire grate, covered in strange drawings.

Bear didn't press hard. He let them argue among themselves; were the rites pagan, some secret church society, or only pranksters looking to frighten folk? The stories became increasingly outlandish, and Bear did wonder if the free ale was continuing to be worth the candle. Elliot's name floated through almost every tale. Still, Bear wondered, was that merely because he himself had raised the man's name?

By the time the landlord rang for closing, Bear had spent quite a bit of coin and been told a lot of gossip, but what was true?

Bear stepped back into the cool air of Minster Street. He pulled his cap low and headed toward the Red Lion Hotel. He hoped that Wolf would seek him out at some point that afternoon. He was sure he'd be very interested in what he'd learned.

Wolf had slipped out of the house, happy to have avoided running into the canon. He made his way to the Red Lion Hotel, but Bear hadn't returned yet. The front desk clerk, a different man than previously, was far less willing to defer to Wolf's assertion of his rank and insisted he cool his heels downstairs rather than letting him into Bear's room.

He'd been waiting over thirty minutes and was almost ready to give up and return to Arundells when, finally, Bear made his way into the reception area.

"Thank goodness," Wolf said rather grumpily. "I wondered if I would wait all day for you to return."

Bear had known Wolf for too long to take offence at his impatient tone. Instead, he indicated that Wolf should follow him up to his room.

What he'd learned that afternoon wasn't something he wanted to talk about in a public taproom.

A few minutes later, they were in Bear's room with the door shut firmly behind them.

"Productive afternoon?" Wolf asked, his good mood almost restored.

"Very," Bear answered. "You? How was church?"

Wolf then told him briefly about the luncheon at the Bishop's Palace with the Earl and Countess of Radnor, and then about his search of the canon's study. He described the discomfiting painting and the writings he'd found in the locked drawer.

As was usually the case with the taciturn man, Bear said nothing while Wolf talked. Once his friend had finished, Bear asked, "So, what did you make of it all? To my ear at least, it's all disturbing, but not proof of murder."

"I agree. Canon Elliot is not the first person to hold devout religious beliefs that glorify suffering. Look at the Spanish Inquisition or the fourteenth century Flagellants. However, it does point to a certain way of thinking about punishment and retribution that I do not believe we can ignore. There is little doubt that Elliot is our primary suspect at this point. He had motive and we now know that he is inclined to violent imagery."

While they had a motive of sorts for the canon, so far, there was no evidence that he had left Arundells at any time the night of the murder.

"Were you and Madison able to find out anything from the stables around Salisbury?" Wolf asked hopefully.

"Yes and no," Bear replied. "We asked at every inn and livery stable, and no one admitted to knowing anything. Just as I was about to give up, Madison tried a stable on the outskirts of town. A stable boy, easily persuaded with a half-crown, admitted a man had hired a fly in the small hours and paid in sovereigns. No crest, no name in the books. He couldn't give me much of a description, just that the man was respectably dressed in a plain dark suit and kept his hat low over his face."

"Elliot certainly would not be foolish enough to hire a fly while wearing his clerical garb," Wolf acknowledged. "Would a lowly stable boy even know what the canon looked like? I doubt it. What time did he say this was?"

"All he could say was 'late.' I doubt the lad can tell the time. He told me that his job is to stay awake and deal with anyone coming from the last trains wanting to hire a fly or dogcart. After that, he can go to sleep. I checked, and the last train arrives around half past eleven, so it was probably before midnight if the boy was still at his post."

Wolf considered Bear's words; they knew Leland had hired a trap at eleven o'clock, and it seemed likely that if it was the canon who hired the fly, he did so not long afterwards. Were they planning to meet at Old Sarum? If so, why not leave together? What were they going to do that needed to be done at that time of night at such a place? Despite Canon Elliot's protestations of the evils of ancient rituals, was he secretly in their thrall?

"Anything else interesting?" he asked.

"Well, I spent some time in one of the public houses off Market Place. I was rather free with your purse, and the stream of free tankards of ale definitely put the gab in the locals." Bear paused, then cautioned, "I heard a lot of gossip and, honestly, I'm not sure how much was just drunken chatter."

Wolf was eager to hear this news, however speculative it might be, and impatiently assured his friend he understood the caveat.

"Bearing that in mind, then," Bear continued. "Here's what I heard." Bear filled him in on everything he'd learned at The Haunch of Venison.

When he was done, Wolf leaned back in his chair, hands clasped behind his head, and considered Bear's words. "Yes, it is gossip. However, I do wonder if this is a case of there is no smoke without fire. We have heard about these supposed gatherings multiple times now, though this is the first time anyone has suggested that Elliot is associated with them. I think I owe Superintendent Wallis a visit. It may be time for us to compare notes. I will go there now."

"Do you expect to find him at the station on a Sunday afternoon?" Bear asked.

"Crime does not stop for the sabbath," Wolf observed. "Moreover, there has been a murder. One would hope that Superintendent Wallis would take such a thing seriously and put in some extra hours. Anyway, if he is not there, I will demand his home address. Bear grinned. "What are you smiling at?" Wolf challenged, though he had an idea what his old friend found so amusing.

"Only that you seem to have made your peace with the demands that the Earl of Pembroke might make that Wolf the thief-taker couldn't." The glare Bear received was all the response Wolf gave. As much as Wolf wouldn't acknowledge it, his friend was correct; perhaps 'made his peace' wasn't quite right, but certainly, Wolf's willingness to take advantage of the benefits his rank and wealth gave him had increased significantly since he first inherited.

Instead of directly answering Bear, Wolf said, "I will meet you back here tomorrow morning." And with that, he left.

CHAPTER 19

Tabitha sat in one of the armchairs in her bedchamber, reading the battered leather journal. She turned another page carefully, the inked lines sloping hastily, as though written in fevered urgency. Leland really didn't have the easiest handwriting to decipher.

Jacob Leland was inconsistent about writing in his journal; sometimes, he wrote daily, then days or even weeks would pass before he wrote again. While some of what he recorded was the minutiae of his life, often he wrote when he had something intellectually interesting to note. It crossed Tabitha's mind that the man might have been consciously writing in anticipation of publication after he made the great academic discovery that was to propel him to fame and fortune.

This journal only covered the past year, occasionally referencing older events. Undoubtedly, the man was obsessed with Old Sarum, Stonehenge, and the idea of ancient rituals being resurrected. She flicked through the pages, scanning the writing and focusing when it seemed pertinent.

An entry from nearly six months ago caught her eye:

The foreman, Edwards, grows restless. He speaks of the bones we've unearthed as if they belonged to him. I suspect he sells to collectors in Salisbury when he has promised me all he finds. I may need to threaten to cut off funds.

Was that what happened? Had Leland threatened to withhold money, and Edwards had killed him?

Then, she came to an entry from almost four months earlier:

I am convinced that the rites are not mere inventions of rustic fancy. They are not limited to Stonehenge but extend their shadow across Old Sarum, where animal bones have been discovered, treated as in sacrifice. I have spoken with someone who tends the cathedral, J, who should not be familiar with such matters. Yet his eyes revealed a strange fervour when I inquired about ancient practices. He showed me a knife, curved and of unusual make, which he said had been found buried in chalk. He would not clarify why he had it, only that it 'awaited the true offering.' I fear him. I fear what he believes must be done. Nevertheless, I am also intrigued; does he hold the key? What can I learn from him?

Leland appeared to have been in Salisbury more recently than they had realised. Who was the man he was talking about? It didn't sound as if it was Canon Elliot, and yet the description of the fervour in the man's eyes sounded not unlike their host on occasion.

Tabitha's heart quickened. She recalled Wolf mentioning that Leland's wound was clean, deep, and not straight. A cold thought settled over her: this "curved knife" might be the very weapon.

She flicked through the rest of the journal and noticed other, less sinister, references to the mysterious J. Was this the man Leland had gone to meet on the night he was killed?

A knock on the door startled Tabitha out of her reverie. She called on whoever it was to enter and was surprised to see the dowager, her maid, Withers, in tow. The old woman hurried into the room, almost pushing Withers ahead.

She looked up and down the hallway after her before closing the door and saying, "I have news. Withers has been particularly sharp-eared."

The dowager took a seat in the other armchair, leaving Withers standing. "Tell her ladyship what you told me," she commanded.

Withers inclined her head. "As her ladyship says, I did chance to overhear some talk in the passage by the canon's kitchen door, milady. His servants gossip when they think themselves unobserved."

Then, Withers lowered her voice, though they were quite alone. "They say the canon is not always abed when he claims to be. A footman swore he'd seen him abroad after Compline, lantern in hand, pacing through the Close like a restless soul. The housemaid added that she's swept chalk from his carpet more than once, though he has no cause to set foot in the masons' yard."

The dowager gave a short sniff of satisfaction. "Chalk in the canon's carpet. Is it not deliciously incriminating? And this is not even the best part," she said with undisguised glee. "Tell her ladyship the rest."

Withers continued, "The scullery girl swore someone cloaked and hooded was admitted through the kitchen door on two occasions. She assumed it was the canon, yet she said the figure moved furtively."

"Ha!" the dowager exclaimed. "I have said from the start that the man is guilty as sin, and now we have proof."

While Tabitha found the servants' gossip intriguing, it wasn't conclusive proof of anything. She knew from her own household staff how quickly a piece of news could spread through the servants' hall, gaining momentum and becoming increasingly outrageous as it went, until, by the time it reached Tabitha's ears, it was unrecognisable from the original snippet.

Despite her scepticism, Tabitha thanked Withers for keeping an ear out. The woman accepted the praise graciously and then excused herself.

In an attempt to distract the dowager from her attempts to be judge, jury and executioner to the canon based merely on tittle-tattle, Tabitha told her what she had found in Leland's journal.

Tabitha and Wolf conducted their investigations with as open minds as possible, recognising that failing to do so could cause them to overlook or even dismiss key clues. The dowager had a somewhat different approach and was often like a dog with a bone once she seized upon a favourite hypothesis.

Given her dislike of the canon, it seemed this would be one of those occasions. She heard Tabitha out, but then proclaimed, "Whoever this mysterious J with the curved knife is, he must be in thrall to Elliot, who is without a doubt the mastermind of this enterprise." Tabitha was tempted to ask what 'enterprise' the dowager believed was being run out of Arundells, but she did not want to add any more fuel to the fire.

Instead, Tabitha said, in a tone she tried to modulate somewhere between placatory yet not patronising, "Perhaps. What is clear is that

Leland has been in communication with J for some time and yet feared him. However, we cannot overlook the comments about the dispute with the foreman, Edwards. And, so far, the only evidence we have of bad blood with the canon is the conversation Wolf and I witnessed over dinner."

Notwithstanding Tabitha's best efforts, the dowager still felt she was being condescended to and scowled. "Let us not forget this canon's shifty behaviour over the last few days," she pointed out. And of course, she was correct; the canon had done more to paint himself guilty than any actual evidence had at this point. Was there something he was trying to hide?

Tabitha felt a headache coming on. As much as she had argued not to be wrapped in cotton wool and to be allowed to participate fully in the investigation, she wondered if that demand had been wise.

Suddenly, the room felt stuffy, and she wanted to get some fresh air. Despite her earlier wish for a nap, Tabitha stood and said, "I am going walk in the Close and perhaps visit the cathedral. I found the cloisters very peaceful and would like to sit in that little garden and think." She didn't offer for the dowager to accompany her and hoped the woman wouldn't invite herself.

Luckily, the dowager didn't make such a suggestion. Not because she was sensitive to Tabitha's need for solitude, but rather because she also wanted to rest. She excused herself and returned to her bedchamber.

The last few days had very much felt like autumn had definitely arrived. Mindful of the likely temperature, Tabitha called for Ginny, donned a coat and hat, and slipped out of the house. The Close really was lovely, lined with grand houses on each side and dominated by the magnificent cathedral at the centre. The sky was slightly overcast, and Tabitha was glad that Ginny had persuaded her to wear her warmer wool coat. Nonetheless, the crispness of the air did help clear her mind.

After walking around the perimeter of the Close, Tabitha felt sufficiently refreshed to venture inside the cathedral. By this time, it was quarter to five. People were drifting out, and Tabitha assumed that Evensong had recently ended. She also assumed that was where the canon had gone following his dramatic encounter with the dowager earlier. She hoped she wouldn't bump into him. Actually, Tabitha hoped she wouldn't have to talk to anyone. She wanted nothing more than to be alone with her thoughts for a few minutes.

She walked towards the cloisters and reflected on everything they had learned that day. What did it all mean? There was the canon's strange behaviour and the discovery of violent words and imagery in his study. Had Jacob Leland done something that prompted Elliot to feel retribution was necessary? And who was this mysterious J who was seemingly connected to the cathedral? Were pagan rituals being performed at Old Sarum and Stonehenge, or was it merely Leland's fevered imagination that hoped to see more in a cluster of old bones than there really was?

Tabitha stopped by a bench in the cloisters. She sat at an angle so she could look out onto the garden and view the rest of the cloisters through the frame of the arches lining it.

CHAPTER 20

There was a serenity in the cloisters that helped Tabitha quiet some of the chaos in her mind. As the tangled threads of the investigation stopped consuming her, other ideas took their place. She had been so worried about the pregnancy that she hadn't allowed herself to consider how her life would change once the child entered the world. Now, she permitted herself to hope, and with that to enjoy the luxury of daydreaming about finally holding a healthy baby in her arms.

For the most part, Tabitha's role models for motherhood were her own mother and the dowager. Both women adhered to a parenting style that delegated most child-rearing responsibility to nursemaids and nannies. Recently, the dowager expressed horror that Tabitha had been in the nursery, sitting on the floor and playing games with Melody and the O'Leary twin boys.

Tabitha realised that Mary and the other nurserymaids would likely still handle most of the baby's daily care. However, she was determined to be more than a mother whose children were paraded before her for inspection and polite conversation for a few minutes each day before being sent back to the nursery. Although she often felt guilty about not spending more time with Melody, especially during investigations, she tried to make their moments together meaningful for both of them. Whether cuddling in an armchair and reading a book or playing lively games with all the children, Tabitha aimed to engage herself in the little girl's daily life as much as possible. She promised herself she would do no less for her own child.

As she realised that she had formed this conviction, Tabitha gasped aloud; how could she have harboured such a thought? She had always maintained that she loved Melody as her own child. Yet she was already differentiating between the little girl and the child not yet born. Tabitha did not doubt the depth of love she and Wolf felt for Melly, but that she could even briefly perceive a disparity between the children shocked her deeply. She would need to be vigilant in preventing such thoughts from entering her mind and influencing her behaviour towards Melody in relation to the baby.

Another concern was that the household staff at Chesterton House would treat the children differently. While all the servants genuinely adored the little girl, their master's offspring would inevitably be considered special, particularly if the baby was male. She and Wolf needed to make clear through words and actions that they loved the children equally and expected them to be treated so.

Ironically, the one person Tabitha wasn't concerned about was the dowager. The elderly woman had such a bond with Melody that she set aside her long-held views on child rearing and spent considerably more time with her than she likely had with her own children. Tabitha suspected she would revert to her usual ways with the baby.

The cloisters lay in half-shadow, the late afternoon sun slanting through the traceried windows onto the worn flagstones. Tabitha had come seeking quiet, hoping that the cool air would clear her mind of the whispers and contradictions that seemed to press in from all sides. For the most part, the serenity of the spot was achieving her aim.

While Tabitha was reflecting and planning for the future, people occasionally strolled through the cloisters; clerics hurried along the corridors; parishioners, who had lingered after Evensong, passed by on their way out of the cathedral. At one point, she saw the bishop in the distance, deep in conversation with someone. She didn't pay attention to who he was talking with until the two men parted ways and realised that Canon Elliot was heading towards her.

Given the canon's obvious reluctance to converse with any of them at

Arundells if it could be avoided, Tabitha was surprised to see the man notice her but not turn to walk in the opposite direction.

In fact, his expression was almost pleasant as he stopped before her and said, "I am surprised to see you here, Lady Pembroke. Are you in need of something or merely deep in contemplation?"

"The latter, Canon Elliot. I felt a headache coming on and longed for some fresh air. After a walk around the Close, I decided to enter the cathedral and enjoy the tranquillity of this spot."

"Indeed. I find myself drawn here when things are weighing on my mind," the man said. Then, after a brief pause, he continued meaningfully, "As indeed they are now, in fact. I must beg your forgiveness. I have been derelict in my duties as a host. However, there is a reason."

What was he about to confess? Tabitha wondered.

She decided to provoke the man and observe his reaction. "I will not lie. Your reluctance to be in our company has been noticed by all in our party. Given the debate we witnessed between you and Jacob Leland, such behaviour has made us wonder if you are carrying a secret shame." This was undeniably provocative, and Tabitha wondered if she had gone too far and revealed too much. Still, it was done now, and she was eager to see how her words would affect Elliot.

A flicker crossed the canon's face. "Shame, yes. However, not for the reason I believe you imagine." He glanced around to ensure they were not overheard, then said quietly, "I have confessed my concerns to the bishop this very day. Now, I believe I must share them with you."

Again, Tabitha wondered whether this was to be a confession of murder. Though she found it difficult to believe the bishop would have heard such an admission and let the canon walk away.

Once Canon Elliot was sure of privacy, he said, "I have seen things. Not once, but more than once. Men abroad in the night, where they had no right to be. At Old Sarum, and again upon the Plain. Lanterns shuttered, voices raised in a chant I could not wholly catch. Previously, I believed that if I spoke, I would be dismissed as fanciful, or worse. So, I kept my silence."

He drew a sharp breath, his gaze fixed ahead, avoiding eye contact. "That silence has weighed on me, Lady Pembroke. It made me cold and caused me to turn from your company. I feared every question would pry at the thing I dared not confess. It must have seemed to you like guilt, but it was only cowardice. I had managed to keep such concerns buried for some time, but Leland's words, and in front of the bishop at that, brought every worry to the surface. The nature of his murder, in that cursed place, surrounded by incontrovertible signs of pagan ritual, made me realise that by not speaking up sooner, I might share some blame for his death."

Tabitha felt the weight of his words. Cowardice was no absolution; it still tainted him. Yet it was not murder. She was not even convinced that the canon bore the blame he assigned to himself; if he had spoken up sooner about his concerns, it seemed likely Jacob Leland would have been even more drawn to Old Sarum, not less.

She sat very still for a few moments, saying nothing. If Elliot had truly seen such rites, and this was at the root of his behaviour towards them, perhaps he was not the murderer, and the field of suspicion widened again.

"What was the bishop's answer?" Tabitha asked.

"The Lord Bishop forgave me for my reluctance to say what I knew. However, he ordered me to make the appropriate amends immediately. This includes going to the police superintendent and informing the earl. I was on my way to do the latter when I came upon you."

Tabitha wasn't sure how to respond. To his own mind at least, the canon seemed to have received sufficient absolution from his bishop, and her personal distaste for Elliot disinclined her to offer her own.

Instead, she said, "I am not sure if Lord Pembroke has returned to Arundells yet, but I am sure he will be there shortly. You should make haste and tell him everything you know as soon as possible."

Canon Elliot nodded in agreement and took his leave of her with almost as much relief as Tabitha felt in seeing him go. While the canon might not be a murderer, he continued to be a pompous prig.

Whatever peace of mind she had found in the cloisters was now shattered. Between the unease she felt about her thoughts regarding Melody and her conversation with Elliot, Tabitha could feel the previously easing headache roaring back with a vengeance.

Tabitha sat on the bench, pondering whether to enter the cathedral's main body and try to seek solace in the solemnity of its ancient walls or to accept her unease and return to Arundells. As she remained there, she heard a faint swish of robes as someone stepped out of the shadows.

It was a man in a black cassock, with a white surplice, his head respectfully bowed. There was something familiar about him, but Tabitha couldn't quite place why she knew him. He offered the usual murmur of greeting, which Tabitha responded to. At first, she thought nothing of the exchange. However, the air shifted as the man passed her, and she caught an unusual scent.

At first, Tabitha thought it was frankincense, the lingering scent of Evensong. Then she realised it wasn't. This was harsher, acrid, almost bitter on the tongue. It wasn't the smell of the cathedral's beeswax candles or incense. This odour was entirely different. It clung stubbornly to the man's cassock as if it had soaked into the very weave. With a start, she realised what the smell reminded her of.

As a girl, she sometimes sneaked into the family estate's stillroom where the housekeeper, Mrs Adams, made preserves and syrups. She remembered wrinkling her nose at a particularly sharp smell. When she asked the kind Mrs Adams about it, she was told it was because of the juniper berries she often steeped in spirits to make a cordial. The man who had walked past her smelled of juniper.

And then she recalled the pungent smell that the superintendent had mentioned clung to Jacob Leland's body.

Chapter 21

At the very moment Tabitha recognised the smell, she also recognised the man it lingered on. He was the verger who had shown them to their pew that morning at Matins. She remembered Wolf mentioning his odd words when referring to the Canon: "Watch yourself there." What had the man meant?

As Tabitha pondered this, a thought struck her: had the verger been hiding in the shadows listening to her conversation with Canon Elliot? The more she thought about it, the more certain she was that the unsettling man had been, but why?

She could see the verger's back as he walked away along the length of the cloisters. Soon, he would step through a doorway and be gone. Without hesitation, Tabitha stood up and followed him.

The verger's footsteps echoed softly along the cloisters, the faint jingle of his keys accompanying the rhythmic tapping of his Verge, the staff he carried to lead the Evensong procession.

Tabitha paused just for a heartbeat before following him, trying to stay close enough not to lose sight of the man, yet not so close as to alert him of her presence. He moved with the ease of someone familiar with every turn and nook. Even as he strode ahead, the sharp scent of juniper still lingered around the verger.

Fortunately, the corridor they had entered was dark and gloomy, making it easy for Tabitha to hide in the shadows. She was glad the coat she wore was navy blue; it helped her blend in better.

The verger went through a doorway. Trying to be as discreet as possible, Tabitha followed, staying close to the wall and keeping as quiet as she could. She saw the man ahead stoop and bend low for a moment.

Tabitha pressed herself against the wall, her pulse quickening. The verger looked around, and then, when he was certain no one was nearby, his hand emerged from his cassock, clutching a long and slightly curved knife. Why would a lay clergy, or anyone associated with Salisbury Cathedral, need such a blade?

At the sight of the knife, Tabitha's breath caught; the police surgeon had said that Leland's wound was curved. First the juniper, then the blade. It was almost certain that the verger had been involved in Jacob Leland's death, but why?

Tabitha edged back, intending to retreat before the verger turned. She needed to return to Arundells and tell Wolf everything she had learned. As she turned, her heel caught a jut of stone, and its sharp crack sounded louder than cannon fire in her ears.

There was no way the verger hadn't heard that. Tabitha held her breath, motionless as the verger's head whipped around. Whatever hope she'd had of remaining unnoticed was shattered as the man's eyes locked onto her with a terrifyingly predatory stare. In the next instant, Tabitha's senses were assailed by the thick smell of juniper as long, bony arms wrapped her in their grip.

A cry barely escaped Tabitha's throat before a cold, parchment-dry hand slammed over her mouth. She wrestled but felt a knife hard against her ribs.

"You should not be here, my lady," a voice whispered, low and almost sorrowful. "You see too much and ask too many questions."

Tabitha would have struggled again, but she could tell the knife blade was pressing against her, and all she could think of was the child growing in her womb, its fragile body protected from the weapon by nothing more than some wool and silk.

She was dragged down the corridor, more terrified than she had ever been in her life. At the end of the corridor, they reached a narrow staircase.

The verger hauled her step by step, almost lifting her off her feet as he forced her down. The cold stone pressed close on either side until they emerged into what appeared to be a vestry, dimly lit by the stub of a candle. He continued to hold Tabitha with one hand, the knife glinting in it, then, with the other, turned the key in the heavy oak door. After pulling her through the doorway, the verger closed the door with a dull thud and locked it behind him before pocketing the key in his cassock.

Even as she was consumed with terror for the well-being of her unborn child, Tabitha had questions swirling around in her mind. She assumed this man was Leland's killer, but why?

Then, Tabitha recalled the words in Leland's journal: *I have spoken with J, who tends the cathedral. He who should not be familiar with such matters. Yet his eyes revealed a strange fervour when I inquired about ancient practices.*

What else had Leland said? The fear clouded her thoughts, but Tabitha fought to remember the words. There was something about a curved blade that had turned her mind to the description of Leland's wound. Then, a cold chill ran through her, which was more connected to her next memory of Leland's words about the knife than to the undeniable damp coolness of the room the verger had dragged her into: *He would not explain why he had it, only that it 'awaited the true offering.' I fear him. I fear what he believes must be done.*

Even as this memory arose in her mind, the verger muttered, "You will do nicely. Very nicely indeed. Surely a woman of rank will make a better offering than a simple milkmaid."

"Offering?" Tabitha couldn't help but ask.

It seemed the verger hadn't realised that he'd spoken aloud. Now, he thrust her onto a wooden bench and replied, "Sit there and try nothing. The slightest movement, and I won't hesitate to use this knife." As if she might need convincing, the man shoved the gleaming, curved blade in her face.

Tabitha's breath caught. Her eyes fixed on the blade's cruel crescent, the potential brutality of its edge illuminated by the candlelight. This was the knife. The very object Leland had feared, the secret he had hinted at but never explained.

The verger stroked the steel with one finger, his lips moving as though in prayer. As Tabitha watched his crazed fervour, she tried to calm her thoughts sufficiently to understand what this man wished from her and the situation he was in

There was no doubt the verger hadn't meant for her to be his prisoner, but it seemed he might have intended to snatch some woman tonight, and she had simply been presented as an opportunity. As she considered this, Tabitha was glad she was his victim rather than some other young woman who might not have the resources to outwit her captor or friends, such as Wolf and Bear, to rescue her.

Even as she had this thought, Tabitha realised how little she knew about the man who had her in his clutches; she didn't even know his name. She understood she had to humanise this situation. At present, the verger regarded her as a means to whatever twisted ends he sought. She needed him to see her as a person, and to do that, she had to try to see him as one too.

Trying to speak gently yet firmly, the Countess of Pembroke said, "My name is Tabitha. What is yours?"

Her words and tone seemed to catch the man off guard. Perhaps he had expected her to throw her title in his face and describe the horrors that awaited him as a punishment for abducting someone so important and well-connected.

The verger was so startled that he lowered his weapon and said, "Frank. Frank Jasper." To Tabitha, these words seemed like a significant achievement. Moreover, now she was sure that Leland was referring to the verger in his letter; J was clearly Jasper.

Tabitha continued in the same steady tone. "Frank, I know you did not mean to take me and now you must be wondering how to extricate yourself from such a tricky situation. Let me help you."

Too late, Tabitha realised that she had said the wrong thing; the murderous gleam returned to Frank Jasper's eyes and she found the knife perilously close to her throat again.

Bringing his face close enough that Tabitha knew he'd eaten raw onions recently, Verger Frank Jasper spat, "You, a mere woman, help me? Ha! As if. You may be rich and titled, but you are still a weak and helpless female, who is good for nothing more than to have the honour of being the true offering. And that will be your precious duty tonight at the stones."

Her heart pounded so loudly she feared he must hear it. Tabitha wasn't sure she wanted to know what "the true offering" signified. However, she couldn't avoid the obvious conclusion: the verger had not taken her merely to silence or to scare her. He intended to spill her blood, to offer her as a sacrifice to whatever gods haunted his delusion.

Of course, the verger did not know that he would be spilling the blood of two. Tabitha considered telling him about the unborn child she carried; perhaps that would make her an unfit offering. On reflection, unsure if that would make her a more or less desirable sacrifice, Tabitha decided to keep that information to herself.

Just as suddenly as the verger had thrust the knife towards her, he now stepped back. Any hope Tabitha might have had that he had reconsidered holding her captive was dashed as the man grabbed a handkerchief from his cassock and stuffed it into her mouth. Then, he took ropes he seemed to have prepared for just such a purpose and bound her hands and feet.

Before he turned and left the room, Verger Jasper said coldly, "Do not bother to try to attract attention; the cathedral will be empty by now." Then, he left, locking the heavy oak door behind him.

The verger had tied the ropes securely. Despite Tabitha's efforts to wriggle her hands loose, she couldn't break free from her bonds. She was tied tightly, and there was little she could do. Tabitha wondered if she would be left alone in the vestry all night and then considered that Wolf would realise that she was missing very soon, if he hadn't already. Sufficient people knew she had walked to the cathedral that it would be the first place he searched.

Tabitha knew her husband well enough to realise he would search every part of the cathedral for her if needed. It was also likely that the verger would consider this possibility at some point. It made little sense to leave her in the vestry for too long, so he would have to move her soon. How could she let Wolf know she had been there? Tabitha wondered.

She was always quite restrained in the jewellery she wore. Besides her engagement ring and wedding band, Tabitha wore a simple emerald ring that her father had given her for her sixteenth birthday. While the ring was very dear to her, the baby growing inside her was far more precious. By wriggling her fingers, Tabitha slid the ring off her finger and onto the wooden bench beside her. She tucked it under her skirt so the verger would not see it when he returned. She hoped Wolf would notice it when he inevitably searched the room.

The candle had burned down, and it seemed that Tabitha sat in the darkened vestry for some time before she heard a key turning in the lock. Any hope she had of being discovered and rescued was dashed when Frank Jasper re-entered the room. He moved across to where she sat. Then, before she realised what was happening, he had thrown a coarse sack over her, lifted her off the bench, and slung her over his shoulder as if she were a haunch of beef.

CHAPTER 22

The streets of Salisbury were quiet, with the only sound being the tolling of the cathedral bell. Every so often, Wolf would hear the murmur of voices as the faithful drifted home from Evensong. On a weekday, the police station would have bustled with activity, but now the streets were mostly empty, save for a stray cart rumbling by the river.

Inside the station, the silence was almost eerie. It was empty except for one man, slumped on a bench, sleeping off the worst of his drunkenness. A constable, the same as at Wolf's previous visit, sat behind the front desk, helmet set neatly before him, flicking through the local newspaper. He looked up, startled at Wolf's entrance. He'd hoped to send the drunk on his way shortly and make it home a bit earlier than usual. Since leaving early depended on Superintendent Wallis finally departing, the sight of the toff from the other day dashed those hopes.

"Are you looking for the superintendent, m'lord?" the constable asked after a moment, rising to his feet. "Though it's Sunday, mind." His tone suggested that the day should protect them all from the intrusion.

Wolf only gave a curt nod. "Tell him I have business that will not wait upon the Sabbath."

The constable blinked, then inclined his head and disappeared into the passage. Wolf stood in the room, listening to the faint echoes of boots down the hall and the tick of a distant clock. He flexed his hands behind his back, his jaw tight. He considered it a good sign that the superintendent was indeed at his post; hopefully, the man was taking the murder very seriously. A few minutes later, Wolf sat in the superintendent's cramped office, tapping his foot impatiently.

The superintendent had not tried to hide his irritation upon seeing Wolf. Sunday was the day he aimed to catch up on some of his paperwork, taking advantage of the peace and quiet at the police station. Violent crime was infrequent enough in and around Salisbury that Leland's murder had taken up most of his time during the week as he moved between the actual investigation and constant interruptions from the mayor, local officials, and various other dignitaries demanding updates on the inquiry. And then, of course, there had been this earl's interruptions and demands on his time.

Wallis had hoped that the meddlesome aristocrat would have lost interest in the case and decided to leave it to the professionals by now. He had even imagined, rather wishfully, that perhaps the earl had returned to London. However, it seemed that neither was the case.

"How can I help you, m'lord?" Wallis said with as much politeness as he could muster.

"I have not heard from you in some days," Wolf said, trying to keep the irritation out of his voice. "Meanwhile, I have learned some things and thought we might compare notes."

For his part, Wallis tried to suppress a sigh. Compare notes? What game did this nob think he was playing here?

As much as the superintendent wished to express a slightly more respectful version of this thought, he was mindful of his promise to the bishop. Instead, he responded, "I am always pleased to hear any intelligence relevant to an investigation. Please share what you have learned."

Wolf debated whether to discuss what he had seen in Canon Elliot's study. Finally, he decided to leave that out of his explanation, at least for now. Instead, he recounted what they had overheard in the marketplace and then the conversations Bear had with the patrons of the Haunch of Venison.

When he finished speaking, the superintendent chewed his lip, debating how to answer. Finally, he said, "M'lord, what would you have me do with market gossip and the ramblings of the local drunks?"

While Wolf hadn't expected Wallis to welcome him into his office and thank him for the information, he was somewhat taken aback by the man's dismissiveness. "Superintendent, are you saying that you do not believe there are gatherings at Old Sarum and Stonehenge?"

"Lord Pembroke, there are always those who believe those sites hold some mystical significance. If I were to send men to interrogate every group of chalk-made, addle-pated cranks who don a robe and howl at the moon, there would be no one left to police the streets of Salisbury."

"I appreciate that superintendent, however, it is not every day that you have a murder at one of those sites that seems to be linked to such rituals. Or am I wrong?"

"You are not wrong. And trust me when I say that we are investigating all possible avenues, including any links with such groups." Even as Wallis said this, he could see that this meddlesome earl would not be easily put off. He searched for a bone he might throw to Wolf that would serve as some sort of appeasement and at least stop him running to the bishop, who might then run to the Chief Constable of Wiltshire.

As he contemplated his dilemma, Superintendent Wallis fussed with the papers on his desk, aligning their corners, before finally sighing and nudging one sheet aside.

Wallis spoke without meeting Wolf's eyes. "There is a matter I've not been entirely forthright about," he admitted.

Wolf's voice was sharp. "Concerning what?"

The superintendent winced. "Concerning Mr Leland. We found a note in his coat pocket when we searched his effects. At first glance, it seemed of little consequence, and I judged it best not to spread alarm until we knew more. However, given your concerns..." He opened a drawer and laid the folded paper flat on the desk.

Wolf leaned forward, snatched it up, and read. The words were spare, and the note was anonymous: *If you would have the proof you seek, come tonight to Old Sarum at midnight. Bring no one.*

As he read, Wolf's eyes showed his furious reaction. "You kept this from me."

"I thought it was some antiquarian's fancy," Wallis protested. "It seemed Mr Leland was always chasing these supposed historical mysteries. And given Canon Elliot's quarrel with him that very evening, well, you can see how it looked. I didn't want to cast suspicion without cause."

"You damn fool," Wolf growled, slamming the note back on the desk. "This is cause. This is the very noose that drew him to his death."

Wallis's face darkened. "Perhaps. Perhaps not. But you have seen it now."

Barely containing his anger, Wolf replied, "And it tells us one thing for certain: someone lured Leland to Old Sarum. Someone who feared what he knew and was, most likely, his killer."

Superintendent Wallis agreed; how could he not? However, he also felt defensive. This earl was implying that the Salisbury police force hadn't made this obvious connection and that they needed his help to do so.

Now it was Wallis's turn to say through gritted teeth, "Indeed! And in fact, that is what my men, and I have been investigating. However, it is also possible that he went to meet one man but was killed by someone else."

It was so obvious that what the superintendent was describing was an unnecessarily convoluted, and therefore almost certainly false, scenario that Wolf almost laughed in his face. One of the key principles of all Tabitha and Wolf's investigations was that the simplest explanation was usually right. Wallis was too sharp not to see this. Instead of pointing it out, Wolf folded the paper and slipped it into his inner pocket.

"You cannot take that," Wallis protested. "It is a key piece of evidence."

"Which I will return once I have confronted Canon Elliot with it. I assume you have not done so yet?"

Now, the superintendent looked somewhat shamefaced. "Not yet. The bishop wouldn't want me to make such accusations against one of his most senior clerics without more proof."

"That may be true for you. However, I have no reason to kowtow to the Chapter. I will show it to Elliot tonight and will let you know what he says."

With that, Wolf stood and took his leave before Superintendent Wallis could think of a suitable retort. As he watched Wolf depart, the superintendent reflected on his next move. He was already walking a fine line: trying to conduct his investigation without outside interference while at least seeming to comply with the bishop's request. Wallis was well aware that he had not been in the chief constable's good books lately, and while he believed he was being unfairly scrutinised, he had no wish to exacerbate the situation.

Finally, he decided that perhaps allowing Wolf to leave with the note wasn't such a bad idea. After all, there was real cause to suspect Canon Elliot. Wallis couldn't escape the conclusion that the bishop had intervened in the investigation specifically to try to prevent the finger of blame being pointed at one of his clerics. He was sure the bishop hoped this earl would exert his influence to this end. Yet, Lord Pembroke was about to confront the very canon the bishop wished to protect. So, perhaps this was all to the good, and the superintendent would be saved from having to do something that might put another blot on his record and hinder his career.

As he returned to Arundells, Wolf's thoughts ran in a similar direction: he understood why the bishop had wanted him involved and, although he felt no duty to protect the canon, he realised that forcing a confrontation with Elliot might incur the wrath of the Chapter, making the rest of the investigation more challenging. Of course, he had only taken on the case at the bishop's request. If the man became troublesome, Wolf had no qualms about packing their bags and heading back to Mayfair. He knew Tabitha might question his willingness to give up, but he was prepared to handle that.

Wolf entered the Close and considered how best to confront the canon. Given the man's reluctance to be in the same room as them, it might require some subterfuge to run him to ground. The more he reflected on the situation, the more he believed that this could be an excellent moment to exploit the dowager's enjoyment of confrontation. He wasn't entirely sure how to best leverage her predisposition towards obstreperous behaviour, but he knew that the dowager always relished engaging in battle.

CHAPTER 23

W hen Wolf returned to Arundells and couldn't find Tabitha downstairs or in her bedchamber, he wasn't worried; he assumed she had gone for a walk. Indeed, when he met the dowager in the hallway on her way from dressing for dinner, she confirmed as much.

"She said she felt like some fresh air and then perhaps the calm of the cloisters," the dowager explained. "For my part, I have never found churches or cathedrals as peaceful as others seem to. They hold far too much threat of eternal damnation for my tastes. But each to their own."

Wolf had suspected that the strain of the investigation had been wearing on Tabitha more than she wanted to admit, so he wasn't surprised to receive this news. However, as the hour for dinner approached, he began to worry. It was unlike Tabitha to be thoughtless.

Wolf dressed for dinner as quickly as Thompson permitted, then descended the stairs two at a time. He had already checked with Ginny and knew that his wife had not dressed for dinner, yet he still hoped to find her in the drawing room, perhaps too tired to conform to the formality of changing clothes.

Entering the drawing room, Wolf saw their host standing by the fireplace, seemingly lost in thought; it seemed he would be joining them for dinner tonight. The dowager sat in an armchair, pretending to read as she did her best to ignore Canon Elliot.

The dowager looked up as Wolf entered the room. "Ah, Jeremy, has Tabitha returned yet?"

Whatever underlying nervousness Wolf had experienced over the past thirty minutes erupted into full-blown panic at her words. "She is not back yet?"

Canon Elliot had turned from the hearth when Wolf entered. Now, he said in a voice full of concern, and something else Wolf couldn't quite pin down, said, "Her ladyship has not returned from the cathedral yet? Why I left her there quite some time ago."

Wolf seized on the man's words. "You saw my wife in the cathedral?"

"I did. We spoke briefly. In fact, we discussed something that has been weighing on my mind, and she advised me to mention it to you. I was planning to do so this evening."

It was all Wolf could do to prevent himself from hurling himself across the room and throttling the canon. Even as he restrained this urge, he reminded himself that the man didn't deny seeing Tabitha. Yet, there was something in the canon's manner that suggested he carried guilt, and Wolf had a feeling in his gut that whatever Elliot wanted to confess would have something to do with his wife's apparent disappearance.

Wolf took a deep breath, then asked, "And you know nothing of why her ladyship has not returned yet?"

"I do not. I saw her perhaps an hour or two ago in the cloisters. She had taken a walk in the Close to ward off a headache and then entered the cathedral in search of some tranquillity."

Given that this was much the same explanation the dowager had given earlier, it seemed the canon was telling the truth, or at least partially.

"The countess said nothing of any other plans?" Wolf pressed.

Elliot shook his head. "She did not. She told me that you would be returning to Arundells shortly, and that if I wished to confess my sins, I should hurry home to do so."

As the canon said this, Wolf focused on the words he'd been too anxious to notice a few moments before. "Your sins?" And now, Wolf's fears overwhelmed him, and before he knew what he was doing, he was across the room, and his hands were on the canon's throat. "What have you done with my wife, you dastard?" he yelled.

"Jeremy!" the dowager exclaimed, leaping to her feet with unexpected agility. "It does no good to incapacitate the man."

Wolf released the canon, realising she was right. However, he refused to apologise; he knew the man was guilty of something and had admitted as much.

Canon Elliot rubbed his throat, even though Wolf had not grasped it with real force. Then, in an aggrieved voice, he said, "Her ladyship was unharmed when I left her. Why on earth would you believe I would have anything to do with her supposed disappearance?"

Taking a deep breath, Wolf tried to control his voice. "Because you have been going out of your way to avoid our company ever since Mr Leland's murder. I am sure that you are involved in his death in some way, and I believe my wife may have voiced her suspicions to you."

The canon sighed. "I had nothing to do with Jacob Leland's death, at least not directly, and I certainly did not lay a finger on your wife. However, I do have something to confess. Perhaps we might all take a seat. For my part, I suddenly feel quite lightheaded."

The last thing Wolf wanted to do was sit and chat as casually as if they were discussing the weather. However, the dowager caught his eye and, with a subtle nod of her head, directed him to the armchair. He knew she was right; there was no use in frightening the canon off.

Albeit reluctantly, Wolf sat. The other man had barely taken his seat when Wolf rose again, crossed to where Elliot was seated, and demanded, "Let us start with this." Wolf took the paper Wallis had given him from his dinner jacket pocket, into which he had transferred it, and showed it to the canon. "Do you recognise this?"

Elliot's hand hovered over the page but did not touch it. "Where did you get this from?"

"From Jacob Leland's pocket. The superintendent chose to keep it from me until tonight. It lured Leland to Old Sarum. Read it."

Elliot's fingers finally closed over the paper. His lips moved silently as he traced the words. His face blanched.

"You think I wrote this?" he asked flatly.

"You quarrelled with him that very evening," Wolf replied. "You spoke against his theories very publicly and passionately. Then this note is found, unsigned, urging him to the very place you claim profane rituals are held. What am I to think?"

Elliot rose to his feet, the paper trembling in his hand. "I may have despised his arrogance, but I did not summon him to his death. Do you believe me capable of such deceit?"

Wolf's gaze was steady, searching. "I believe you have been withholding truths. According to your own words, you confessed as much to my wife in the cloisters. And now she has vanished. Tell me, Canon, if not you, who had reason enough to lure him there?"

Elliot's mouth moved silently for a few seconds. Then he threw the note back at Wolf. "I have seen things," he whispered hoarsely. "I tried to warn as much. Earlier, I confessed to the bishop and then to her ladyship that I had seen men abroad at night, where they had no right to be, performing strange rituals and chanting. I stalked them and tried to discover their identities. My confession was that I was frightened that if I spoke without proof, I would be dismissed as fanciful or of losing my mind, even. And so, I said nothing for far too long."

The man appeared sincere, but Wolf was still sceptical. "And what about your violent disagreement with Mr Leland that night? You were upset at discussions of such rituals happening even years ago. Yet now you want me to believe that you have witnessed them yourself?"

The canon bowed his head in shame. "I thought that his interest in such matters would only stir up trouble. The current fascination with the occult, so-called clairvoyants, and such things, does not need more fuel added to it, and that is what I believed Mr Leland was going to do."

"Can you not see how that provides you with a perfect motive to kill the man?" the dowager asked harshly.

Elliot pressed his hand to his brow. "God forgive me, I should have spoken sooner. If I had, Leland might still be alive."

"And what of my wife?" Wolf almost shouted at the man. "You swear you know nothing of her disappearance?"

"I do not," Canon Elliot said. Then, he paused, unsure how much more to say before continuing. "However, I have worried for some time that some of this pagan fetishizing may emanate from within the cathedral itself."

At these words, the dowager sat up straighter. "Wait, the man might be telling the truth. I was with Tabitha in her bedchamber earlier, and she was reading me an extract from Mr Leland's journal, and it said as much."

The dowager had scarcely finished speaking before Wolf was out of the room and rushing up the stairs towards Tabitha's room.

Out of breath, he burst into the room, catching Ginny off guard as she was busy putting away clothes. "The journal? Where did she put Leland's journal?" Wolf knew Tabitha had been nervous about keeping the journal at Arundells while Canon Elliot was their primary suspect. He also knew she kept very few secrets from her maid.

Ginny had been anxious for some time now, ever since her mistress had failed to return from her walk. Although she knew her place as a servant, she had been Tabitha's maid for many years and felt very protective of her mistress. When Tabitha hadn't come upstairs to change for dinner, Ginny debated when she should seek Wolf out. Now, she looked at the worry etched on his face and realised her concerns had been justified, and that he was even more worried than she was.

"Has something happened to her ladyship?" Ginny asked in a panic, dropping the clothes in her arms.

"I believe so. And I need to see the journal she was reading earlier."

As Wolf suspected, Ginny knew exactly where Tabitha had secreted the journal and hurried to retrieve it. Wolf couldn't wait even a few moments and began reading the recent entries immediately.

"What can I do to help?" Ginny asked.

Wolf looked up from the pages he was scanning as quickly as possible. "Run to the Red Lion Hotel and fetch Bear. And tell him to bring the weapons."

CHAPTER 24

T abitha had placed a bookmark on the page where Leland referenced J and the knife, so it wasn't difficult for Wolf to find that page and understand the passage's significance. He grabbed the book and returned to the drawing room, where the dowager sat alone.

"It seems the canon felt the need to be alone after your little tiff," the dowager said sardonically. "Did you find the journal?"

"I did," Wolf replied. "And now I need to speak to Elliot again."

In her own way, the dowager was concerned about Tabitha. Now, her dispassionate mask slipped just enough for her to say in a much gentler voice, "You will find her, Jeremy. Tabitha is a strong and resourceful woman and will do what she can to mitigate whatever situation she has found herself in."

While her words were intended to comfort, Wolf couldn't help but find them depressing; if even the dowager was worried, he ought to be very concerned.

Wolf left the room and headed for the canon's study. He hoped the man had fled the room and not the house. He entered the study without bothering to knock; Canon Elliot no longer deserved such a display of respect.

Inside the room, the canon was sitting at his desk, beneath the disturbing painting which, in the glow of the oil lamp on the desk, was illuminated in a rather ghoulish manner.

The door slammed shut behind Wolf, rattling the glass panes of the windows. Canon Elliot looked up suddenly, surprised. When he recognised his visitor and saw his angry face, his expression shifted to one of fear for his safety. Silence settled over the study, broken only by the tick-tock of the clock on the mantelpiece. Canon Elliot sat stiffly, his hand resting on the desk where the note sent to Jacob Leland lay, filling the canon with increasing waves of shame.

He looked down at the note lying before him in rebuke. His lips moved before he knew it, whispering:

"Not my hand... never by my hand."

But the truth offered no comfort. He had seen enough to arouse his suspicions; suspicions he had believed he must investigate alone, fearful of possible mockery and even disgrace. He had caught the scent of herbs not used in any service sanctioned by the Church. He had heard murmurs in the cloisters of words out of place in a house of worship.

If he hadn't known, he had at least guessed something. Yet he had kept silent.

The canon's shoulders sagged under the weight of the memory and the realisation. Leland might have survived if he had spoken, challenged, or confessed his suspicions. The scholar's arrogance was infuriating, yes, but arrogance did not warrant such a fate. And now, a woman was missing, another consequence of his inaction and cowardice.

Elliot pressed his hands together, his fingers trembling. "God forgive me," he whispered. "I feared ridicule more than truth. I feared the bishop's rebuke. And now a man is dead, and a woman..." His voice broke. "And a woman may yet be offered up."

It was as if he suddenly did not see Wolf before him. Elliot sank back into the chair, head bowed beneath the painted martyrdom of St Stephen, whose uplifted face seemed to mock him.

"Coward," he breathed. "Coward twice over."

If the woman could be found, his name might yet be cleared. But how could he achieve true absolution, for he had seen sights and knew something was seriously amiss, yet still chose to say nothing.

Wolf observed all this in silence, at least for a few moments. Then, he crossed the room to the desk and threw the journal before the canon.

In a strained voice, Wolf said, "Read this and tell me what you know."

Canon Elliot read the entry in the journal and gasped, "It cannot be!"

"What cannot be? Who is J?" Wolf demanded. He wanted to grab the canon by the collar of his black evening coat. He believed this weak and dissembling man held the key to finding Tabitha and wanted to shake it out of him. Still, Wolf knew he had to control his emotions and at least try to get the canon to cooperate.

"It may be Frank Jasper, the verger," Canon Elliot whispered. "I thought I saw him lurking in the shadows while I was speaking to Lady Pembroke. At the time, I wondered why the man wasn't busier considering that Evensong had just ended. However, now I believe he may have been listening to our conversation." Then, almost to himself, he said, "How can it be? He has always been so dutiful and deferential; seemingly so devoted to the Chapter and all it stands for. How could such a man have been corrupted by pagan rituals?"

As much as Wolf was a man of action and wanted to begin the search for Tabitha as quickly as possible, he couldn't help but want to understand the canon's words. "So, whatever suspicions you had, they were never about this man?"

Canon Elliot looked truly pitiful as he spoke. "I must own the truth to you, Lord Pembroke," he said again, voice low. "I thought I knew where the corruption lay, though I dared not speak it," he added tremblingly.

Wolf crossed his arms to hold back the urge to throttle the man once more. "Then speak it now. Whom did you suspect?"

Elliot's hand moved to his clerical collar, as if the white band were choking him just as Wolf had done earlier. "One of our own. A younger canon, Michael Ashwell. He has always been overly fond of old books and antiquarian speculation. I have seen him in the cloisters long after Compline, muttering to himself in bits of Latin that sound less like prayer and more like incantation. He lingers in the Chapter library, poring over manuscripts no one else bothers with. To me, it seemed a sign of dangerous curiosity, of pride in unholy knowledge."

Wolf's eyes narrowed. "So, you saw innocent scholarship and made it into some kind of pagan sorcery?"

Elliot flinched. "I feared the worst. And in fearing it, I convinced myself it must be true. Better, I thought, to believe a man of learning strayed into folly than to imagine one of our humbler brethren was so debased as to embrace heathen rites. Ashwell had the learning, the opportunity, the temperament. He seemed... likely."

Wolf studied him in silence, his expression grim. "And all the while the verger stood beside you, bowing, fetching your surplice, leading visitors to their seats."

The canon closed his eyes briefly, as if struck. "Yes. That is my shame. I looked for sin among the learned and never thought to see it in one so dutiful, so insignificant. Ashwell was guilty of nothing worse than eccentricity, yet I judged him. Meanwhile, the true evil went unseen beneath my very nose."

Wolf's voice was like flint. "And now my wife has paid for your blindness."

Elliot bowed his head, his lips moving in a prayer too faint to hear.

The sight of the man praying caused Wolf to lose the last of his patience. "This is not a matter that prayer will fix, but rather we need action. The only help you can provide at this point is to tell me all you know of this verger and where we might find him."

Elliot appeared to have aged a decade since Wolf first confronted him. The Canon clasped his hands in front of him, his whole body shaking, and he responded in a trembling voice, the words spilling out as though a dam had finally burst. "It is the nature of a verger that he is everywhere and nowhere. He alone holds the keys to every door and is the keeper of every lamp. He might be in the treasury or the library. He keeps all the keys on his belt at all hours. If he has hidden her within the cathedral, she might be in so many possible hiding spots. Oh, why was I so blind? How can I receive absolution for this sin?"

It seemed the canon was about to embark on another round of self-flagellation over his role in Tabitha's disappearance. Wolf had no patience for his apologies and was sure he had no time for them.

At that moment, there was a knock on the door. The canon ordered whoever it was to enter. The door opened, and to Wolf's great relief, Bear stood in the doorway. Ginny must have flown to the Red Lion Hotel for him to have returned with her so quickly.

Wolf had forgotten that the canon had not seen Bear before and only realised this when the man started, with his eyes growing wide with terror at the sight of the enormous and rather terrifying giant standing before him.

"Canon Elliot, this is Albert Caruthers, my private secretary and friend," Wolf explained tersely. His words didn't seem to do much to comfort the canon, who continued to shake. Wolf had no interest in consoling the canon and instead addressed Bear. "Did you bring the weapons?" When the other man nodded yes, he continued, "I believe Tabitha was taken from the cloisters in the cathedral by the verger, a Frank Jasper."

Turning back to Elliot, Wolf asked, "Do you have keys for the cathedral?"

"I have some, but not all," the canon replied. Wolf was unconcerned; he would take his lock picks with him.

If the canon had hoped to hand over the keys and wash his hands of the situation, he was to be disappointed. "Then, let us go," Wolf said. "Canon Elliot, you will show us the way." For a moment, it looked as though the canon might try to refuse. Then, he looked from Wolf's angry face to Bear's terrifying one and thought better of it.

CHAPTER 25

Tabitha had not screamed when the verger first took her because there hadn't been time before his hand had clamped over her mouth. Now, slung over his shoulder and wrapped in a coarse sack, she felt helpless and terrified of what the man had planned for her. The sack smelled faintly of flour and old straw. The handkerchief was still stuffed in her mouth, so Tabitha had no choice but to breathe through her nose. Given this, she gave thanks for the small mercy that the sack didn't smell worse. Her world shrank to the darkness pressing against her face and the rhythm of the verger's boots ringing in her ears. Where was he taking her, and would there be an opportunity to escape? This was all she could think of.

The verger carried her rather unsteadily, one arm beneath her knees, the other across her shoulders. The sack shielded her from the feel of his hands but didn't drown out the sound of his laboured breathing. It was the breathing of a man unaccustomed to manual labour any more intense than polishing candlesticks. Tabitha noted this. She could even feel the thump of his heart and hear the faint clink of keys in his pocket. She heard these keys opening doors and sensed the slow ascent of the verger walking up the steps with his added burden.

After a few minutes, Tabitha sensed a change in the temperature around her ankles, which were nearest to the sack's opening; they must be outside.

"Help me get this into the cart," Tabitha heard the verger say curtly. Was this her chance? Might this other person be unaware of what was in the sack and be a potential saviour? She tried to move as much as the ropes tying her would allow, hoping this would alert whoever it was that the sack contained a living woman.

"Stop that!" the verger's harsh voice said nastily. "It won't help. This man won't assist you. He's a half-wit who does whatever I tell him." This was followed by a laugh that sent shivers down Tabitha's spine. She felt herself hoisted off the verger's shoulder and roughly thrown into what she assumed was the cart.

Someone said something to the horse, who was impatient with the wait so far. Then, Tabitha heard a noise above her as the verger drew the tarpaulin over the hood, tucking it neatly.

Before climbing up to the seat beside the driver, he turned and said, "You will be kept safe until the appointed hour. Then you will see and understand the magnificent role you are to play." Tabitha tried to answer, but nothing but a muffled sound emerged through the sack. The verger laughed again. "The stones will answer," he murmured. "They will have their remembering."

The cart lurched forward as Tabitha was carried away from the cathedral. More than anything at that moment, Tabitha feared for her unborn child; while the verger hadn't thrown her very far, she had landed on the cart floor with a hard thunk. Her hands were tied in front of her body, and so Tabitha did her best to rest them against her stomach to try to communicate to her baby that she would protect it in any way she could.

They drove out through a gate that opened onto the Downs. Town fell away behind them; the air grew cool enough that Tabitha was strangely grateful for the protection offered by the heavy sack. The world beneath the tarpaulin was dark and stifling, and she wasn't sure how long they had been driving. After the first few minutes, she decided she would gain no information while they were travelling and should instead focus on trying to relax and calm her pounding heart, if only for the baby's sake.

They must have left Salisbury because the cart jolted forward with a shudder as it sped up, knocking the breath from Tabitha's chest. What she could tell was that they must be driving over rough ground now; she could feel the cart bouncing around in a way it hadn't initially. Were they heading towards Stonehenge or Old Sarum? Tabitha wondered. She did not doubt that one of those sites was her ultimate destination.

The rough boards pressed into her side, and the coarse weave of the sack scratched against her face, suffocating her. She tried to shift, but her bound wrists and feet made that almost impossible. The smell of old grain and horse sweat mingled with the sour reek of damp straw, overwhelming her, and she had to fight her gag reflex.

Tabitha was accustomed to travelling in the padded comfort of the Pembroke carriage. However, lying on the bed of this wooden cart, she felt every rut in the road and every bump and turn. The horse plodded at a faster, though still relatively slow, steady pace, its hooves striking the road in a dull rhythm. Tabitha wondered if she could measure the passing of time by that relentless cadence. She wanted to try to gauge how long they had been travelling so she could understand where she was being taken.

Deprived of sight, her ears became more attuned to the world around her. She heard the creak of leather traces, the driver's muttered curses, an occasional comment from the verger, and the rattle of a lantern swinging from the board overhead. Once, faint voices echoed, perhaps villagers, as the cart moved through the outskirts of a hamlet, but the horse did not stop. Soon, even those sounds faded, leaving only the wind whistling softly through the sackcloth. How long had they been travelling? Tabitha wondered. Despite her best intentions, she had lost track of how long she had been lying in this cart.

Tabitha saw a tiny speck of light and realised there was a hole in the sack. She shifted her head, scraping her cheek raw, in an effort to move closer to that small opening. Even after she finally repositioned herself slightly to glimpse beyond the sack, the sides of the cart still blocked most of her view. Nonetheless, the hole allowed some much-needed fresh air, which she gratefully drew in through her nose.

At some point, Tabitha realised she must have fallen asleep, but she was clueless about the duration of her slumber. She had lost all sense of time. All she knew was that she was being carried further away from Salisbury, Wolf, and safety, heading towards whatever grim purpose the verger had in mind for her.

Suddenly, the cart came to a halt. Tabitha could hear the verger speaking again to the other man, presumably the driver. She felt herself being grabbed by the ankles and pulled. The sack scratched against her cheek as the verger hauled her into the night air. The ground beneath her boots felt soft.

The sack was wrenched away, and Tabitha was hit in the face by the chill of the night, as the sudden brightness of the nearly full moon made her blink. The moon hung large and round above the horizon, not quite full but bright enough to turn the Salisbury Plain to an almost magical-looking silver. Tabitha heard the faint cry of an owl somewhere in the distance. In other circumstances, the scene might have been eerie and beautiful. However, the sharp tang of juniper that clung to the verger reminded her of the horror of the situation.

Looking past him, Tabitha saw low, swelling mounds scattered across the open land, resembling the backs of giants buried beneath the turf. Some stood alone, others were in ragged clusters. Their slopes gleamed white in places where chalk broke through the thin skin of grass, and their shapes cast long, eerie shadows. What could these be?

Then, Tabitha remembered reading about the barrows on Salisbury Plain that antiquarians believed were ancient gravesites. From what she recalled, they thought that chieftains or warriors were buried beneath them, sometimes with weapons or treasure. Was this where the verger was taking her? The thought was terrifying.

The verger stooped and untied the ropes that bound her ankles. "You can walk yourself in there," he snarled. Tabitha wondered if she could make a run for it. As if sensing her thoughts, the verger pulled out the knife and held it just beneath her chin. "And don't think of trying anything silly," he added.

The verger's grip tightened as he steered her towards the nearest mound, with a gaping, dark opening. As the verger pulled her towards the low burial mound, Tabitha tried to stay calm and take in all the details of her surroundings she could. If she were able to escape at some point, it would be important to have a sense of the direction they had come from. The mound they were moving toward was low and squat, its narrow entrance half-hidden by gorse and years of overgrown weeds. The verger drew aside a single lintel-stone and entered, pulling Tabitha roughly behind him.

The hollow beyond smelled of old earth, lichen, damp wool, and the faint tang of something older: the scent of chalk that had been pressed and preserved for centuries. The chamber inside the barrow was small, worn down by time. A thin shard of moonlight slanted in through the shaft, and the stone walls glistened with dew.

Looking around her, Tabitha blinked to make sense of the shapes she could discern in the gloom. The rough-hewn chamber had a low ceiling and an uneven, chalk-strewn floor. Verger Jasper reverently placed the long, curved knife on a flat stone near the entrance. With horror, Tabitha remembered the words in Leland's journal as he described the knife he'd seen: *"it 'awaited the true offering'."*

The verger pushed Tabitha onto the damp ground, then crawled in after her and rebound her ankles. He then tied another rope around her waist to tether her to a heavy rock that appeared to be anchored into the earth. Satisfied she couldn't escape, he took a bundle he'd been carrying, a small heap of what smelled like more juniper tied with black thread, and placed it next to the knife. To Tabitha's horrified eye, the stone with those items arranged upon it almost resembled an altar prepared for an unholy mass.

The verger turned back towards Tabitha. "I will leave you now and return tomorrow. When the full moon is in the sky, the stones will open, and the debt will be paid."

Tabitha couldn't help herself and cried out, "You cannot leave me here. Can you not at least leave bread and water?"

Her captor chuckled. "It is best that you fast before the offering is made. It will enhance your sensitivity and make the sacrifice that much more potent." And with those chilling words, he turned and left, replacing the lintel behind him.

Alone in the barrow, Tabitha's lungs filled with the cold, ancient air, and her hands felt numb from the many hours tied together tightly. The first thing she did was try to get her circulation going by moving her fingers and wrists, even in the small circles she could barely manage. The curved knife lay almost within arm's reach, its steel shining not with menace now but with promise. If only she could reach it, she might be able to untie her bonds.

Outside, the verger walked away beneath the moon, chanting a strange, private liturgy. He believed he had done what needed to be done, and he left his victim to the night and the barrow.

CHAPTER 26

With Canon Elliot in tow, Wolf and Bear crossed the Close, cutting across the grass rather than sticking to the paths. Wolf wanted to run but knew he had to conserve his energy for what might be a very long night. A few windows in the Close houses showed a candle or two, nothing more. It was Sunday night, and most residents of the Close had ended their Sabbath in quiet contemplation or other suitably subdued activities.

At the north porch, Elliot paused. "If he's used the cathedral," he said, "the signs will be small. He knows which doors open silently and where to enter and exit without drawing attention."

The canon almost seemed convinced of the futility of their search. "We will find them," Wolf said determinedly.

Elliot unlocked the side door beneath the porch. The hinges creaked softly. They stepped into the dim building. The moonlight shining through the high glass windows illuminated the pale stones that made up the well-worn floor of the cathedral.

"Let us try the library first," the canon said. "If he meant to hide her, surely, he would choose a room with a door he could lock. It is next to the muniment room, and so we should try both places." Wolf nodded his agreement. It was frustrating, but they were reliant on the canon at this point.

Elliot led them along the north aisle, then turned through the transept door into the cloisters. The air was colder under the arcades. He guided them eastward. "The muniment room is close by," he murmured. "The library is beside it, and the Chapter House just beyond." His keys jingled in his hand. The noise was jarring to Wolf's strained nerves, and it was all he could do not to shout at the canon to keep them quiet.

"This is the muniment room," the canon said quietly, pointing to one of the doors. "The records of the Chapter are kept here. If the verger intended to hide her inside, he could have easily slipped in under the pretence of checking the cupboards. The room would not be used at all on a Sunday and would be a perfect place to keep someone prisoner, at least for a few hours."

Elliot bent down to the heavy oak door and turned the iron key with difficulty. The bolt finally gave way, and the noise was louder than Wolf preferred in the silence; for all they knew, the verger was still with Tabitha. In preparation, Wolf drew his revolver, and Bear did the same. The canon noticed the weapons and appeared ready to comment critically about guns in a cathedral. Then, he looked at Wolf's expression and thought better of it.

Wolf led the way into a square chamber lined with presses and shelves. The air was dry and stale, with a faint smell of parchment and dust. A small, grated window let in a sliver of moonlight, but the lantern Elliot held was necessary to search every corner.

They couldn't hear anything. "Tabitha?" Wolf whispered. There was no reply. Undeterred, he was determined to scour every possible hiding spot. Canon Elliot seemed determined to stay safely by the door; his only contribution was to hold the lantern up high. The other two separated to check the room as quickly as possible.

After inspecting every nook and cranny, prising open every trunk, and even peering behind the heavy curtains, Wolf admitted gruffly, "She's not here." Wolf said, standing. His voice was clipped, with barely a hint of the desperation he felt. Bear grunted in agreement.

They left the room, and Elliot closed the door firmly behind them, locking it, his hand trembling only slightly. He drew a deep breath and gestured across the landing. "The library, then. Some of the clerks come here during the day, but at night it is always empty. And again, on Sunday, it is highly unlikely that anyone visited."

Wolf nodded once. "Open it."

The Canon moved to the opposite door and inserted another key into the lock. This one turned more smoothly. He pushed the door open, and the scent of old bindings and paper wafted out. Rows of presses and long tables filled the space, shadows extending between them. The canon lifted the lantern and cautiously entered the room after Wolf and Bear.

The two men searched everywhere, but it was soon clear that no one was there.

"What if she was somewhere in the cathedral, but he has already moved her?" Wolf whispered to Bear, who could hear the terror in his friend's voice.

"Then we will track them down and find her," Bear promised.

At the Chapter House door, the canon tried one key, then another. The third turned, and the big door swung open, revealing a many-sided chamber spreading out before them, empty and cold. Desks were arranged beneath the windows, and chairs were tucked in neatly. Nothing appeared to have been disturbed.

Even so, Wolf didn't want to overlook any potential hiding spots. "Quickly," he said.

Again, the two friends split without discussing it; Bear went right, Wolf left. Wolf kept his eyes low as he moved, scanning the floor first, then the furniture. He checked the baseboards, the spots where a foot or hem might brush, and the shadows under the benches. He found nothing. He wasn't sure what clue he was seeking, but the room had nothing unexpected to offer.

After that, Elliot led them down another corridor to a small anteroom where clerks worked during the week. Wolf was aware of how long their search was taking, and he began to panic. Were they wasting time? He caught Bear's eye, and his friend gave him a reassuring smile, perhaps guessing Wolf's thoughts. Wolf returned it half-heartedly, but he took a deep breath and forced himself to slow down: panic made men miss what was right in front of them.

The search of the anteroom and then the treasury yielded nothing. Some rooms the canon had a key for, others Wolf had to waste more valuable time picking the locks. Either way, the search of every room was fruitless.

They decided to search the nave next. While it hadn't been their first choice of locations to search, Canon Elliot advised them that the cathedral was old and had been constructed over many years. Many spots might have seemed like good hiding places.

The nave felt very different at night compared to earlier that day when they attended services. The pews appeared as dark shapes and the choir screen cast a deep shadow. Wolf now had the lantern, holding it high, aiming to light up any potential spots worth checking. Wolf marvelled that only that morning, he and Tabitha had sat here, listening to the bishop's sermon.

Elliot stepped back and to the side, observing the cathedral with a practised eye and pointing out spots Wolf and Bear might otherwise have missed. They moved along the south aisle, examining each chapel. In the first, the floor was spotless. In the second, a few grains of sand marked where a mason had worked earlier in the week. In the third, there was a smear of something lighter on the pier at knee height.

"Someone brushed this," Wolf said. He ran his nail through the smear, and it lifted. Chalk again. He looked at the base where a skirt might drag and found a single strand that might have been the colour of the dress Tabitha had worn that day.

"A thread from her dress?" Bear asked.

"Could be. Could be nothing." Wolf put it in his pocket anyway. He didn't want to say the words aloud, but they couldn't ignore the fact that Sunday was the cathedral's busiest day, and it was likely that any threads, buttons, or other detritus they found in the nave and its chapels were left by one of the many parishioners who thronged it only hours before.

They walked down the nave to the crossing. Wolf stepped into the middle and turned slowly in a circle, listening. He could hear nothing but his own breath and the faint noises of the night outside. He scanned the transepts, up to the tower arch, back along the aisles. The organ loft sat above them.

Desperate now, Wolf called out louder this time, "Tabitha? Are you here?" There was no response; only the echo of his voice bouncing off the thick stone walls. Frustrated, he realised that the cathedral was enormous and that it might take hours to search every possible spot. They needed to focus more.

Turning to the canon, Wolf said, "You mentioned the vestry. Where is that?"

Elliot led them eastward towards the crossing from the nave. They passed beneath the tower arch, the choir screen looming dark ahead. He kept to the south side, turning toward the transept where smaller doors broke the continuity of the wall. At one such door, plainer than the carved portals of the nave, he paused with his keys. "The vestry lies through here," he murmured. Wolf crowded close, every muscle tensing. He held the lantern high enough to illuminate the worn steps that led down. At the bottom, they reached a heavy oak door with a lock that Wolf had to pick.

Again, he took the small bundle of tools from his pocket and unrolled it on the floor by his knee. Three picks, a tension wrench, a slender probe, a short blade. This lock looked more formidable than the ones he'd had to open so far. Wolf selected a wrench and a pick without looking at them. Elliot glanced away, as if it offended his pious sensibilities to witness a trick usually used by thieves and scoundrels.

Wolf set the wrench, checked for pressure, and eased the pick in. He tried to feel his way through the lock: one pin, two, a lighter third. It had a stubborn fourth pin that set with a little click until finally, he turned the wrench and the lock opened. He stood and pushed the door open.

There was something different about this room; it was an odd, bitter smell: juniper, if he'd only recognised it. Yet, that wasn't the only distinctive scent present. Wolf sniffed the air and caught a faint but unmistakable odour. It had notes of violets, sweet and powdery, too refined for this place. His chest tightened. Tabitha had been here. The scent of her perfume clung stubbornly to the air, proof that she had spent time in this room at some point that afternoon. There could be no other explanation for why such a female perfume would linger in the air of a cathedral vestry.

The room wasn't large, but it was quite packed with the paraphernalia of cathedral life. A drawer held rope, cut and coiled. The blades used for trimming wicks lay cleaned and put away. On a peg, a cassock hung with a shadow of chalk on one cuff where a man had brushed against a wall.

"We should search the cupboards," Wolf said, unsure what he hoped to find. Now that they had finally found a room that he was certain his wife had spent time in, Wolf didn't want to miss any detail that might help them find her.

Bear tugged open the cupboards. There were stacked linens beside folded surplices. At the bottom of one cupboard was a crate of candles.

"Behind the table," Wolf said next. There was a narrow gap. He ducked his head and looked. Nothing but a scuffed skirting board.

"Nothing here," Bear said after going through the drawers. "A few pins. A broken collar stud." Then, he noticed a wooden bench at the far end of the room and saw the glint of something on it. He pointed it out to Wolf, who crossed the room quickly, holding the lantern before him.

As he caught sight of Tabitha's ring, Wolf's heart beat faster. "She left this ring for me to find," he said firmly. "Tabitha was taken from here and wanted me to know it." He reverently held the ring in his hand before slipping it into his waistcoat pocket.

"But where did he take her from here?" Bear asked, articulating the question that shattered Wolf's moment of elation at the definitive clue.

"He knew he would have to move her soon enough," Canon Elliot pointed out, trying to be helpful and redeem himself. "The cathedral will be full of people early tomorrow morning. He had to take her out tonight."

While the canon had said nothing particularly revelatory, it did make Wolf think. He led the way out of the vestry.

They left the cathedral through a small side door near the vestry, with Elliot locking it behind them out of habit. The air outside felt sharper, and the Close was even quieter under the nearly full moon. They hardly needed the lantern to see. Even so, Bear lifted it, casting light across the flags and onto the strip of grass beside the path.

"There," he said.

Wolf crouched. A scatter of straw lay caught against the stone step, the kind you'd find in a cart bed, not in a vestry yard. He pinched a stalk between his fingers and frowned.

Bear moved to where Wolf was crouched and brought the lantern closer to the ground. Two parallel ruts sliced through the turf, pressed deep enough to appear damp. One wheel had left a broken rhythm, biting harder every few feet, as if the rim was warped.

Bear sniffed the air. "A horse went this way quite recently," he said. "I can smell the sweat and leather."

The tracks led towards the lane at the edge of the Close. Wolf stood up, jaw clenched. "He had a cart waiting. But where has she been taken?"

CHAPTER 27

The trio stood in the shadow of the cathedral. The deep grooves of cartwheels cut through the turf and disappeared into the lane beyond. For a long moment, no one spoke.

Finally, Bear said, "We've seen enough. He's taken her. Best we get the carriage and ride out."

"Ride where?" Wolf snapped. His fists were clenched at his sides. "We don't know which way he's gone." His words belied his true emotions; his first instinct had also been to act. However, if he had learned anything from Tabitha during their time together, it was that reckless activity was usually pointless. As much as every fibre of his being screamed to jump on a horse and do something, Wolf knew they had to be more thoughtful and strategic.

Bear didn't have as much exposure to Tabitha as his friend did and was much more inclined to act for action's sake. "North," he growled. "Where else? Out to Salisbury Plain. Stonehenge, Old Sarum, it's one or the other. We'll cover ground if we start now."

Elliot shifted uneasily in the gloom. "In darkness? Across the Plain?" he shook his head. "Those tracks may lead to Old Sarum, or to Amesbury and beyond. If we choose wrongly, we waste the night. You'll find neither the ruin nor the stones in pitch black. And even if we could, we have no idea where he might be holding her. Trying this in darkness is madness."

Bear raised the lantern high enough to reveal his scowl. "So, we stay here and potter about while this madman spirits away her ladyship?"

"Don't twist my words," Elliot said sharply. "I want her safely returned as much as you. But galloping blind, with no light but the moon, is folly. You'd break your neck or miss the very trail we're meant to follow."

Wolf pressed the heel of his hand against his forehead, fed up with the bickering. Every muscle urged him to run and at least do something, as Bear wanted. Still, Canon Elliot's words spoke to his analytical mind; a wrong decision and they might lose Tabitha altogether. He crouched and touched the rut again, as if it might give him the answers he sought.

"Do you believe she might be in the city then?" Bear asked Elliot after a silence.

"She could be," the canon admitted, "in some cellar or shed. But the marks show a cart left the Close. Would he trouble with a cart if he meant to keep her very near?"

Wolf stood again, jaw clenched. "Then we have two options. We search Salisbury, covering every corner we can think of before dawn. Perhaps we will find some sign if he has hidden her in the city. If not..." he looked to the north, though the sky was dark. "...then we follow at first light. The tracks will be clearer, and the horses will last the day."

Bear let out a grunt that could have been a curse or an agreement. "I don't like waiting."

"Nor do I," Wolf replied, his voice rough. "But if we ride now, we will chase shadows. Better to hold till dawn than lose her in the dark." He touched his friend's shoulder. "Trust me, Bear. No one hates the thought of Tabitha spending the night as this man's captive more than I do. I am just trying to do as I believe she would advise me if she were here."

The lantern light illuminated Wolf's face, pale with the strain of managing his impulses. He buttoned his coat as if to armour himself. "We need to consider where in Salisbury they might have gone. If we cannot find her here, we will set out at sunrise."

Wolf wished he were a good enough horseman to hire steeds for himself and Bear; there was little doubt horseback would be the quickest way to travel if they needed to head out at first light. However, neither man had a good enough seat for that to be practical.

Given this, he added, "At some point, we will need to find Madison and tell him to ensure the horses are well-rested and the carriage is ready to leave at dawn." Then, turning to Canon Elliot, he said, "We will be taking you with us. You know this verger and have witnessed some of these rituals." Elliot didn't look pleased with this command but held his tongue.

"Now, what do you know of the verger?" he asked. "Tell me everything."

Between the illumination of the full moon and the lantern, Wolf could see the canon's face clearly enough to notice the shamefaced expression crossing it. "I do not know much," Elliot admitted. "Even though Frank Jasper has been the verger for many years, my primary interaction with him is in the cathedral and Chapter House."

"Well, let us begin with what he does to earn a living. I believe that vergers are laymen. Is that correct?" Wolf asked.

Canon Elliot was relieved to be able to answer this question. "Indeed! He is no priest, no canon. A layman only, but a trusted one. The Chapter relies on him to ensure the order of the cathedral. He unlocks the doors at dawn and secures them at dusk, lays out the vestments, trims the candles, and keeps the place tidy. During services, he leads the dignitaries to their seats, manages the collection, and keeps the choirboys from fidgeting."

"Quite!" Wolf said impatiently, wanting the man to get to the part they didn't already know.

The canon heard the testiness in Wolf's tone and hurried to get to the point. "Here in Salisbury, like in many cathedrals, the role of verger overlaps with that of sexton. He oversees the gravediggers, ensures the grounds are kept in order, and that funerals are conducted properly. If bones emerge from the soil, he is the one to dispose of them. If a stone slab cracks, he finds the mason."

Wolf contemplated this information. A graveyard could serve as a suitable hiding place, although the thought of Tabitha possibly being shoved into a grave or vault made bile rise in his throat. Momentarily setting that concern aside, he asked where the verger lived.

"I believe the verger lives modestly in one of the cottages just outside the Close wall. Endless Street, I think," the canon answered. "Many of the staff do the same: the porter, the cleaners, the masons' boys. It is close enough for Verger Jasper to be summoned at any hour, yet out of sight."

"Do you know which cottage?" Bear asked.

The canon shook his head, then recalled something. "I believe the verger is an avid gardener and often boasts of his prize roses. Perhaps if we look for those, it may lead us to the right cottage?"

It seemed thin evidence on which to base breaking into a house, but it was all they had, and so Wolf allowed it might be helpful.

He inquired about the graveyard, and the canon explained that Jasper was responsible for maintaining the Close graveyard rather than the entire city's burials. "New interments are generally directed to the London Road Cemetery outside the city, but the historic tombs, chest graves, and memorial slabs within the Close still require attention. However, I believe he also has oversight for St Thomas's churchyard, which, while not far, he might have considered distant enough to need a cart."

Wolf felt certain the canon could have jumped to the most relevant detail more swiftly; the man was verbose as well as pompous. Biting back a remark to this effect, he replied, "Then let us head to St Thomas's."

The lane north from the Close was still at that hour on a Sunday evening. Wolf kept his pace brisk, Bear close beside him, the canon hurrying to keep up, even though he was the only one who knew where they were headed. The spire vanished behind them, and ahead, the smaller tower of St. Thomas's Church rose above the Market Place.

Arriving at St Thomas's, Bear raised the lantern higher. The iron gate creaked as Wolf pushed it open. The churchyard of St. Thomas's was not a wide, open space like Cathedral Close, but a cramped plot enclosed by walls and railings.

Inside, the ground was uneven, scattered with headstones that leaned at odd angles as if the earth had shifted beneath them. Many were so weathered that their inscriptions had become illegible, eroded by lichen; others were better preserved, clearly engraved with the names of merchants and aldermen who had died over a century ago.

A narrow path of worn flagstones led to the church porch, but the grass grew long elsewhere, with nettles pressing against the rails. A yew tree spread heavy branches in one corner. Iron railings enclosed a few family plots, their gates rusted, one hanging ajar.

Wolf and Bear moved cautiously among the graves and plots, listening for the faintest sound beyond their breaths. Canon Elliot kept back; as far as he was concerned, he had done his duty by leading them to the churchyard.

Wolf drew his revolver once more and held it at his side. "Check every corner," he said quietly. They started with the chest tomb closest to the path. The lid had slipped, leaving a dark gap. Bear lifted the lantern, and Wolf looked inside. Damp earth and rotting leaves. Nothing more. The two men moved on.

Bear crouched by a family vault embedded in the wall to test the iron gate. Rust crumbled under his fingers, but the bar held firm. He pressed his shoulder against it until it groaned open slightly. Lantern light revealed only the edge of a coffin lid, covered in mould. He closed it again, and Wolf clenched his jaw; this could take hours.

The sexton's shed was next, a lean-to against the churchyard wall. Wolf easily picked the lock. Inside, ropes hung from nails, a shovel leaned in one corner, and a broken wheelbarrow occupied the other. He pushed through every corner, turning over boards and rags. Wolf even checked in places so small it seemed absurd to imagine the verger had secreted Tabitha there. He didn't want to risk missing even one clue.

"Not here either," Bear said, lowering the lantern.

Last of all, the two men examined the porch. Wolf forced open the wooden door, and they searched the narrow vestry cupboard and the shadows behind the stacked chairs. Nothing but dust and the smell of old hymnals.

They left the porch, and Wolf stood motionless among the stones, the lantern light casting shadows that made the graves appear quite foreboding. He looked around desperately, his hand curled into a fist. "She's not here," he said. "The cart wasn't for bringing her across town to this place. So, if not here, where?"

Bear nodded, his face set hard. "We should check the man's home. It seems an unlikely spot to choose; far too obvious, but we may find a clue."

Wolf agreed, if only because he had no better idea. And maybe it wasn't as unlikely as Bear thought. After all, the verger didn't know they had deduced his identity from Leland's journal.

They left the churchyard, the canon trailing behind. Wolf snapped the gate shut and turned towards the road. "Where do we find Endless Street?" he asked Elliot.

CHAPTER 28

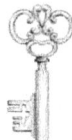

C anon Elliot led them through the High Street Gate into the town. Soon enough, Endless Street stretched before them, flanked by cottages and shuttered shops, the stillness of the late Sunday evening broken only by their footsteps. Most front gardens were bare at this time of year, the soil turned, and stalks cut back, leaving only weeds and withered remnants of leaves.

"Many of the cathedral staff live here," Elliot said, his voice low. "The verger never spoke of family, only of his roses. Prize roses, he called them. Given that, I have no idea if he lives alone."

Wolf slowed as the lantern light fell on a narrow garden separated by a leaning trellis. While the other plots lay stark, this one was a riot of late-summer colour. Against the wall, the canes of a cream-coloured rose twisted upward. A cluster of deeper crimson flowers clung stubbornly near the gate, the air faintly sweet with their scent.

The canon stopped. "I'm surprised to see so many roses blooming in September. But then, I know little of such things," he added.

Wolf glanced up at the shuttered windows. "Let us hope that this is his cottage." No lamps or candles were glowing in any of the windows, but given that it was now past midnight, that was hardly surprising. Wolf knew he had no choice but to break into the cottage and deal with any occupants, if it came to that.

Tightening his grip on the lantern, Wolf said, "Let us see what secrets he keeps inside."

Wolf paused briefly as he wondered whether they should approach via the back door. Then, he considered the time of night, its darkness, and complete stillness. And what if some curious neighbour happened to look out of the window? They'd see a cleric and two well-dressed men walking up to the cottage. What could possibly be suspicious about that?

Having made the decision, Wolf lifted the garden gate latch and led the way up the front path. The front door had a simple lock, and it was a matter of only moments before Wolf had opened it. Gently, he turned the handle and stepped inside, his gun at the ready. Bear followed him.

The canon lingered in the doorway. "I will remain here. As a lookout," he added. "A canon of the Chapter cannot be part of an illegal entry."

Wolf was tempted to deliver a sharp retort, but the reality was that the man had been unhelpful in the search of the cathedral, and there was no reason to imagine he'd be any better in the verger's cottage.

"Fine," Wolf replied. Then, addressing Bear, he said, "Close the door and leave him... keeping watch." These last words were spoken with heavy sarcasm. "The moonlight is enough illumination; I am going to put the lantern out."

It was true; with the curtains open, the bright light of the moon streamed into the small cottage and, at least for the time being, was enough to see by. The cottage was small and neat as a pin. A short passage ran from front to back. On the left, they could see a small parlour, on the right, a cramped kitchen with a range, a table, and a dresser.

Wolf nodded to Bear. "I will start upstairs. You take the kitchen and parlour." This was not a random decision; they still weren't sure if anyone else lived in the cottage, and Wolf considered that if there was, and they scared that person from their bed, it would be far less terrifying to encounter him than Bear.

Bear made his way into the parlour. It contained two rather uncomfortable-looking chairs placed in front of the hearth. Bear could tell even from his spot in the doorway that there hadn't been a recent fire. There was a table against the wall beneath the window. On it sat a writing slope.

Bear assessed the room; nothing suggested a struggle of any kind. Everything was in its place, yet the room lacked homeliness. There wasn't a painting or a knick-knack in sight. For a man who loved flowers, there were none cut in a vase, brightening the room. The armchairs had no cushions either for decoration or comfort. The place was as spartan as a monk's cell.

Crossing the room, Bear began with the writing slope. Inside were nibs and sealing wax. There was also a small, battered booklet, its cover creased and thumb-marked. "Old Moore's Almanack," Bear read aloud, then flipped it open. Pages of tables and loose notes on the weather, eclipses, and moon phases spilt out. He looked through the book and noticed that one page had a corner turned down. Flipping to that page, he saw it was for September, the month they were in.

The neatly printed entry read: *Full Moon, 25 September*. But beside it, in a cramped hand, was written *Monday, 26 September – true night: offering*. Bear didn't want to think about what that might mean.

He collected the papers that had fallen from the almanack and spread them out on the table. The first sheet was a crudely hand-drawn plan, with circles in pencil labelled with small notes. One line extended from the outer circle to the margin, marked "N.E." Another had a note: "moonrise." The words "altar stone" were underlined three times along the bottom edge. There were numbers beside the northeast. Bear set it aside.

Another paper contained two paragraphs with headings in Latin, although the text was in English. Phrases repeated included: "blood to the earth," "renewal at the standing stones," and "the land answers." Lines were underlined. Written at the bottom of the page was: "the *true* offering binds past to present."

Bear opened a side compartment of the slope and pulled out a small, folded map of the Plain. Two routes from the Close were marked in pencil. One went north towards Old Sarum. The other turned east past Amesbury to Stonehenge. The Stonehenge route had minor points marked along it, each with a time. A third piece of paper held a list of items: "rope 2 lengths; brazier; coals; candles; flint; chalk; knife; juniper; bowl." Each item was ticked.

A second drawer contained an envelope of clippings. Bear went through them. Articles about Stonehenge, barrow excavations, and even one about the discovery in Pembrokeshire. One was a brief notice about Leland's upcoming lecture. Another was a commentary speculating on "Druid rites" and "blood on the stones," with several parts underlined. A small scrap of paper sat between the clippings with a single line: *If the bones speak, the earth listens.*

From the final draw, Bear drew a small wooden box, the kind used for communion wafers. Inside, on a square of linen, lay a curl of pale hair tied with a faded blue ribbon. Beneath it, a card in the same neat hand: *Peter Jasper, 1888–1896.*

Bear studied the box and the hair within. "A child," he said softly. "He lost him two years ago."

Upstairs, Wolf found very little. He was relieved to discover that no one was asleep in the cottage. While the parlour was austere in its decorations, the bedrooms were even more so; it was almost as if no one slept in them. If Wolf hadn't opened a wardrobe and found a few clothes hanging neatly, he might have wondered whether the verger used either bedroom.

The one item that implied a person lived in this cottage was a Bible next to the bed. Wolf picked it up and noticed sheets of paper slipped in between some of the pages.

Opening the Bible to one of the marked pages, he found a pamphlet, its cover half-torn. *The Old Faith of Albion: A Treatise upon the Sacred Stones of Britain.* The margins were crowded with writing. One phrase had been underlined twice: *The ancient rites must be renewed so that the land may live.*

He turned another page. A sheet of foolscap had been pressed between the leaves of the Bible; a letter that was never posted, it seemed. The heading read simply *Mr Leland,* and the ink had blotted at the start of the last line.

You do not understand. The Church has forgotten the true covenant. I have seen the signs at the altar, in the chalk and the blood of the birds. It was never meant for bread and wine alone.

Why hadn't he finished the letter and sent it? Wolf folded the letter carefully and slipped it into his pocket.

Returning downstairs, he found Bear in the parlour, examining the notes. Gravely, Bear showed him what he had discovered.

"A child, taken too early. Is that what this is about somehow? Does he somehow think he can bring him back?" Wolf wondered incredulously. "Through the old rites. He twisted grief into faith."

Wolf felt chills as he reached a terrifying conclusion: the verger intended to perform a pagan ritual and offer up a sacrifice.

Watching the horror dawn on his friend's face, Bear said, "It might be the blood and bones of a sheep or goat he is talking about. Didn't Leland's journal talk about animal bones?" Wolf knew it was possible his friend was correct, but he had a horrible feeling it was not to be a farmyard animal that would be offered up to the pagan gods on the Monday night.

"Have you searched anywhere else?" he asked. Bear shook his head. "I saw a cellar door under the stairs. Let us try that just in case."

Walking out into the corridor, they found the door and a key hanging on a hook beside it. Wolf felt a flash of hope that he quickly suppressed. Was it possible they'd find Tabitha in the cellar?

"Try it," Wolf said.

Bear took the key and opened the door. Steps led down into a small cellar. Bear went first, lantern high, gun ready. Wolf followed. The space under the stairs was cramped, especially for Bear. A few shelves held jars and boxes. A brazier stood in the corner with a small bag of coal beside it. Two coils of rope hung on pegs. Wolf ran his hand along the rope. Leather straps were on the shelf. A small earthenware bowl sat on the ground beside the brazier. Next to it lay a folded bundle of cloth, bound with string. Wolf untied it. Inside were candles, thick and plain, some with faint marks on their sides: shallow scratches, perhaps symbols copied from somewhere else.

Wolf observed grimly, "The man seems quite ready for whatever he has planned." He looked around the cellar again. No discarded gag. No torn fabric he could link to Tabitha. No ring, no hairpin, nothing pointing to someone having recently been held here. He spoke his disappointment aloud. "He did not bring her here."

The two men went back up the stairs. Wolf crossed to the small cupboard by the door. Spare boots. A cloak. A belt with a bunch of keys. He took the keys and turned them over in his hand. Some were for old doors, some new. One long bit matched what he had seen on the vestry. Another looked like a gate key. Was there any point in taking these? He'd been able to pick any lock they'd come across, and taking these keys would alert the verger that someone had been there, if he returned. Wolf left the keys where they were.

"We should check and see if there's a garden shed," Bear said. "An avid gardener is bound to have one. Then I think we're done here."

They crossed the small kitchen and stepped out into the back garden. At the end was a little wooden shed. It was also locked, which briefly gave Wolf hope that they might find Tabitha inside. The lock was easy to pick, and quickly he had lifted the latch and pushed the door open. Inside were gardening tools, a wheelbarrow, and a small stack of boxes. Wolf opened the top box: charcoal. The next: more candles. The third: small bundles of herbs tied with string, labelled by month in the same cramped hand-writing as the papers upstairs. He replaced them as he had found them.

He checked the floor. There were no recent-looking scuff marks or cloth scraps. It was the cleanest and neatest shed Wolf had ever seen. He paused and gazed around him. Then, feeling disheartened, he left, and they shut and relocked the door.

Back in the kitchen, Bear sighed. "There's no sign she was ever here."

"No," Wolf said. "He hasn't used this place to hold her. He uses it to plan. Let's take those papers with us. Now we know for sure that whatever he's planning will be tomorrow night." Then, looking at the clock on the kitchen wall, he amended, "I should say, tonight. We do not know the exact time or spot, though. What we need to do is to find her before he starts his macabre ritual."

They gathered the map and the papers. Wolf closed the writing slope and pushed the chair back into place. Then, they left the house, locking the door behind them.

At the gate, Bear paused. "There is no reason to believe that anything will happen to Tabitha before nightfall. I think we need to return to Arundells and get a few hours of sleep." As he expected, he saw that his friend was ready to disagree. Putting a gentle hand on Wolf's shoulder, Bear said, "We will need all our strength when the time comes. It will not help Tabitha for us to force ourselves awake for no reason."

Wolf knew he was right, yet everything in him revolted at the thought of taking to his bed while Tabitha was being held captive somewhere.

Because he couldn't argue directly against Bear's logic, Wolf pointed out, "We still do not know precisely where this ceremony is to take place. Also, we need to explain what is happening to Superintendent Wallis."

"Something we cannot do in the middle of the night," Bear pointed out. "Also, it is better if we look at these diagrams and notes with clearer heads." Reluctantly, Wolf agreed. For his part, Canon Elliot looked very relieved that he was to be allowed to return home to sleep; he'd worried he was expected to trail around after the other two men all night.

They walked back along Endless Street in silence. The city was still. Wolf pondered the facts: a map pointing somewhere, a prepared kit, and dates written clearly. There was no sign of Tabitha in the cottage, so where was she?

As they passed under the arch and into the Close, Wolf was determined to allow himself no more than an hour or two of rest before rising to examine what they had discovered.

CHAPTER 29

The darkness pressed on Tabitha like a weight. She wasn't sure how long she had been in the barrow, but she knew it had been hours. Had she heard chanting from outside, or was it merely fear causing her to imagine terrible things?

At one point, she had fallen asleep, waking with a stiff neck from the uncomfortable position she was dozing in. She shifted against her bonds, the rope chafing at her wrists, the chalk floor cold through her skirts. The air inside the barrow was close, and with every breath she drew, the damp earth mixed with chalk dust, mould, and something mineral seemed to seep more deeply into her lungs.

Tabitha tried to slow her breathing. Then, she raised her bound arms and attempted to press her sleeve against her mouth, though she knew the cloth of her coat did little to protect her. Moreover, she couldn't stay in that position for long.

Her thoughts drifted, as they often did recently, to the child within her. "What I breathe, they must breathe also," she said to herself, a twinge of fear prickling along her spine.

Dr Pauls had warned that foul air could weaken the blood and that noxious vapours might leave an infant frail from the very first breath. She remembered everything she had been told when she failed to bear

Jonathan a child. Her own mother had suggested that shocks, terrors, and corrupt air might have caused her to lose the babies she had managed to conceive.

She placed a hand on her belly, trying to stay calm. "You are safe," she whispered, though she was unsure she believed it. If the miasma could harm her, might it not also threaten her unborn child? The thought tormented her, more painful than the ropes binding her wrists and ankles. She endeavoured to steady herself, knowing she had to stay strong and keep her wits about her. She must persevere for her baby's sake until Wolf could rescue them.

The thin line of moonlight filtering through the opening to the barrow was enough to illuminate the chamber sufficiently to see the chalky pallor of the walls pressing close around her. The chamber was small, barely wide enough for her to stretch her legs, and the roof so low she could not stand upright even if she had been free. The stones lining it were rough and damp. Still, she was thankful to lean back against them.

Tabitha shifted against her bonds, and her shoulder brushed loose chalk. A trickle of grit ran down her sleeve. She could just about make out marks on the stone, scratches, perhaps the tools of antiquarians who had broken into this place years ago. A splinter of bone lay on the floor, half-buried in the chalk dust. She twisted her face away, trying not to think about the possibility that it might be human remains.

The silence was absolute, broken only by the sound of her own breathing. She felt as if she were sealed alive in a grave. Tabitha closed her eyes and pressed her hand to her abdomen. She must not succumb to terror. For her child's sake, she must endure. She knew Wolf would find her; he had to.

She drew the rope around her wrists against the rough wall, causing chalk dust to fall. With a deliberate scrape, she left a streak on the stone. Could she write something and leave a message? The position she had to be in to do so was very uncomfortable, but she persevered and scratched WOLF into the chalky wall. Then, shifting again, somehow, she pulled a thread loose from her sleeve and let it fall.

Tabitha didn't know if Wolf would ever find this spot, but if he did, she wanted to know she'd been there, just as she'd done by dropping her ring in the vestry.

Closing her eyes, Tabitha tried to control her thoughts. Panic would sap her strength. She tested the knots at her wrists. They were tight, but not impossible to loosen. The ropes cut into her skin as she twisted, but she managed to make the bonds a little looser.

Opening her eyes, Tabitha had an idea. She didn't know how long she had before the verger returned, so there was no time to waste. She twisted her shoulders until the tether around her waist scraped against the edge of the anchoring stone. The flint in the chalk wall caught the fibres with a faint rasp. Her heart leapt. Again, she arched her back and pulled hard. Pain seared across her skin, but the rope rasped once more, and this time she felt something give way.

This could take some time. Time she did not have. Tabitha thought of Wolf and the child she carried and worked faster, sawing the rope back and forth against the sharp stone, ignoring the discomfort and even the pain. Her sweat mingled with the damp of the barrow, helping to soften the fibres. Just as she began to think it was pointless to continue, the tether parted with a muffled snap, and Tabitha collapsed forward, free of the rock though still bound by hand and foot.

Unsteadily, she dragged herself across the gritty floor. Her knees knocked against the chamber wall, but she carried on until her wrists brushed another jutting flint. She ground the rope against it, teeth clenched, arms trembling with the effort. One strand frayed, then another.

"Hold on," she whispered to herself. "Just hold on."

At last, with a final twist, the cord snapped. Her wrists were free, raw and burning. She tore at the knots on her ankles with numb fingers until they also loosened. Depleted from the effort, Tabitha lay still, gasping in the stale air. Then she pushed herself upright, shaking, bruised but free.

The barrow was dark and silent. Tabitha swallowed hard. Now she only had to make her way out and cross the plains. She didn't know how far she was from Salisbury, though she knew she'd been in the cart for hours. Perhaps there was a nearer village she could head to and find help. What she knew was that she had to try.

As she crawled towards the entrance of the barrow, Tabitha could see the curved knife resting on the stone beside the bunch of juniper. Should she take it with her? The idea of being armed with a weapon seemed sensible, but the knife was large and unwieldy, and Tabitha wasn't sure she was comfortable moving quickly while holding it.

Ultimately, Tabitha decided to leave the knife behind. It unsettled her so much that she couldn't bear the thought of touching it, let alone carrying it with her for hours. She crept towards the barrow's entrance on all fours because she couldn't stand upright inside it. Even going past the knife made her skin crawl. She was relieved to find that, although the verger had moved the lintel-stone partly in front of the entrance, it wasn't hard to move.

Tabitha staggered out of the barrow, one hand pressed to the cold chalk of the mound for balance. The air outside was sharp and damp with dew. Suddenly, she realised it was almost sunrise, and that she had been inside the barrow all night. She drew deep breaths of the fresh air, eager to fill her lungs after the staleness of her prison. Tabitha stood there, her body trembling, the remnants of rope still dangling from her wrists and waist as she contemplated what to do next.

The fields stretched wide before her, with nothing else to see in any direction. Tabitha turned slowly in a circle, trying to get her bearings. To the east, the sky showed a faint orange edge, the promise of sunrise. Wherever she looked, the fields undulated in places where there were barrows.

Tabitha didn't know which way to go. Every direction looked the same, fields merging into fields, chalk down into chalk down. But at her feet, the ground was marked by twin ruts cut deep into the soft earth, pressed by a heavy cart. She crouched, fingers brushing the grooves. These must be from the cart that had carried her here. Her breath caught. Should she follow them or go the other way, away from the verger? She might stumble into them again if she turned back along the route they had come. Yet if she struck out blindly across the fields, she might walk in circles until exhaustion overtook her.

She closed her eyes, recalling the journey to the barrows. She remembered that at some point, she'd heard the sounds of village life, however faintly. If she could reach that village, she could beg for shelter. She might even find a farm cart heading for Salisbury on the road. The thought steadied her. It was better to take the chance of passing through a place where she had heard signs of life than to lose herself completely on Salisbury Plain.

Pressing her lips together determinedly, Tabitha set off to follow the ruts.

As she walked, the sun began to rise. There were no sounds, save for her own footsteps and the occasional cry of a waking bird. The Plain stretched pale under the lightening sky, the grass wet with dew. It was a frosty morning, and every breath Tabitha drew filled her lungs with cold, fresh air that helped to clear her head. She was grateful for the coat she had been wearing when the verger grabbed her. Now, she pulled it close around her and fixed her eyes on the twin lines before her, not daring to look too far ahead.

The sun had fully risen now, illuminating the sky with pinks and golds. Tabitha wasn't sure how long she had been walking. Her legs ached, and her shoes were damp with dew. The exhaustion she had been feeling for weeks now had subsided, replaced by a wild energy born of the thrill of escape.

Tabitha stumbled more than once on concealed flint beneath the grass. Still, she carried on, forcing herself to count her steps and focus only on reaching the next rise, the next bend in the track.

As she walked, Tabitha tried to focus on happy thoughts. She imagined herself entering the hamlet from which she had heard sounds and pictured a kind farmer's wife giving her a blanket. Perhaps the farmer would offer to take her back to Salisbury. More than anything, she envisioned herself safe with Wolf's arms around her and their baby. All she had to do was keep moving.

The creak of wheels reached her before she saw them, jolting her out of her reverie. Tabitha stopped dead in her tracks. Her heart was pounding as she turned towards the sound, hoping it was nothing more than a farmer out early in the fields. She could see a cart approaching along the same track she was walking, the ruts guiding it unerringly towards her. Her breath caught. Could it be? Had Providence sent her deliverance so soon?

Tabitha shaded her eyes against the low sun, squinting to see the cart, its silhouette sharp against the rising light. A horse plodded steadily ahead, tossing its mane. She felt a rush of relief so powerful it made her knees weaken. She raised a hand, half-ready to call out, her voice rising in her throat.

Then she saw the figure seated on the cart's plank.

The shape was unmistakable: stooped shoulders, a cap pulled low, sitting beside another man holding the reins. Even from a distance, she recognised the verger's countenance as he leaned forward.

The relief in her chest suddenly turned to ice.

"No," she whispered. Her hand dropped. The cart kept coming, the creak of wheels growing louder with each heartbeat. Where had they come from, and had they already visited the barrow and realised she had escaped?

Without another thought, Tabitha turned and ran.

Her skirts tangled around her legs as she sprinted, the ropes still dragging from her waist slapping her side. The grass was slippery with dew, slowing her with every stride. She gasped for breath, her lungs already burning from exertion.

Behind her, the horse snorted, hooves pounding as the cart rattled faster along the track. It was pointless. She was no match for it. The cart drew nearer, and the sound of its wheels roared in her ears. Tabitha tried to veer off the path, cutting across the field, but the ground rose sharply, slowing her. Her shoes skidded on chalk, and she stumbled, nearly falling.

A shadow loomed over her as the horse snorted fiercely from the gallop, foaming at its bit. The cart pulled alongside. A hand shot out, gnarled and strong, closing around her arm with bruising force. Tabitha screamed and struggled, clawing at his sleeve, but the verger only tightened his grip, hauling her bodily onto the cart. She kicked, twisted, and nearly tumbled back to the ground, but he pinned her fast against the plank seat.

"Thought you were clever, did you?" His voice was harsh, and his breath foul with juniper smoke. "Did you think you could run from what is written? The old gods will not be cheated."

Tabitha emitted a wordless cry, struggling, but her strength had ebbed. The verger snapped the reins, and the horse surged onwards. The cart jostled along the track, carrying her back across the fields. She slumped against the wooden rail, despair crushing her chest. She had escaped the barrow, but not him. Not yet.

Every so often, Tabitha twisted, testing the verger's grip, but his hand was gripping her arm like a vice.

"You will not run again," he muttered. "The full moon waits for you tonight. And you will be the offering it demands."

CHAPTER 30

Wolf struggled to fall asleep; he tossed and turned, his mind too full of fears for Tabitha to rest. At one point, he was tempted to give up trying and get out of bed. However, he kept hearing Bear's words: "We will need all our strength when the time comes."

Finally, somehow, he managed to fall asleep. Despite his intentions, he didn't wake until dawn. He had deliberately left his drapes open so the morning's first light would wake him. At the first sign of daybreak, Wolf's eyes snapped open, and he immediately cursed himself for not waking earlier.

The previous evening's search had been carried out in his formal evening wear. Now, he put on the most comfortable clothes he had brought with him. He wished he had thought to bring his thief-taker attire, but it had never occurred to any of them that they would be conducting an investigation. He did not ring for Thompson to help him; he had no patience for the man's fussing and his relentless cravat retying.

As soon as he was dressed, Wolf gathered everything they had found at the verger's cottage and went downstairs. Just as with Bear's advice to sleep, Wolf knew he should eat something, despite having no appetite. He was up so early that the staff hadn't laid out food in the breakfast room yet. They were horrified when Wolf made his way to the kitchen to request some toast and coffee. A maid offered to bring some to him as she encouraged him to leave the servants' domain.

While waiting for his breakfast, Wolf laid out the papers again and tried to make sense of what he was looking at. They needed to answer two key questions: was that night's ritual to take place at Stonehenge or Old Sarum, and where was Tabitha being kept until then?

Given the men working on the excavation of Stonehenge, Wolf couldn't imagine the verger easily hiding a prisoner there unnoticed. Was there anywhere at or near Old Sarum that would be more suitable? Of course, he thought despondently, the verger could be holding Tabitha anywhere.

He had just been served his coffee and toast when Bear entered the room, closely followed by the canon. In truth, Elliot would have liked to find a reason not to rejoin the search that day. However, he felt sufficient guilt for the role he'd played and was nervous that the bishop would be less inclined to show him even less mercy once he discovered that the Countess of Pembroke had been abducted.

Wolf was pleased to see Bear and mildly surprised that the canon had willingly joined them. He was grateful to see the man, if only because he believed Elliot could help them identify the most likely location for the verger to perform his Druid ritual. It was reasonable to assume that Tabitha was being kept somewhere close to that spot, and Wolf didn't want to waste any more time searching in the wrong place.

What did shock Wolf was when the door to the breakfast room opened again, and the dowager entered. He had never seen her up and about at such an early hour. His first instinct was to say as much, but his nerves were strung too tight to risk engaging in a sparring match with the woman.

Despite his resolve not to allude to the early hour, his shock must have shown on his face. "There is no need to act quite so surprised to see me up and about, Jeremy," the dowager said tartly as she seated herself at the table. "I was very worried last night when you did not return with Tabitha and insisted that Withers wake me early this morning. Now, tell me everything you have learned."

Although the dowager could sometimes hinder an investigation, Wolf respected her intelligence and strategic mindset. It might be useful to tell her everything and gain a fresh perspective.

First, he explained everything they had learned from the canon's confession. While the dowager did not comment, she shot the man a withering look that made him cower in his seat.

Wolf didn't give a detailed account of their search of the cathedral. Instead, he said, "We searched everywhere, but found nothing until we reached the vestry. There, I discovered Tabitha's ring, which she must have dropped deliberately to alert me."

"Clever girl," the dowager replied approvingly. "Where else did you look?"

She listened to the account of searching the St Thomas churchyard and the verger's house. As Bear explained what he found in the verger's writing slope, Wolf laid the papers on the breakfast table.

The dowager read the verger's handwritten phrases and gasped. Wolf wasn't sure he'd ever seen the woman as genuinely aghast as she was now. Perhaps the only other time had been when Melody had been abducted.

Now, her hand went to her throat in shock. "Surely, he does not mean what this seems to imply?" she asked, unable even to bring herself to say the words.

"We do not know," Wolf confessed. "It is possible that this sacrifice is nothing more disturbing than a goat. However, we cannot dismiss other possibilities." He struggled to articulate his worst fear. "Perhaps he seized Tabitha opportunistically. Perhaps she overheard or guessed something. I am trying not to jump to the worst conclusions," he added cautiously.

Yet, how could he not? There was every reason to believe that the verger had murdered Jacob Leland. If so, why would he hesitate to kill again?

"What can I do?" the dowager asked.

"I do not know," Wolf acknowledged in a voice thick with desperation and fear.

"You will find her, Jeremy. I have no doubt of that," the dowager said, covering his hand with her own. "Where do you plan to look first? These notes seem to suggest that tonight's so-called ceremony might be at either Old Sarum or Stonehenge."

Indeed, Wolf agreed. Turning to Canon Elliot, he asked, "Do you have any insights into why this man might choose one place over another? After all, you have been observing these rituals, have you not?"

The canon looked sheepish. "I only saw one. I had heard rumours and gossip for some time and suspected that something was taking place. However, I only managed to witness one of these ceremonies happening, and that was at Old Sarum."

"So, that is where you believe we should focus the search?" the dowager inquired anxiously.

Before the canon could reply, Wolf said, "There is one line underlined more than once: *renewal at the standing stones.* It can only mean Stonehenge, can it now?"

Elliot pressed his lips together briefly, then replied, "Perhaps. The phrase would definitely suggest it. But you must understand, there is more than one place nearby to which these words might apply."

Wolf looked up sharply. "Explain." He was worried that he was encouraging the canon to embark on one of his lengthy and pompous diatribes. Yet, this man was by far the most knowledgeable of all of them on the topic of local history.

Perhaps aware of his audience's limited patience, Canon Elliot did his best to get to the point quickly. "Before Salisbury Cathedral was built, there was another at Old Sarum. The ruins remain. Not only the walls, but the very bases of columns. Some still stand, worn and broken though they are, rising from the chalk. Antiquarians call them fragments, but a man with a mind for pagan symbolism might see them as standing stones."

Wolf frowned. "Columns from a cathedral, or stones from a heathen temple. Can it really be all the same to this man?"

"Yes." Elliot's voice dropped. "You see, there has long been a dispute among scholars. Some argue that the cathedral's builders raised their piers upon stones older than Christendom itself. A fanciful notion perhaps, but it endures. Others insist that what appear as crude monoliths are merely the weathered remains of Norman craftsmanship."

Despite his best efforts, the canon's explanation still felt overblown to Wolf. Trying to be patient, he allowed the man to speak because he wanted to understand what might be going through the verger's mind, and the canon seemed the person best placed to illuminate that.

The canon went on, "We antiquarians write pamphlets and argue in our societies about it. However, to a mind like the verger's, the doubt is enough. He can convince himself that the very foundations of the old cathedral are pagan in origin and that to stand among them is to stand where the ancients once made their sacrifices."

When the man finished speaking, Wolf felt more conflicted than ever. He didn't know, nor could he know for sure, which site was correct, and they didn't have the time to waste going to the wrong one. He put his head in his hands in despair. He had to make the right choice; Tabitha and their baby's life depended on it.

Then, a tart voice cut through his bleak thoughts. "You men can argue your antiquarian theories all you want in the safety of your libraries and lecture halls, but you are missing the simplest truth."

Wolf turned to the dowager impatiently. "And what truth is that?"

With a certain smugness, she replied, "That the whole of England, for the last half-century, has treated Stonehenge as its pagan theatre." She lifted her chin, her eyes bright with scorn. "The poets, the journalists, the gentlemen antiquarians with more money than sense have all made a fetish of it. Every young man who imagines himself touched with ancient mysteries dreams of parading about those stones by moonlight. Old Sarum is a local curiosity for sure, but Stonehenge is a shrine. It is the only place that would flatter a mind swollen with delusions of grandeur."

Elliot bristled. "The ruins of the cathedral are no less..."

"Oh, hush," she snapped. "Old Sarum is a heap of broken masonry. No one writes breathless verses about Old Sarum. But Stonehenge, well, that is the stage on which a madman might cast himself as a high priest, calling upon gods no one remembers. If your verger wishes to play at sacrifice, he will choose the stones every society lady has swooned over since Victoria's coronation."

Wolf drew a long breath as he made the momentous decision. He looked once more at the scrawled words, *renewal at the standing stones*, then said with a confidence he didn't truly feel, "Stonehenge. Her ladyship is right. He must mean Stonehenge. And that is where we shall find him and my wife."

The dowager's lips curved into the faintest of smiles. "At last, some sense."

CHAPTER 31

Having decided where to look, Wolf faced yet another problem: how to get there. The previous night, he'd told Bear they would take the carriage. However, now that they had fixed on Stonehenge, Canon Elliot felt it necessary to point out that the carriage was wholly unsuitable for traversing Salisbury Plain in any thorough manner.

"You can certainly take a cart," Elliot said. "That would do better on that terrain than your grand carriage, but it won't be fast."

Wolf sighed; he knew what they had to do, but wasn't happy at the idea. "Bear, find Madison and tell him we need horses to ride instead of the carriage. Oh, and tell him that you and I are to be the riders; I assume he will know what that means."

Bear gave his friend a look of rueful acknowledgement of the situation they faced; they needed horses that weren't too spirited for the two less-than-expert riders, yet young and sturdy enough for the task ahead. Luckily, Madison was a far more competent rider than either his master or Bear, so at least one of them could have a steed that could ride like the wind if it became necessary.

It had never crossed Wolf's mind to take the canon with them. Still, the man said in a panicked tone, "I should tell you that I am not up for the task of riding across the Plain, milord."

As much as Wolf never intended for Canon Elliot to join them, his refusal even to offer was irritating. Wolf was unwilling to allow the man to sit comfortably in his study, sipping tea while they were all out trying to save Tabitha from a situation he was at least partially responsible for allowing to happen.

Wolf considered ordering Elliot to mount a mule just to force him along, but he quickly realised the self-defeating futility of such a command.

Instead, he said, "I have a different task for you, canon. I wish you to escort her ladyship to the police station. We need to alert Superintendent Wallis to the situation and request the help of his men to search Salisbury Plain. It is far too large an area for the three of us to hope to cover alone."

Then, turning to the dowager, he said, "I am sure it goes without saying, your ladyship, that anything other than the superintendent's complete cooperation is unacceptable."

Wolf could have sworn that the dowager almost licked her lips, eagerly anticipating the skirmish to come.

"I assume you, Jeremy, that the superintendent will be sending all of his men to assist you," the dowager said with a gleam in her eye.

Confident he was sending the perfect person for this particular task, Wolf said that he imagined the superintendent would arrive at the station between seven and eight in the morning. According to the grandfather clock in the corner of the room, it was already 7 a.m.

"Then, let me dress accordingly while you arrange suitable transport, canon. I will meet you downstairs within the hour." The look on the canon's face indicated that he didn't appreciate being ordered about like an errand boy, but he was astute enough to keep his thoughts to himself and merely nodded in acknowledgement of the command.

Bear was attending to the horses, the dowager was informing Superintendent Wallis, and Wolf knew what was left for him to do. "Canon, do you have an Ordnance Survey map of the area?" he asked. As an antiquarian with a particular interest in local history, he imagined this might be something Elliot owned.

It seemed Wolf's assumption was correct. While the dowager left to bedeck herself with diamonds and furs to intimidate the superintendent into full compliance, Elliot led Wolf to his study.

Elliot bent down to a cupboard in the corner of his study and returned with a long roll of paper bound by fraying tape. He untied it with fingers that shook more than he cared to admit and spread the sheet across his desk. The early morning light through the window caught the crisp lines of the Ordnance Survey: roads, rivers, villages, all marked in neat black lettering on a pale background. Salisbury lay in the centre, with the cathedral noted as a tiny, printed symbol, while to the north and west stretched the expanse of the Plain. Just looking at it laid out before him reminded Wolf of the herculean task they faced that day; the area was vast.

Wolf leaned closer, tracing the familiar names with a fingertip. Old Sarum, its earthworks marked in short, parallel lines. Further still, Stonehenge, circled next to the words, *Druidical Temple*. Besides these, a scatter of barrows was spread across the paper, annotated with little crosses.

From beneath the survey sheet, Elliot drew out another, older and browned with age, its lettering uneven, its execution more enthusiastic than precise. This was no modern chart but one to satisfy an antiquarian's fancy: long barrows carefully shaded, circles sketched boldly, the word "Templum" written in Latin where Stonehenge stood.

"Do you see?" Elliot murmured. "Even our maps cannot agree. The survey calls them temples, though it dares not say to whom. The antiquarians made them the altars of Druids. I tell you again, the verger would not distinguish one from the other. To him, they are all standing stones."

Wolf frowned, his eyes narrowing on the vast space of the Plain. "And to us, they are a huge expanse in which he might hide her ladyship." He rolled the map back up with a snap of the paper. "We will not sit here debating fancies. Whatever the antiquarians scrawl, I believe that he means Stonehenge. That is where we will find my wife." Wolf said this with a certainty that he wished he felt. What if he was mistaken?

As far as Canon Elliot was concerned, he'd voiced his opinion and could now wash his hands of the search details. He would escort that old harridan to the police station and then be done with the entire business.

Left alone, Wolf traced the turnpike heading north, the broad road that led toward Amesbury.

Old Sarum was situated quite near the city, a jagged oval of stones and ruined walls. Wolf let his hand rest on that spot of the map briefly, pondering his decision. It was too close. If the verger had only intended to spirit Tabitha away there, he could have done so in half an hour on foot, under cover of darkness. Why the cart? Why the effort to bind her and drive through the night? No, Old Sarum was a blind. Yet even as he considered this, Wolf second-guessed his own logic.

Finally, Wolf decided that, depending on the size of the force Superintendent Wallis sent, there was no reason not to send some men to monitor Old Sarum at nightfall. Relieved by this pragmatism, Wolf's eyes moved further across the sheet, following the road as it stretched onto the pale expanse of the Plain.

If Stonehenge was where the man intended to take her, then the direct road from Salisbury to Amesbury was the quickest route, suitable for a carriage at speed. But was it too exposed? A cart carrying a bound woman might have chosen a different way. Even if she was hidden, would the verger want to travel so openly where locals might remember the tall, thin, rather distinctive-looking man?

Wolf's eyes narrowed on the thinner lines crossing the Plain. There were green lanes and drovers' tracks, carved deep into the chalky soil by centuries of hooves and wheels. One ran north-west before bending east; another curved through Winterbourne Stoke. A dozen routes converged at Amesbury, and from there the Plain opened out towards Stonehenge.

That was the key. Amesbury was the funnel through which all the traffic had to pass. If they headed straight there, perhaps they could still intercept the verger, or at least discover which track the cart had taken. Farmers rising at dawn, shepherds with their flocks, even a lone labourer would have noticed a cart moving at such an hour. Someone must have seen it. Or at least, that was Wolf's fervent hope. Of course, even as he thought this, he reminded himself that the verger had snatched Tabitha the night before and likely moved her under the cover of darkness. So, perhaps no one had witnessed anything.

Shaking off such thoughts, Wolf's mind moved with the precision of a man long experienced in pursuit from his years as a thief-taker. With Bear and Madison, they would leave via the north gate of the Close, take the turnpike to travel at a decent pace, and push their horses as hard as their limited riding skills allowed. Amesbury was little more than eight miles away. Even at a cautious pace, they could reach it within an hour and a half.

He made a mental note of the route: Salisbury to Amesbury; from Amesbury, eastward across the Plain to Stonehenge; and if necessary, from Stonehenge further out to the scattered barrows. Wolf folded the map with a definitive gesture. His decision made, he would find Tabitha before it was too late.

CHAPTER 32

It was fortunate that the dowager always travelled with sufficient jewels and other trappings of rank and fortune so that if she were suddenly to have cause to interact with royalty, she would not lack for grandeur. This preparedness stood her in good stead for the task ahead.

"Withers," she called out as she re-entered her bedchamber, "I will need my diamonds and mink stole." Was a tiara a little much? The dowager pondered this question for a moment. She decided that a country policeman, whatever his rank, could be sufficiently overpowered by even an inferior choker of rubies, let alone the glorious diamonds that were more suited to a grand ball than a Monday morning in a small market town.

Thirty minutes later, the dowager was lavishly adorned with jewels and furs, confident that she would easily achieve her goal.

By the time the dowager descended to the ground floor, the canon had secured the finest transport he could at such short notice. When she saw the brougham waiting outside Arundells, the woman ignored the canon's effort and sniffed derisively.

The ride to the police station was sufficiently brief that neither the canon nor the dowager felt the need to force themselves to find a topic of conversation. Instead, they sat in silence, each lost in their thoughts about the task ahead of them.

For his part, the canon wished to perform his duty by delivering the dowager to the police station as swiftly as possible. He realised that etiquette might require him to wait and return with the woman. Still, he had no intention of escorting her into the building, let alone to the superintendent's office. Casting a quick glance at the dowager's profile, he consoled himself with the thought that this imperious old woman didn't need his help to lord it over Wallis.

It never occurred to the dowager that she would need or desire the canon's company as she carried out her commission. She thought even less of the man than she did of most of his profession.

When the brougham pulled up outside the police station, the dowager noticed the canon hesitate to exit the vehicle and remarked, "You may help me down and then can wait for me here."

As much as the canon had no desire to accompany the dowager, he bristled at being ordered about as if he were a footman, or less. He was tempted to give a sharp retort, but then he realised he would be cutting his nose off to spite his face, and instead, nodded in agreement.

The dowager swept into an empty police station. Aside from a constable behind the desk, it was too early in the morning for the room to be filled with drunks and pickpockets. The constable looked at the terrifying-looking old toff approaching him and immediately regretted agreeing to swap shifts with Johnson.

"You may inform the superintendent that the Dowager Countess of Pembroke will see him now," she said in her most imperious tone as if Wallis were calling on her rather than the other way around.

It never crossed the constable's mind to do anything other than nod his head and scurry off to warn his superior.

It seemed the warning had been fully delivered and acknowledged when, a few minutes later, Superintendent Wallis himself entered the room. Wallis approached the dowager and gave a quick bow. He had no idea what relation this woman had to the bothersome earl, but his constable had been rattled enough that it seemed wise to start the encounter with as much deference as he could bear.

"Your ladyship. I am told you wish to speak with me?" Wallis said.

"I assume you have an office where we might speak in private," the dowager replied.

"Indeed. Please follow me." Glancing over at the constable, Wallis added, "Brown, see that some tea is brought in."

The only police station the dowager had ever visited was the one in Brighton the previous year. She hadn't been particularly impressed then, and she wasn't now. She was tempted to run a finger along the superintendent's desk to highlight the dust build-up, but didn't want to spoil a perfectly fine pair of gloves.

With just a sniff of distaste, the dowager took a seat on the hard wooden chair with the air of a martyr ascending their death pyre. If the superintendent noticed any of this, it didn't show on his face. Instead, he tried to adopt an expression of polite authority. Wallis didn't know what this woman wanted, but something told him he was about to be treated as if he were a boot boy.

"Let me come straight to the point," the dowager said. She then gave a terse account of Tabitha's predicament, their certainty about the verger's role, and their belief that he had taken her somewhere on Salisbury Plain with the intention of performing some sort of ceremony at Stonehenge that night.

Superintendent Wallis sat motionless behind his desk, hands folded, his expression neutral as he listened to the dowager's account. Finally, when it seemed she had finished, he explained, "My lady, I understand your concern, but I cannot simply send my men across Salisbury Plain as you suggest. We have only twenty constables in Salisbury for all shifts, and half are needed for their rounds within the city during the day. I can't strip the streets bare to follow the earl and his friends on a wild goose chase."

As soon as these words left his mouth, Wallis regretted his turn of phrase. If he was honest, his men had exhausted every lead open to them in the death of Jacob Leland, and he should have been eager for this new information. However, cognisant of the bishop's clearly stated wish for the investigation to be kept as far from the Chapter as possible, Wallis was disinclined to take these toffs' word that the culprit was even the lowly lay verger of the cathedral. He certainly would not take all his men off the streets of Salisbury without proper authorisation from the Chief Constable of Wiltshire.

The dowager's eyes narrowed. "Do you value my daughter-in-law's life less than keeping the streets free of drunkards on a Monday afternoon?"

Wallis flushed. "It is not a matter of value, but of numbers and jurisdiction. Much of that country lies under the county constabulary, not the borough force. I have no standing to deploy men across every mile of the Plain."

"Then, send as many men as you can and communicate with the county immediately. Or do you prefer to explain to the magistrates why you delayed while a woman was being carried to her death?"

The superintendent hesitated, his gaze drifting to the window. "Even if I did, my lady, the Plain can be treacherous. Chalk and flint make poor footing. To send unarmed constables on foot after a desperate man would be folly."

The dowager leaned forward, her gloved hands gripping the edge of his desk. "Do you wish for it to be said that the Salisbury police stood idle when action was most needed? Do you truly wish that?"

Wallis swallowed hard, but his voice was resolute as he replied, "I will send word to the county and contact the Chief Constable, but that is all I can do, for now."

The dowager was shocked that she couldn't subdue this man more easily. However, from his tightly pressed lips to clenched jaw, he didn't seem like a man likely to be easily swayed.

"See that you do," she said coldly, somehow straightening her already impeccable posture. "We have no time for hesitation. If anything happens to her ladyship, I will consider the blame to lie with your inaction and will report as much to the Home Secretary himself."

When even this threat failed to move the man, the dowager stood and said, "The earl is setting out immediately. See that you send whatever men you are able to assist him as soon as possible." With that, she turned and left the room.

Superintendent Wallis watched her leave, pondering what to do next. Ultimately, he decided to send a telegram to the chief constable in Devizes, leaving him to determine the best course of action. He knew that his superior planned to retire within the year and was not overly concerned with Whitehall politics anymore. Let him decide whether to pull officers off the streets. Superintendent Wallis wasn't going to let these aristocrats playing at detectives thwart his plans for promotion to chief constable.

For her part, the dowager returned to the brougham feeling frustrated, a mood that could be only somewhat alleviated by berating someone else. She snapped at the canon, "How long do you expect me to stand here before you hand me in?" The man hurried to obey her command before enduring a ride back to Arundells that felt even more oppressive than the earlier journey.

By the time they returned, Wolf and Bear had already left. The dowager only hoped that Superintendent Wallis would reconsider his decision or, at the very least, be commanded to do so by his superiors.

CHAPTER 33

Bear returned sooner than Wolf had expected, with Madison and three saddled horses in tow, two carefully selected for their steady temperament. Wolf trusted Madison's judgment, but even so, he wasn't looking forward to a hard day of riding on challenging terrain. He had no illusions about his riding skills. As a boy visiting Pembrokeshire to spend time with his grandfather at the family estate, he had some experience with horses, but no one had ever taken the time to teach him properly.

They had taken some bread, cheese, and apples from the canon's kitchen, along with a flask of ale. It was going to be a long, strenuous day, and they would all need some sustenance. Madison took the provisions from Bear and strapped them to his saddle.

Wolf shifted awkwardly in the stirrup as he mounted, trying to find his balance. Bear was worse, his colossal frame hunched as if the animal might buck him off at any moment. Madison had said these horses were slow to startle and even slower to bolt, but that knowledge did little to calm Wolf's nerves. Still, he knew this was a better choice than taking the carriage and would do whatever he needed to find Tabitha in time.

"Keep your heels down and your hands light," Madison had instructed his master. "Let the horses do the work." Wolf did his best to follow his servant's instructions.

As they rode out onto the road east of Salisbury, Wolf repeated Madison's words to himself like a catechism. The horse moved at a steady trot, head down, but every jolt made him tighten the reins until the poor beast flicked its ears in irritation.

Bear cursed under his breath as his mount shied at a bird rising from the hedge. "Never thought I'd envy Madison his seat," he muttered.

"He has had years of working with horses," Wolf said tersely. "We will manage."

Madison rode behind them, very comfortable in the saddle. The servant silently observed that the earl and his private secretary looked like men who would have given all the coin in their purses for the stability of four wheels.

The road climbed a rise, and soon enough, Salisbury Plain opened wide before them. Wolf felt his stomach tighten. To a confident rider, the terrain might offer the freedom to canter for miles, but to him, it was an endless expanse with many chances for the horse to lose its footing and throw him. He forced himself to breathe and keep the reins loose.

"We'll never search it all before night," Bear said, his voice flat, eyes on the vast stretch of ground ahead.

"I know," Wolf said despondently. "But we have to do what we can. I have mapped out the hamlets and farms listed on Elliot's map. We should start with those."

Bear agreed. "Then let us begin here," Bear added, nodding towards a farm track below. "Perhaps the farmer who lives here noticed something."

Wolf gladly seized the excuse to stop riding. A few minutes later, he dismounted stiffly, grateful to plant his boots on the ground and leave the horses with Madison. If he was this stiff after such a brief ride, how would he feel by the end of what was likely to be a very long day?

Despite his relief at dismounting, there was little else about the break at the farm to comfort Wolf; the farmer's wife was friendly, but knew nothing of any usual sighting of a cart. She went out to the barn and called her husband in, but he wasn't any more useful.

Back in the saddle, they pressed on to the chalk grassland. At one point, they encountered a shepherd. As good as it had felt to get off the horse at the farm, getting back on was even worse than never dismounting in the first place. Considering this, Wolf called out to the shepherd from where he was. When the man approached, they inquired about a cart possibly travelling faster than he might expect. He paused for a few minutes, weighing whether there might be any coin in it from these clearly well-heeled men and their servant. Finally, the shepherd reluctantly admitted he had seen nothing untoward and went on his way.

They made their way along the edge of the Plain, stopping at every cottage and pasture where smoke still drifted from a chimney. Most of the men they questioned were half-curious, half-amused by the sight of the three strangers, two of them clearly uncomfortable on horseback.

At one smallholding, an old shepherd leaned on his crook and squinted up at them. "Cart in the night, you say? You'll not be the first to hear one that isn't there. Wind plays tricks out here." He offered a toothless smiled and turned back to his dog.

Further on, a dairyman claimed he'd seen lights on the ridge the previous evening. "Lanterns, swinging back and forth," he said with relish. "Could've been smugglers, or maybe some lads fooling about. Never know what they're up to." Wolf asked exactly where he'd seen the lanterns, then thanked the man and gave him a coin in thanks.

Another man insisted he'd heard chanting. Bear muttered that he'd heard less nonsense in London taverns, but Wolf pressed for detail.

"Voices," the farmer said, "soft, like a hymn, coming from the barrows. Frightened my boy half to death." His boy, when asked, admitted he'd been asleep and heard nothing.

Each story grew taller. Lights that changed colour, shapes moving between stones, a cart that vanished into thin air. Wolf listened, noted what he could, and felt his patience fray. These men wanted a story to tell their wives at supper, not to help him find Tabitha. He buried his irritation as best as he could as he tried to separate truth from fantasy.

By late morning, the horses were lathered, and Wolf's temper was short. "They will have us chasing ghosts until dark," he muttered.

Bear shaded his eyes against the glare of the early afternoon sun. "Surely someone must have seen something real."

They came upon a stream at one point, and Madison suggested that they dismount, let the horses drink and rest. Wolf hated the idea of stopping, even for a short while, but he knew it was the sensible thing to do.

After hours in the saddle, he was so stiff that he wasn't sure how he would get back on the horse.

The horses were permitted to drink and graze, while the three men sat and ate their simple fare. Wolf would have overcome his soreness and mounted the horse again as soon as he'd finished his last bite of bread, but Madison said the horses needed a bit more time. Though he was a servant, he was also the expert, so Wolf deferred to him and waited a little longer.

When he finally hoisted himself back onto his horse, Wolf couldn't imagine staying on its back for many more hours. Then the thought of whatever terrifying, dangerous situation Tabitha was likely in made him berate himself for his softness and spur his horse forward.

After riding for about another thirty minutes, they encountered a middle-aged workman mending a section of wall. He glanced up briefly when they approached and continued working. A flock of sheep grazed nearby.

Taking pity on his master, Madison dismounted and approached the man. "We're looking for a cart," he mumbled. "Perhaps late last night. Two men, driving hard."

The man nodded towards the valley below. "I didn't see naught last night, but I did early this morning. One man, tall and skinny, all dressed in black, looked like the devil himself he did. They were driving that horse so hard it was foaming at the mouth."

"Did you see where they were headed?" Wolf asked eagerly.

"Not then. I went back to my work. But a few minutes later, they came back and drove off in that direction. Seemed to have a woman with them that time."

Wolf gasped; this must have been the verger with Tabitha. What had happened? Had she escaped from them and been caught again? He scoured the man's face. He appeared to be speaking the truth with no hint of the storytelling that had characterised so many of their conversations so far.

Giving a single nod, Wolf tossed the man a coin. "Thank you."

The man tipped his cap in thanks. "Not my affair what fools do at break of day," he said. "But if you're following them, you'd best do it soon. They were in a hurry, and it's been many hours since I saw them." The man pointed ahead, indicating where he had seen the cart go.

Wolf turned to Bear and said with undisguised relief. "Then we are on the right road at last."

They kept riding in the direction the man had indicated. At one point, Madison signalled they should stop, and he dismounted his horse with an ease Wolf envied.

The man bent down, inspecting the ground. "I think these are cart tracks," he said. "Though it doesn't mean it's the cart we're following."

Wolf recognised that his caution was sensible, yet he couldn't help feeling a flicker of hope at this sign that they were possibly making progress. Madison remounted, and the men pressed on, doing their best to follow the ruts they hoped were made by the verger's cart.

Wolf and Bear rode side by side, the wind at their faces, both men uneasy in their saddles. The horses Madison had chosen for them were calm, slow to startle, and forgiving of their poor riding. Even so, each step felt uncertain to Wolf. He kept his weight too stiff, and his knees locked against the saddle. Beside him, Bear looked no more comfortable, hunched forward, jaw clenched, his huge hands gripping the reins too tightly.

"Madison said the horses were steady," Bear muttered as his horse stumbled slightly on a patch of rutted ground. "He didn't say they'd test a man's patience." A Londoner through and through, Bear had spent even less time on horseback than Wolf had.

"They will carry us if we do not fight them," Wolf said with more certainty than he felt. "Try to sit still. Let the horse do the work."

Bear gave a thin smile but said nothing more.

CHAPTER 34

Tabitha didn't know how long it had been since the verger had recaptured her. Caught in his grip, she had screamed into the wind until the man threatened to stuff her in the sack again and throw her into the back of the cart.

They had driven across the Plain for a while before the cart stopped at a shepherd's hut. She had been bundled inside, with her ankles and wrists bound again. Any hope she had of escaping once more was crushed when it became clear that the verger wouldn't leave her alone again. The simple man who had driven the cart was given a cudgel and told to watch her.

That had been hours earlier. The sprint to freedom earlier had sapped Tabitha of energy, and she eventually gave in to her tiredness, closed her eyes, and slept. When she woke, the driver hadn't moved from his position. Rather disconcertingly, he sat staring at her, almost motionless, with the cudgel by his side. Tabitha didn't want to imagine what he'd been instructed to use it for.

At one point, the man reached into the bag at his side and pulled out a loaf of bread. Watching this, Tabitha realised how hungry she was. The verger had stuffed the handkerchief back in her mouth, so instead, she nodded toward the bread and made some incoherent sounds.

The man had torn off a lump of bread that he was slowly chewing. At first, he watched her attempts to communicate with him indifferently. Then, just as Tabitha was about to give up, he ripped off another piece of bread and brought it to her.

He took the handkerchief from her mouth and said, "If you scream, I'll have to put it back in."

"I won't scream," Tabitha promised. "Though I cannot eat it with my hands bound." At this point, she wasn't planning to attempt another escape; she just wanted some sustenance for herself and the child within her womb.

After considering her words, the man bent and untied her hands. He handed Tabitha the bread, stepped back and said, "Eat it quickly. I don't want him to see that I did that. Sometimes, he's not a nice man."

As she greedily tore chunks of bread and ate them, Tabitha considered the man's words: He's not a nice man. Was there something she could do with this?

"Do you have anything I could drink?" she asked. "I have not had a sip of water since yesterday afternoon."

The man looked uncertain, but then turned and grabbed an earthenware bottle, which he handed to her. Though the water inside wasn't cold any longer, it was fresh from a nearby stream, and Tabitha gulped it down. She hadn't realised how parched she was until the liquid slid down her throat.

When she had quenched the worst of her thirst, she said in a gentle voice, "My name is Tabitha. What is yours?" The man blinked, his face uncertain, and she wondered if she had gone too far.

Tabitha thought he wouldn't answer and would simply retie her hands when he said, "My ma called me Edward, but everyone calls me Eddo."

"Well, thank you for the bread and water, Eddo. That was very kind of you."

"I have to tie you back up," Eddo said apologetically. "He told me he needed you for his suromeny." It took Tabitha a moment to realise that the man was mispronouncing ceremony.

Once she understood, she replied cautiously, "Did he tell you what this ceremony is?" Eddo shook his head. Tabitha continued, "He is going to hurt me during it."

Eddo appeared genuinely taken aback by her words. "No. Mr Jasper works in the cathedral. Ma always told me to listen to the churchmen because they were always right."

"Well, normally they are. Your ma was correct. However, he is different, and he is going to hurt me with that big knife he has."

Tabitha saw genuine concern flicker across Eddo's face and felt a moment of hope. Then, just as quickly, she heard a sound outside.

Whether it was the verger returning, the sound startled Eddo enough that he said gruffly, "Have to tie you back up, miss. Sorry." And with that, he shoved the handkerchief back in Tabitha's mouth and retied her hands before she had a chance to say anything more.

Tabitha believed she could have persuaded Eddo and that the simple man might have let her go. Now, as he finished binding her hands, she felt utter despair, and tears rolled down her cheeks.

"Don't cry, miss," Eddo said with genuine concern. "He's not going to hurt you. He just needs you for the suromeny." Even with the handkerchief in her mouth, Tabitha groaned in frustration. If only she could have persuaded Eddo of the truth.

Sometimes she heard voices in the distance and wondered about the chances of a shepherd returning to his hut and rescuing her, but no one arrived. Once, Eddo stepped outside the hut, the earthenware bottle in his hand. Tabitha assumed he'd gone to refill it. As the door shut behind him, she tried to get to her feet but couldn't.

All Tabitha could do was hope that somehow Wolf was on her trail. She must have fallen asleep again, because when she opened her eyes, the verger had joined Eddo.

At least she thought it was the verger. The person before her was the right height and build, but he was wearing a hooded cloak, and she couldn't see his face. The fabric was coarse, the colour somewhere between soot and earth. The cloak covered what could have been the verger's cassock, but now it was cinched at the waist like a monk's cincture. Chalk smeared along the hem of the cloak. There was something incredibly ominous about the attire.

Eddo stood behind the verger, looking far more doubtful than he had earlier. "Sir," he said nervously. "She's ever so scared of the suromeny. I told her you're not going to hurt her. You're not, are you?"

Without turning, the verger spat. "Eddo, there's a reason you're fit for nothing more than digging graves and weeding the churchyard while I serve as sexton. Now do your job and leave everything else to me. This lady's blood must spill tonight if the resurrection is to begin."

"Blood?" Eddo cried. "I told her you weren't going to hurt her."

The verger spun around and slapped Eddo around the face. The man whimpered in fear and retreated to the corner of the hut. Tabitha was grateful for his attempt to help her, but clearly Eddo was too simple and too under the verger's spell to be her saviour.

From what Tabitha could see through the small, dirty window in the hut, the sun was beginning to sink in the sky; how long had she been held captive here?

"Ah, you are awake," the man in the cloak said. The unpleasant snarl could only belong to the verger. "Let us prepare you for your glorious sacrifice."

Tabitha longed to scream, but all she could do with the gag in her mouth was weep. The verger approached her and unbound her ankles. For a fleeting, deliriously hopeful moment, she thought he might free her. Then, the man roughly pulled her to her feet and began pushing her towards the door.

"You must be clean before the light," he said as he shoved his hand in her lower back.

Outside the hut was the stream where Eddo must have filled his bottle. With Eddo commanded to follow behind, the verger pushed her towards the stream and then forced her to her knees. Dropping beside her to his own knees, he spoke, almost as if in a trance. The words made no sense to Tabitha, but after a few words, he pushed her head down. Then he dipped a cup he had pulled from his cloak, filled it, lifted it over Tabitha's head, and let the freezing water fall on her arms, face, and hair. The rivulets ran dark down her neck, soaking the collar of her gown and making her shiver. When the verger was finished, he stood up, breathing heavily, and nodded as if satisfied.

"Hold her," he commanded Eddo, who knelt beside Tabitha and placed a hand on her back, though he let her raise her head.

"I'm so sorry, miss," Eddo whispered. "I'm so sorry."

Despite her dire situation, Tabitha turned her head and did her best to indicate with her eyes that she forgave the simple-minded man.

The verger had fetched a folded length of white linen from the cart. At first, Tabitha thought it was an altar cloth, but when he shook it out, she saw the shape of a surplice, long, thin, and yellowed at the cuffs. The verger approached and slipped the surplice over Tabitha's head. The fabric clung damp against her wet coat and gown.

"It is fitting," he hissed. "The moon will see you as pure."

Tabitha stood still, water pooling at her feet, feeling utterly hopeless.

Addressing Eddo, the verger barked, "You can stay here. It is clear you are not worthy of being part of the ceremony."

Then, the verger pushed Tabitha towards the cart, where he stuffed her again into the sack and bound her ankles, before tossing her in the back once more, as if she were a load of potatoes.

The sun was setting when the verger finished his ritual cleansing. The last thing Tabitha saw before the sack was pulled over her head was the most beautiful golden and pink sky she had ever seen. Tabitha wondered if that would be the last sunset she would ever see. If it were, it was indeed a beautiful one.

Then, the cart started moving. Tabitha wasn't sure of the duration of the journey, but it wasn't long before they stopped. She was pulled out of the cart and hauled over someone's shoulders. They walked for a few minutes, and then Tabitha felt herself being lowered onto what felt like a cold rock. The sack was pulled off her, and she realised she must be at Stonehenge. She also realised there were other figures, also in hooded cloaks, staring at her. The handkerchief was taken out of her mouth, though she remained bound.

Tabitha realised she had very few options remaining to her. She did not doubt that Wolf had spent the entire day and night unsuccessfully searching for her. She had clung to the hope of rescue, but that hope was gone.

Realising she had to do whatever she could to save herself, Tabitha cried out, "I am with child! Please, do not hurt my unborn baby." Would it work? She hoped so.

Suddenly, the person standing over her pulled back their hood, and the verger's face sneered at her. As unpleasant as she had found his face before, the sight of the fanatical delight she now saw there terrified her.

The verger paced before her, knife glinting in his hand, his voice low and menacing.

"You carry more than yourself? Life within life. It was ordained! The chalk has thirsted long, but it shall drink twice now with mother and child. Two offerings in one."

Tabitha felt her stomach tighten with fear and fierce protectiveness. "You call it an offering. I call it murder."

He smiled faintly, eyes distant. "No, not murder. Completion. The stones will wake, and your name will be remembered long after the canons and bishops are dust. As your blood seeps into the chalk, know that your life could have had no greater purpose than this sacrifice. And from death will come life."

Then, he gently placed his hand beneath her head, like any lover would, and lifted her up. Another hooded figure approached, holding a goblet handed to the verger, who took it in his free hand.

Horrified, Tabitha realised why she recognised the goblet; it was the chalice used during the cathedral's Eucharist the day before. Even through her fear, the sight of the chalice was particularly jarring. She remembered Bishop Wordsworth reverently lifting it. She thought of the countless lips that had touched it in faith and how its purpose was now being twisted.

The verger lifted the chalice towards her, the gesture disturbingly priestlike. His lips moved silently at first, as if rehearsing a prayer, and then the words came, low and certain: "*Accipe calicem salutaris.*"

Tabitha froze. She knew the phrase; she had heard it from the pulpit, spoken with reverence as the chalice was lifted towards the light. As the verger recited the words, the syllables felt heavy, each deliberate, and his voice quivered not with devotion but maniacal rapture.

Then, he pressed the rim toward her lips. Tabitha tried not to drink, but the liquid was forced into her mouth. She tasted the wine that was sweet, then sharp, with a faint medicinal tang.

As she was made to drink the wine, the verger spoke again, almost tenderly, "Drink!"

Tabitha tried to turn her face away, but his grip on her chin was unyielding. "*Accipe*," he repeated, the single word sharp and authoritative. To refuse was pointless. She drank, and as the warmth spread through her limbs, she began to feel drowsy.

CHAPTER 35

W olf had hoped to find Tabitha well before any macabre ceremony began, but as the afternoon lengthened with no solid lead on her whereabouts, he faced the reality of the situation: they would have to make for Stonehenge.

Based on what the canon had intimated and the gossip in town, there was reason to believe these Druid rituals involved more people than merely the verger. Wolf was nervous about how large a group they might find gathered. While he and Bear were armed, firing into a crowd, particularly one with Tabitha at its centre, was something he'd wanted to avoid. However, now it seemed there was little choice.

After a long day on horseback, Wolf wasn't even certain how prepared he and Bear were for a fight. Under other circumstances, they would have wanted nothing more than a hot bath and a comfy bed to sink into. Yet, they somehow had to push themselves and their horses further and consider the possibility of fighting their way to Tabitha before remounting to escape.

As much as the thought of all this made Wolf sigh, for at least a moment, there was no flicker of doubt that this was what needed to be done.

One last concern needed to be addressed, though. "Madison, we have been unable to find her ladyship and need to head to Stonehenge. Undoubtedly, there will be some sort of altercation, which you are not obliged to join us in. You have already done more than necessary by riding with us all day; I will understand if you wish to turn back now. Perhaps Lady Pembroke has been successful in rousing the Wiltshire Constabulary, and we will find police officers waiting for us."

In truth, Wolf had quite low expectations about this; he assumed that if Superintendent Wallis was willing to send men out, they would have come across them at some point during the day. However, Madison didn't need to know this.

Madison pulled his horse to a halt, then turned in his saddle and replied, "From the first moment her ladyship arrived at Chesterton House, she was always kind, thoughtful, and gracious to every servant there. I'm not going anywhere, though I could use a gun if you have a spare."

Wolf wasn't sure if his driver knew how to use a weapon, but he handed over the extra one Bear had the foresight to bring along with him.

"Thank you," was all he could bring himself to say to the servant willing to risk his life for his mistress. Yet, it was said with a sincerity that Madison couldn't miss.

The moon had risen high by the time they reached their destination. Wolf hadn't realised how far they had ridden across Salisbury Plain and how long it would take to arrive at Stonehenge. As it was, he was grateful for the cannon's ordnance map. Without it, they might never have found their way.

Wolf drew rein just short of the ridge and raised a hand for the others to halt. The three horses stopped together, breath misting in the cold air. He leaned forward in his saddle, squinting. "There," he whispered.

Across the grassy expanse, the stones of Stonehenge loomed ominously against the sky. Even from this distance, Wolf could see movement: figures drifting among the monoliths, the flicker of torches, and the brief gleam of metal. The muscles of his jaw tightened.

"There's a lot of them," Bear said quietly. "A dozen, maybe more."

Wolf said nothing. Stiffly, he slid down from his horse, boots softly crunching on the chalk, and crouched behind the rise. The others followed, tethering the horses to a patch of gorse. The wind carried the low murmur of voices, woven together in a rhythm that was almost a chant.

The men moved silently to the edge of the ditch and peered into the hollow where the henge stood. The scene below was the stuff of nightmares: a ring of hooded figures moved slowly around the outer circle, their robes pale grey in the moonlight. A small brazier was lit inside the circle.

A tall, thin man, who must be the verger, stood bareheaded among the stones, guiding them with brief gestures. Torches were driven into the ground, each sputtering in the wind. In the centre rested a large, horizontal stone that acted as the perfect altar. And on that stone, lying motionless, was Tabitha.

Wolf's breath caught. She was dressed in white with her hair flowing loosely across the stone. Her face was turned slightly towards the sky, eyes closed. Wolf felt unbelievable pain wash over him; she was dead. Then he thought he saw the slight rise of Tabitha's chest with each shallow breath.

"They've drugged her," Bear murmured.

"Probably laudanum," Wolf said, his voice low. "She won't wake easily."

The verger moved to the front of the stone and raised both arms. The chanting paused and then resumed, now slower and more deliberate. Someone began to beat a small drum. The sound was ominous.

Madison swore softly. "What in heaven's name are they doing?"

"They've made her the centre of it," Bear said. "Whatever this is, Tabitha's the point."

Wolf muttered in despair, "And there are too many to take head-on. Twelve, maybe fifteen."

"Closer to twenty," Madison said with certainty. "Look to the outer circle; there are more of them."

Wolf took another look. On the other side of the outer circle, he saw a cart drawn up near one of the sarsens. Maybe it was the cart they'd been trying to follow all day. Beside it were some other carts, their horses stamping impatiently, reins loose, and their flanks dark with sweat.

Near the carts, two men were organising bundles of candles, cloth, and a coil of rope. One man had his hood thrown back; his hair was cut short, and his face was plain. They were labourers, not zealots. How had the verger persuaded such men to take part in his ceremonies? Whatever their motivation, it made no difference; there could be no doubt that they realised by now that they were about to become accomplices to murder. Surely, if the men had been tempted to stop the verger, they would have done so by now.

Bear shifted beside him. "We can't rush them. We'd be cut down before we got near her."

Wolf nodded slowly. His mind ran through what he had: each had a pistol and half a dozen cartridges per man. In addition, they each had a knife. This was enough for intimidation, not for waging war. They couldn't risk failing and being captured themselves, or worse.

"They think they're unseen," Madison said. "If we could startle them, perhaps spook the horse, cause a commotion, we might scatter them long enough to reach her."

Wolf considered it. Madison's idea had merit. Presumably, these were townsmen and farmhands, not soldiers. Their courage would break easily if they believed something had gone wrong with their ritual.

"Bear," he said, "how far can you throw a stone?"

"Far enough."

"Then find a few and move closer. When I sound an owl's hoot, Bear will send the first one through that brazier. Madison, circle east, and when you see the commotion and the men nearby are distracted, cut their horses loose. Try to encourage the beasts to stampede into the circle. Remember, our goal is to create a distraction so we can grab Tabitha," Wolf instructed the other two.

Madison nodded. "Aye."

Below them, the verger started speaking again, louder now. The words rose and fell in a rhythm that resembled liturgy. He held a long, curved knife in one hand, its edge catching the light from the brazier each time he turned. Wolf felt his stomach twist. This was the knife Leland had written about in his journal.

The verger's voice was clear even at that distance. First, some words that sounded like Latin. Then, in English, "The light renews what the world forgets. The gift returns balance."

The others echoed the final phrase. "The gift returns the balance."

Bear muttered, "They're stark raving mad. All of them."

Wolf agreed. However, as he watched the verger trace a line with the knife across the air above Tabitha's body, he realised that the men's state of mind was irrelevant; they were caught up in mass suggestion. The verger had persuaded them to be bound by some ancient madness.

It terrified Wolf to watch the verger wield the ceremonial knife he intended to murder Tabitha with, yet he forced himself not to look away. Wolf noticed that the gesture was slow, deliberate, and not yet deadly. The verger was performing, savouring the rhythm of the ritual. Hopefully, this meant they had time.

Wolf dropped back behind the ridge and crouched. "We will wait until he steps away from her; I cannot risk him acting in desperation. I get the sense that this ceremony is still in its early stages." He hoped he was right. "When he shifts away from Tabitha, we move. Bear, you take the left, draw their attention if they turn. Madison, stay in the shadows and come up behind the cart. I will make my way to Tabitha. Once I have her, we run and mount the horses. No fighting unless we must."

"And what about the verger?" Bear asked. "We know the man has already murdered at least once. Do we let him escape?"

As much as Wolf wanted to be the one to hold the man to account for his crimes, he knew that the only thing that mattered for now was to save Tabitha. Bitterly, he replied, "Leave him to Wallis. It seems he could not be bothered to send his men to help us. So, we do what we can alone, and he can track this madman down later. Or not. It is no longer my concern."

Bear nodded and went to find stones large enough to disrupt the ceremony, while Madison made his way towards the carts and horses.

Wolf glanced once more at the henge. The chanting had resumed, the rhythm steadier now. A low hum supported it, the men's voices merging into a single note that made the air vibrate. The torches sent their smoke upward into the still sky.

He could see Bear in the shadows, rocks in hand, moving to a better position from which to throw. He hoped Madison was also in place and ready.

They waited. Minutes dragged by. The cold seeped into Wolf's knees where he crouched, but he hardly noticed it. His focus had narrowed to the movement of one man among the stones. Suddenly, the verger moved away from Tabitha, leaning over the brazier to dip the blade into the smoke. He lifted it out again, the metal dark with soot, and turned towards the altar.

"Now," Wolf whispered to himself. Then, he gave the signal to Bear and Madison.

From his position, Bear stood, drew back his muscular arm, and threw the first stone. It arched through the moonlight, striking the brazier dead centre, and causing a shower of sparks to fly. The chant ceased. Some of the robed figures cried out.

At the first sign of sparks, Madison slapped the horses he'd freed and sent them galloping in a panic into the circle of stones.

The second stone followed, striking a torch and knocking it to the ground. The fire flared up, catching a dry patch of grass and sending a ribbon of flame creeping across the circle. Confusion erupted. The horses, already spooked, now panicked, neighing wildly; in one case, rearing onto two legs and fearfully striking at the cold night air.

The verger's congregants screamed and broke apart, their courage failing them even more quickly than Wolf had hoped. Few shared the verger's absolute fervour strongly enough to stand their ground amid the chaos. The ditch gave way to open turf, and the moonlight was bright enough to guide them as they ran away.

In that moment, Wolf seized the opportunity the chaos gave them. His soreness and exhaustion forgotten, he leapt up, and his boots pounded the ground as he sprinted toward the altar. Bear's heavier steps followed closely behind. Up ahead, the robed figures were shouting and scattering. The verger spun around, the knife flashing in his hand, trying to make sense of what was happening to his holy ceremony.

Wolf reached the edge of the stones and didn't hesitate. He burst through the ring, grabbed the first man he came upon, and drove a fist into his stomach. The man doubled over silently. With his revolver ready, Wolf's only aim was to save Tabitha.

"Bear!" he shouted. His friend was already there, swinging his fists and knocking man after man to the ground. Madison stepped out from the shadows near the cart, knife in hand, after cutting through the ropes that tied the horses.

Wolf reached the altar. Tabitha lay still, her face pale and lips parted.

The white of her gown gleamed in the moonlight. He placed a hand on her throat. There was a pulse; weak but steady.

"Thank heavens," he whispered. He slid an arm beneath her shoulders and started to lift her.

A shadow fell across the stone. "Leave her," the verger said.

Wolf pivoted. The man stood just six feet away, knife in hand, eyes shining with a fury driven by pure conviction. "She is the offering. You interfere with what must be."

Wolf shifted his weight, keeping his body between Tabitha and the knife. "You will not touch her again."

Around them, the rest of the circle had broken. Some followers had fled outright; others lingered at the edge, unsure. The sparks the fire had ignited licked higher, painting the stones orange.

"You do not understand," the verger said. "This will set it all to rights."

Wolf shifted Tabitha in his arms so he could raise his pistol, the barrel steady. "No, this will end it."

Neither man moved as their eyes met. Then the verger lunged, the knife held before him. The gunshot cracked across the Plain, loud as thunder. The knife clattered against the stone. The verger stood a heartbeat longer, eyes wide with disbelief, and then folded forward onto the turf.

Bear caught up beside Wolf, breathing hard. "You alright?"

Wolf lowered the pistol. "She's alive."

Madison ran up, panting from the exertion. "The rest are gone, running towards Amesbury."

"Good," Wolf said. "Help me with her."

They gently lifted Tabitha, wrapping the surplice securely around her to keep out the cold. Her head rested against Wolf's shoulder, breath shallow but even.

Behind them, the brazier hissed and guttered out. The smoke rose straight into the moonlight. The stones loomed silently, their long shadows stretching west.

As they crossed back over the ridge to where the horses waited, Wolf glanced over his shoulder. The grass hadn't been dry enough for the flames to do more than sputter out quickly. The stones were returning to their solitary stillness. Whatever madness had gathered there dissolved into the night.

Wolf tightened his grip on Tabitha and kept walking.

Epilogue

T abitha had not stirred since Wolf and Bear had carried her in, although she had murmured once or twice, words blurred by laudanum. The house had moved quietly around her: the dowager, stirred from her bed by the commotion, had immediately taken control, directing servants in low tones, ensuring that Tabitha was undressed and gently washed after the horrors of her capture.

Once Tabitha was in her nightgown, lying comfortably beneath the covers, the dowager sat by the younger woman's bed, her dressing gown wrapped around her, gently stroking her hair.

"What did that monster do to her?" she asked, as much to herself as to Wolf.

"The true horror was what he intended to do to her," Wolf replied. He stood at the foot of the bed, praying for his wife and unborn child to be unscathed from the ordeal.

"And that superintendent never sent any men to help?" the dowager asked in disgust.

"None that we ever encountered," Wolf acknowledged with a sigh.

"Well, I will be having words with the Home Secretary on our return!" the dowager informed him. Wolf shrugged; did it matter at this point? He would have to report the verger's death at some point. However, it was the furthest thing from his mind now.

The dowager and Wolf remained by Tabitha's side throughout the night. As exhausted as Wolf was, he would not allow himself even to doze.

Eventually, through a crack in the curtains, Wolf saw that the sun was beginning to rise. He was determined to send for the doctor at first light. In fact, he would have summoned him as soon as they returned, but it was uncertain what the man could do until Tabitha started to emerge from her laudanum-induced stupor.

Now, as a faint ray of sunlight entered the room, Tabitha shifted beneath the coverlet. Her brow furrowed; her breath came unevenly, as if her mind were fighting its way back through layers of fog.

Wolf had been standing at the end of the bed, trying to fight sleep. Now, he hurried to stand beside his wife and took her hand. "Tabitha," he said softly. "You are safe."

Tabitha's eyelids fluttered, opened momentarily, and then closed again. She turned her head slightly toward the sound of Wolf's voice. The movement was slight, but relief shot through him with a warm burst.

The dowager stood. "I shall send someone to fetch the doctor."

After the dowager left the room, Tabitha's eyes opened again, initially unfocused. She blinked at the ceiling, then at the window, as if trying to identify the source of the light. Her lips moved. The word that emerged was faint and uncertain: "Wolf?"

Wolf's throat felt rough as he choked out, "Yes. I am here."

Tabitha's gaze shifted towards him. "The stones..."

"It is over," he assured her. "You are at Arundells and are safe."

Tabitha's eyes closed again, a tremor passing through her. "The baby?" That was the question Wolf couldn't answer. His only reply was to squeeze her hand and attempt a smile.

"A boy has been sent with a note telling the doctor to make haste," the dowager said from behind him, her voice soft but firm. "I will go and dress and meet the man downstairs." Although she'd said this, the woman didn't leave the room. Instead, she approached the bed and said in the gentlest voice Wolf had ever heard her use, "I am so happy you are safe, my dear. Rest and the doctor will be with you shortly." Then, she turned and left.

Thirty minutes later, although it felt like an age to Wolf, footsteps echoed in the corridor. The door swung open to reveal a middle-aged, grey-haired man who looked as if he had been woken from sleep and dressed hastily. This must be Doctor Hayes, Wolf thought as he moved aside for him next to Tabitha. The doctor approached the bed without ceremony, setting his bag on the table.

"Well," he said kindly. "I hear you have had quite an adventure." He touched Tabitha's wrist, timed her pulse, then leaned closer to examine her pupils. "Good, she is responsive. How long since she stirred?"

"Perhaps thirty or forty minutes," Wolf said.

The doctor nodded, satisfied. "I believe her body's done with the laudanum. She'll be weak as a kitten and headachy for a day or two, but she's past the worst of it."

He examined Tabitha thoroughly, focusing especially on her abdomen, his movements brisk and professional. "No sign of uterine distress. The pregnancy appears undisturbed."

The dowager, who had silently followed the man into the room and stood by the door, drew a slow breath. "Thank heaven."

Tabitha's eyelids fluttered once more. "Can I sit up?"

"Not yet," the doctor replied. "Lie still a little longer. You've given everyone quite a fright."

Turning to Wolf, Dr Hayes said, "She'll make a full recovery. Keep her in bed for two days, warm and quiet. Milk and broth only. No visitors and no more excitement."

Wolf inclined his head. "You have my word."

The doctor gathered his bag. "I'll look in again at noon. The danger's past, but exhaustion's a stubborn thing. Let her rest and call me if there is any change for the worse, though I do not expect any," he added.

When the door closed behind him, Wolf turned to look at the dowager, tears in his eyes. She smiled wanly back at him, wiping away the tears that even she couldn't prevent from falling.

Tabitha stirred again and opened her eyes fully. She gazed at Wolf's face, as if wanting to be certain she wasn't dreaming, then sighed and allowed her eyes to close again.

Wolf sat down and leaned back in the chair, his weariness finally taking hold.

"Go and sleep now, Jeremy," the dowager said softly. "I will sit with her." He wanted to argue, but had never in his life felt so sore and tired.

Three days later, after Tabitha had moved from the bed to sitting in an armchair downstairs by the fire, the doctor announced that she was well enough to travel. While he would never admit it, Wolf had been so stiff from his time on horseback that he was glad to have a few days to rest and recover.

He'd decided that the superintendent could cool his heels for a few days, but after the doctor left, he sent a note around to the police station. It was terse, but gave all the necessary details. The note described Tabitha's ordeal and the scene at Stonehenge. He explained that while rescuing Tabitha, the verger had been shot.

Sometime later, he received a response.

Wolf scanned the superintendent's note once before reading it aloud to Tabitha and the dowager. "It seems Wallis sent men to recover the body at Stonehenge, but there was none to be found. They are working on the assumption that the verger survived and escaped. The Wiltshire Constabulary has initiated a county-level manhunt. Given that the man must be badly injured even if he lived, one would hope he would not be difficult to track," he added.

"It is a shame Wallis could not rouse himself to such an effort to help you save Tabitha," the dowager said in a vinegary tone, making no effort to disguise her disgust at the superintendent. Hearing her, Wolf wasn't surprised that the man had chosen not to visit the house, even though he must have heard some rumours of what had happened. Salisbury wasn't a big town, and the canon's entire household had been turned upside down ever since Wolf had burst through the door in the wee hours of the night, holding Tabitha in his arms.

The following day, Wolf carried Tabitha to the carriage, even though she assured him she could walk. He placed her inside and wrapped a blanket around her legs. He'd debated whether to have Madison drive them the entire way back to London, but Tabitha had assured him she was strong enough to sit in the first-class section of the train and that all she wanted was to be home.

Canon Elliot had made himself scarce during Tabitha's recovery, but the guilt was deeply etched on his face every time they saw the man. He had apologised numerous times for his role in Tabitha's ordeal, so much so, in fact, that she had finally assured him she bore him no ill will. The bishop had sent a note requesting an audience so he could also apologise in person. However, Tabitha had not felt up to the self-flagellation of yet another cleric and had sent a note in return, assuring him it wasn't necessary.

As she settled back into the comfort of the Pembroke carriage, Tabitha placed her hands on her abdomen. Despite the doctor's assurances that all seemed well, she couldn't help but worry about her baby. She made a vow that Wolf would not have to worry about wrapping her in cotton wool for the rest of her pregnancy; she would be the one thinking only of keeping this baby safe.

~

WONDERING HOW TABITHA BROKE THE NEWS TO WOLF? SIGN up for my newsletter to find out SarahFNoel.com

~

WANT A SNEAK PEEK AT BOOK 13, A CONSPICUOUS WOMAN? Keep reading...

THE AGE OF THE MOTOR-CAR HAS DAWNED, AND WOLF IS determined to embrace it. When he acquires one of the new mechanical marvels and enters the London to Brighton Motor-Car Run, Tabitha is less than enthusiastic, but resolved to meet him at the finish line.

At Wolf's insistence, she travels by train with the Dowager to await his arrival. But what should have been a day of triumph soon turns to dread when tragedy strikes the course, and Wolf finds himself accused of a fellow driver's death.

Refusing to stand idly by, Tabitha and the Dowager embark upon their own investigation, uncovering rivalries, jealousies, and whispered scandals among the competitors. Chief among them is Lady Arlene

Archibald, a woman from Wolf's past whose reappearance threatens to complicate matters in every possible way.

As engines cool and tempers flare, Tabitha must summon every ounce of wit and patience to uncover the truth before her husband's reputation and their future are wrecked beyond repair.

Afterword

Thank you for reading An Anointed Woman. I hope you enjoyed it. If you'd like to see what's coming next for Tabitha & Wolf, here are some ways to stay in touch:

SarahFNoel.com
Facebook
@sarahfNoelAuthor on BlueSky
sfnoel on Instagram
@sfnoel on Threads

If you enjoyed this book, I'd very much appreciate a review (but, please no spoilers).

ABOUT SARAH F. NOEL

Originally from London, Sarah F. Noel now spends most of her time in Grenada in the Caribbean. Sarah loves reading historical mysteries with strong female characters. The Tabitha & Wolf Mystery Series and its spin-off, The Continental Capers of Melody Chesterton, are exactly the kind of books she loves to curl up with on a lazy Sunday.

Visit Sarah's website (sarahfnoel.com/) to join her mailing list, connect with her on social media, and see what's coming next!

www.ingramcontent.com/pod-product-compliance
Lightning Source LLC
Chambersburg PA
CBHW060212180626
46813CB00007B/2796